THE
LATE NIGHT
MUSE

THE
LATE NIGHT
MUSE

Bette Pesetsky

HarperCollins*Publishers*

FIRST EDITION

Designed by Irving Perkins Associates

Library of Congress Cataloging-in-Publication Data

Pesetsky, Bette, 1932–
The late night muse/Bette Pesetsky.—1st ed.
p.   cm.
ISBN 0-06-018302-0
I. Title.
PS3566.E738L3   1991
813'.54—dc20   90–56367

91 92 93 94 95 PS/HC 10 9 8 7 6 5 4 3 2 1

For Jackie

CONTENTS

Take all away—
The only thing worth larceny
Is left—the Immortality
—EMILY DICKINSON, 1876

Some people say that life makes the artist. Others
say that the artist makes the life.
—BERNADETTE AMY BERNE, 1959

How does anyone know that they are destined to be
remembered? I read that Hemingway's third-grade
teacher was interviewed, and she had this perfect
recall of what he was like then, his test scores, his
conversations. Others can present for their archives
such a complete accumulation of their existence—
all those early scribbles, arithmetic papers,
invitations to the dance, movie stubs. Where did
they save them? Weren't their apartments ever too
small? And how did their mothers know? I mean you
can't collect this stuff retroactively, can you?
—BERNADETTE AMY MARRKEY, 1985

PROLOGUE

————■□■————

This will explain how my archives came into existence—the leavings of a twentieth-century artist—and the truth of my journal.

Sick: a departure from health

Consider fascia, a transparent membrane—a caul for muscles, one you could pull thin and taut, something burglars could wear over their faces to distort and disguise the nose, the mouth, the eyes. Not my fascia. Mine was unforgiving and has perhaps burned itself away. My doctor said that wasn't what had happened at all. How did unforgiving come into it? And Clive demonstrated for me with a miniature plastic man and Saran Wrap. "Do you see?" he said.

"Of course."

"What did you think was going to happen?"

"To the plastic man—nothing. I think I'm going to die."

"Bernadette, can't you ever be serious? You've been doing splendidly. A woman to admire. Look at you—you can still do your housework. You do your own housework?"

"Someone comes in."

"Anyway, you can cook. You have the energy for your children—crackerjack mother—you take care of your husband. You are doing swell, Bernadette."

I got into the swing of it. "I can still write poems."

"What?"

"Poems."

"Surely—poems. Must let me read your poems—sometime. Now sweetie, let's see you squeeze this ball."

Consider my doctor, Clive, as I did this morning when I decided to fill out his five-page form. It's been lying on the dresser, the edges of each page fingerprinted by lipstick. "What's that?" my husband, Martin, asked, and peeked at it, flipped one page.

"From Clive," I said.

Martin was already stripping off his pajamas. "You see Clive today?"

"Yes."

"How you getting there—Toby?"

"No, she's bringing me home. Violet—the woman in twelve-C—has to take her mother to the dentist, so she's taking me, too."

Martin headed for the shower. The water hissed.

I've been with the good Clive for four years. Not my best four years. Clive was a man born to doctor. Never mind the short stature, the thin face, the manner of condescension. He inherited me when he acquired Amberson's practice. Amberson died in the classical way. At the ninth hole of Upper Hills Golf and Tennis Club in horse-country New Jersey, the doctor, just before teeing off, clutched his green Izod shirt and collapsed. His score at that point was two under par. Amberson was age fifty-seven.

Clive bought the practice from Amberson's widow. She was a face in a photograph on her husband's desk, a photograph tilted toward the patient. Like background music. I never thought about her. In the picture she looked pleased. The practice must have sold for a mint.

The new owner of my medical records, my tests, and my X rays sent me a letter—happy to have me as a patient, truly overjoyed. My husband Martin said no way. No way was I going to be a patient of some guy whose qualifications were enough money to buy someone's medical practice. So Martin looked him up.

Martin knew all the right places to look up physicians. *American Men of Science, Hector's Guide to Best Physicians of North America, New York State Registry of Physicians*. Martin compared medical schools, residencies, postgraduate training, board certification, publications in refereed journals. He's all right, my husband said. Young, but a first-rate background. Clive is on the cutting edge.

My arms ached.

My back ached.

I fell twelve times last week.

But I halved that. Six times, I said.

The importance of having selected the right physician

The form—such crisp white paper, five crackling white pages—was handed to me at my last appointment. "Be a sweetie," Clive said, "and fill it out for us." I was of two minds about this form.

I've carried that phrase with me for a week. I heard it in the Food Emporium. I'm of two minds about him, one woman said to another as they strolled side by side down the aisle. I understand, the other woman said, either he will or he won't. She wore a hat that I'm certain she bought at a benefit for the Fashion Institute. A silver gull perched on the brim.

My two minds—either I will or I won't. I will—although the other, the second mind, might still win. The first time I met

Clive, he shook my hand heartily. He leaned across the desk to
do that. He preferred to be seated, because from head to bottom
of torso he seemed taller. I was pleased that my palm was warm
and dry, although the fingers were a trifle numb. "We're in this
together for the long haul," he said. His nails tapped a Spanish
dance across my records. A stack of paper in a manila folder, the
papers attached by a thick metal clasp. The edges of the top
sheets were curled and gave off paper dust. All those tests results,
all those data had melded and become their own person.

"We are entering a therapeutic partnership, Bernadette,"
Clive said, and quickly looked down, checking the accuracy of
the first name. There's no intimacy in first names, I would have
told him.

He was making contact with Amberson's people. He hadn't
changed the waiting room, but the inner office—once the
property of Amberson—was not recognizable. The ecru walls
had given way to a stabbing whiteness. I recognized the desk
lamp from one of my husband's books. A genuine Paiolo iron
base with inserts of blue glass circa 1930.

But that wasn't what upset me, despite the fact that I hated
the lamp on sight. Next to the desk—that battleship of
walnut—was a pedestal of Carrara marble on which was balanced a familiar telephone.

"We have that," I said.

"What?"

"We have that—my husband has that—the telephone."

He looked startled. I thought perhaps I had given him a
headache. "You have *this* telephone. I had this imported."

"Its twin sister then. Big, isn't it? Amsterdam."

"Yes."

I understood how he felt. I thought of apologizing. I felt that I
should offer him something—he looked so disappointed.

"We have other stuff like that," I said. "We have a Hansen chair circa 1934 that's uncomfortable as hell and a 1928 glass-topped table designed by Sinvelli with a large saber-sized crack in it."

"A Hansen chair? Really."

I had done the right thing. Clive looked pleased. We were collectors. Otherwise, it might have appeared that we had bought the telephone as a conversation piece. You know, when someone walks into your room and says, My God, what is that?

Martin had placed the Sinvelli table in the far corner of the dining room and the children were forbidden to approach. Without that crack, Martin swore, we couldn't have touched it. With the crack—it cost eleven thousand dollars.

The telephone, though, we bought new. I used to dream about that telephone. . . . August day. I felt heatstroke, felt salt deprivation. I felt the results of sampling at a dozen tiny food stalls. My face stained red, cheeks puffy, belly a bloated curve.

We were in Amsterdam, our first trip to Europe, and walking back to the hotel, back to our economy-class rooms. Suddenly, Martin said wow. The store was on the Kalvertstraat. Martin had my arm, and then we were inside this tiny white-chrome shop. What did I see? I stood next to the window. Eye level with the desiccated bodies of flies plastered like miniature mummies and left to dry on the window.

I thought I would puke right there on the chrome and white counter. Did Martin read my thoughts? He paid no attention to me. He looked at the monster telephone displayed on its own clear Plexiglas pedestal, stared at it as if it were something to be prized by itself—a great white telephone with a base of two circles of glossy plastic separated by a frieze of miniature Corinthian pillars. What had I thought? I thought it was a conversation piece. Then the clerk appeared. Hey, did this plastic man really see what he had? He told my husband that the diameter of the telephone base was thirty-six inches. Feel the weight, the clerk said. My husband did. It could fit fashionwise anywhere, the clerk said, it is that styled. Bernie, Martin whispered to me. My God, Bernie, it's marvelous. The clerk heard, he stood that close. I've two others, he said. He made three in all—the artist from Groningen—just three.

The price—my God—the price of one telephone was beyond belief. My hands circled one of Martin's bare arms. Surely he felt that I was sick. My hands moist. I was sweating, cotton shirt going transparent.

I had already taken two steps back. The clerk sensed that I could still turn off the deal. So he had to get me. Hear this, he said. He plugged in one of the white telephones and made it play its phoenix sounds. The noise rushed at me. Buy one, I said, buy one, and for God's sake, let us go.

Clive harrumphed, stared upward at the freshly painted ceiling, avoided the telephone, and recovered. I, after all, was a patient—with valid insurance. "Bernadette," Clive said, "I want you to know my philosophy. I treat the entire person."

"Pardon?"

"You'll never be a part to me, Bernadette. Not an arm or a leg. Do you use a nickname?"

"No."

"All right, Bernadette. Tell me, what do you do?"

You're supposed to answer questions like that quickly. Rat-tat-tat. What do you do? Mother of two, husband an accountant. Define yourself, provide identity—do not use the celluloid folders in your wallet.

"I am a poet."

I noticed that he wasn't taking notes.

"Poet," Clive repeated, and then, "What's the most important thing that ever happened to you, Bernadette?"

"Writing poems."

"Well now," he said, "so many ladies say the birth of their children."

"Isn't that interesting. What's the most important thing that ever happened to you?"

He wagged a finger at me. "Gotcha. A fair question. You're a quick one, Bernadette. A fair question." He was pleased. After all, now he had a turn. He bounded to his feet, height forgotten. "Did you notice my framed pictures on the wall when you came in?"

I turned around.

"Wait, wait," he said. He took my hand and escorted me to the wall. Framed newspaper clippings—a double row. The sunlight glinted across the glass. Newspaper photographs of groups—one head boldly circled in red crayon in each picture. "That's me," Clive said. "Me in Chicago. Me at the ramparts at Columbia. Me at a sit-in at NYU. Here I am on the Washington march. My political involvement during my student days, Bernadette. Exciting times, important times. I was there, I can say with pride."

"Certainly were."

I stared at the image of a younger Clive lost in the bunkers of the sixties.

Clive reached up and patted my shoulder. "Well now, Bernadette, tell me in your own words how do you feel?"

"Not too bad," I said. "I have my ups and downs."

That was four years ago.

Learning to love your sickness

The form was for today—perhaps for an epidemiological study. You know, women between the ages of twenty-five and forty— good women. Women of means, supportable women, stuffed with food supplements and vitamins. Still—unaccountably sick. Women slipping away. Deteriorating women. Muscles growing brittle.

On the other hand—no, the second mind. Yes, in terms of the second mind—assuming that I was still of two minds. Clive could be writing a paper. A strong purposeful paper for a re-spected refereed journal. And he was too lazy to reread those charts—those detailed histories of ailments that had changed and altered, through the layer upon layer of records. Easier to ask fresh.

I loved the part about the name, the address, the Social Security number. All those tags of identification. Patient's maiden name. My mother's name. My father's name. Unknown. No, that would never do. That used to be a problem. Schools hated that—when fatherlessness was a designation rather than a common curse. Made a list of possible names—tried them out. Chester Berne, Arthur Berne, P. T. Berne—in honor of the late Barnum—Franklin Berne, Sid Berne. Then I settled— Richard T. Berne. I used that throughout high school. Dick. Daddy Dick.

Who made up this form? Clive maybe. They bloody want essay answers. No machine-graded balloons to darken with a number 2 pencil. Fill in how many times? Once a week, twice— more.

The questions in this form have been designed to yield information that will help us to help you. How do you perceive your illness? Think back to the first time you thought you were ill. Describe the sensation. (Use space 1.)

Dear Space 1, How did I know when I was ill? Scratch ill. Sick. Plain sick. How could I have known? And maybe I am wrong. Who's to say that this was the moment? Wasn't the moment when you—no, the late Amberson—said, We are not sure, but we think . . .

Still, Space 1, perhaps this was the first time. Consider the circumstances. Perhaps it was the heat—coming before its time. Weather out of season was always noticed, changed everything—the body vibrated to an unaccustomed cycle. Anyway, hot for April. It was after Passover, before Easter, and somewhere in the middle of Lent. I had a crazed teacher named Spenser who mailed a note to my home. Bernadette is too introspective, he wrote. I was fifteen and termed lazy, indolent, and does not work up to potential. He actually suggested fresh air. I couldn't believe that anyone would suggest fresh air. I showed the note to my friends. What a jerk, they declared. We ceremoniously burned the note in an ashtray outside the girls' locker room.

I was Drama Club. I say that because it defined me—externally. I spent my afternoons painting scenery. I liked painting scenery. I was a junior in the high school where the spring play was *Our Town*.

I imagined that all over the Bronx schools were turning out *Our Towns* where students sat on chairs on stages and shivered in imaginary cemeteries while waiting for the Messiah. Me? I was crew. I painted clouds on cue. My cousin Helene lived on the Island and went to a private school where they put on *Antony and Cleopatra*. We never got too big an audience for Shakespeare. When we did Shakespeare it was for class—people who had to be there.

These were the circumstances. Dawn Pinell, a girl with reluctant although real talents, was invited to go swimming by a boy in his second year at Columbia—they would go to City Island, never mind the month, it was ninety degrees, no one would be on the beach, they'd have a great time. One performance, he said, what would one performance mean? In his voice was such a tender ache. What could she do? She went upstairs and packed a red genuine plastic–covered cosmetic case with all that she would need, then down the stairs, across the courtyard, to the street and the borrowed station wagon, a rich amber with side panels of metal painted to simulate wood.

I saw her get in that car. I suppose I could have called out, reminded her of obligations. But it was three o'clock in the afternoon. None of my business where she went. I did say that I was crew, didn't I? Oh yes, and we, the flotsam and jetsam set, were understudies. That's how it happened. Dawn of the voice of melody, girl of the mournful eyes, the bearer of blossom-yellow hair—did not show up. Old man Kelly said that I must go on as Emily. He looked at me in despair—flat-chested crea-ture, wild hair, a face of angles. Now, nothing happened—not the obvious, at any rate. I didn't startle the audience with my acting. I went onstage as Emily. A boy named Russell was George. He frowned at me. I could imagine the contrast, seeing me as the object of his love instead of *her*.

But that's not what I want to emphasize. I went onstage, took my position as the dead Emily. I must have sat there—poor Emily. I responded, lines came the way they do from a reflexive memory. I say I spoke my lines, I say I was there—but I do not know that for certain. I try to fit myself into Emily's dress, try to be George's wife. I was close enough to George to see his porous face alive beneath a cruelly applied powder. Then, you see, I felt something. Like a sizzle. A blizzard of numbness had embraced me. I immediately lost interest in Emily's fate—dark though it was. Whatever was happening to me was far more interesting. I tried to hug it close. A violent fire, more piercing than adolescent orgasm. Beguiling—come slip with me. No, I did not actually vanish. But I wasn't there—not really there. I felt as if I were in a trick, the magician just out of sight. I believe my voice grew tremulous, my motions slowed and stilled by these physical feelings. Yes, they were physical. To the audience—the slowness, the outward tremble, the careful voice—even to the hand that reached out delicately to prod George's arm for balance—that was acting, they believed. Oh, she is truly Emily. Then that audience applauded. The play was over, I was finished being Emily. Dawn Pinell, chastened and faintly sunburned, returned for the next performance.

Everyone said I was fine. Good sport, the drama coach said. There was a cast party every night of that week—unofficial. That evening I went to Billy Chasen's, where I smoked, drank a bottle of beer, and sat with friends. I didn't do anything obvious like query, How did I seem? They would have taken that as fishing for compliments. No, I kept that experience to myself. I would have been thought strange. I had no objection to being thought strange. In fact, I encouraged the view. You are left alone that way. But deliberately strange, not this. This was recorded in the poem "The Lightning Understudy in *Our Town*." It was, however, slightly disappointing. Not that I didn't value the poem, but most of the experience—the lightning or sizzling or blizzard event—had occurred somehow without my knowledge. I waited all that month for it to happen again—but it didn't. I thought it through—hardly difficult. Fear, I decided. Despite my denials—I must have been afraid. It must have been a daze of fear. The question never settled was whether that was stage fright or a true sickness. (Examine the ambivalence in this poem written immediately after the performance.)

The Lightning Understudy in *Our Town*

Listen, Emily is not dead. Only virgins
die so easily. Tumbling from childbirth.
Therefore, Emily, your death was merely temporary,
sitting in a cemetery from curtain to curtain.
I fled from you, unafraid. In hot April

from the place where the dead converse, speaking no
mysteries. But recitals of daily life. I need not
hear what happened once, for I was there with mirrors.
While Emily spoke of the familiar. Something whistled
free in me. It was important, the soul twitching,
whiter than white. A blazing but with names. Then the
false-husband turned away as the dead bride's face sang
with rich blood. Never mind. The burning was enough.
Listen, Emily is not dead. I cannot believe that
it could be that easy. So to prove the lie I left
you. Distributing myself in explosive, uncontrollable
bundles. This, I think, might be death after a time.
A revolution has occurred. I embrace and hug this
shimmering pain, an electric orgasm performed by no hot
hand. Note meanwhile how Emily wears a dress that is
mine, has arms and legs that are mine. I grant her their
use. I swear there was a moment when Emily whispered to
me. Burning flies down and leaves. Wait, death
could be exciting. I ride the roller coaster to the
revolution on the stage. Listen, Emily, you are not dead.

—BERNADETTE AMY BERNE, 1963

*When were you absolutely certain that you were ill? Describe your
reactions to this realization. Please be frank with us. Remember that all
information is confidential.(Use space 2.)*

Clive, are you joking? Absolute certainty as in cross-my-heart-
and-hope-to-die. Who the hell knows? But I don't mean to be
recalcitrant. Patients should be cooperative. So shall I come
close? Is close enough? If close is enough, then I vote the park. I
must skip years. The park was seven years later. I make the
connection from a dimly recalled second of piercing. That's

possible. One touch of lips brings forth a knowledge of other such touches.

Almost every neighborhood has a park. Sometimes a tiny one. But I swear—one exists. Walk eight, ten blocks in any direction in the city. See, a park. Some of them you wouldn't want to go into—but parks nevertheless. I was in this park. It's gone now, the land recycled into a building. Rather a nice building. This park was too small for children, the bald trampled ground with a tonsure of weed-grass, sticky and alien to the touch. I suppose it was basically a weirdos' park, a place for paranoid old ladies saying their rosaries. But I was trying to write, and I wanted not so much quiet—as aloneness. Noise didn't bother me. I could ignore noise, forget sounds. But I wanted the noise of strangers. You didn't have to attend to that noise.

Anyway, I decided this park was safe. There were no trees, no hedges. Clear space. Ten, twelve benches, scarred by hearts scraped into green paint—*L.M bi/m adores W.N., E.R. loves T., C.M. loves Me.* This shard of a park was narrow and saber-tipped at one end.

Early evenings—straight from my job—before it grew dark, I could have a half hour or so to write in my notebook. I was twenty-two, and my time not answerable to anyone. I didn't truly notice who was around—all right, I guess I did. The chattering women. Three of them, callused and shrunken by time, their bodies and legs squashed and crushed by a different gravity. A man in a turban pretending to be Indian. A truly classic bum who walked back and forth farting and belching.

But then I began to recognize that a certain man sat on the opposite end of my bench every day. He was middle-aged, his body pouched above his waist, he wore a black turtleneck, his lips faintly scabbed supported a cigar, and a sour scent extended a half-inch outward. He was near me, beside me. Always on my bench. I would sit down and he would materialize. Now, he didn't touch me, no flasher, nothing. So I decided to ignore him—maybe I was in a fantasy with him.

Then one afternoon, an icy twilight, I felt a surprising tingle. My fingers, my arms, my elbows. I hadn't taken anything. The sounds of the city—those toots and rumblings, machinery coughs, swishes—grew suddenly louder as if they vibrated within me, answering and answering. Still, I was never one to give in to some bodily discomfort. Look, the light was good. And I had been thinking about a poem—maybe the origin of these sensations was my mood. My mood was foul, maybe that brought on the pain. If it was pain—I'm not certain that it was pain. Then I decided to leave. Might as well stop. I'd go to a bar, have a drink, see what was happening. I stood up, ignoring the paresthesias. Ignore, and whatever goes away—that's what I believed. Perhaps my muscles had fallen asleep. That was an illusion I liked. Nighty-night, muscles, or rather rise and shine. Either way. My shoes—I wore black flats, firm-heeled shoes. So I slipped on nothing. My ankles became pudding-soft. I dropped, I spilled, I tumbled in that awful way of public falling. My notebook skittered into a puddle of city slime. I believe I reached out my hand toward the man on my bench.

"Hey," the man said. He jumped up and ran to the narrow dagger end of the park. Leaving me to my contagion—of falling. My breath came hard, accompanied by the nauseous taste of bile. I waited, I counted, I went through the names of presidents in order, and then I pushed my hand palm downward on the dry talc-smooth earth and stood up. I found my notebook—ripped off the covers and shoved the paper into my purse.

I headed straight for a neighborhood bar called Allegro, where I met a man who quoted Wallace Stevens. I never mentioned my experience, we spoke about poetry. He was a graduate student, he didn't know for sure but he thought he'd do his dissertation on aspects of self-realization in the poetry of Frost. We left together, and outside the bar I saw the man from the park again. A nifty coincidence. Pervert, I yelled. Go back to Weirdos Park!

After midnight, I considered the possibility that I was sick. Could be. I sat down and concentrated on my notebook.

Weirdos Park

Once there was a weirdos park
An angel sat there, what a girl
What a knockout. Where a sunburst was
Shade from a building. AT&T. And sound was
Sputters. Where people sought refuge from the
Sane. Twirling their dreams. Very verbal.

I went to weirdos park. Despite
The rumors. A rape occurred they said
In some January. No one knew the girl.
And a murder. Two men in a struggle.
In some June. The man was named John.
And an abortion. Just lift your skirt
In some October. And if you touch the ground,

Instant lockjaw, long white worms like snakes,
And rainwater puddles that never dry and never
Freeze. In weirdos park, a street asylum, gather
Your fetuses while you may. In weirdos park
Blood drips, and unconcerned the inhabitants draw
Apart. I called out in weirdos park, an unseen
Voice. Failing to note weirdos have nothing in
Common. I sat upon the ground, while harpies
mumbled prayers for the departed, instant victim
As promised to those who would frolic beneath my
Skirt, also to lockjaw, to worms, to beer cans,
In weirdos park where cardboard coffins whistle.

In what way has this illness affected your ability to handle everyday tasks. Try to be specific. (Use space 3.)

Be specific. All right. If I were a waitress, I would cough in your soup—inadvertently, of course. If I handled electrodes—fear me to place them on your body. Affect my daily tasks?—no more than any deteriorating system can. Do I tremble when lighting a cigarette? Perhaps that is emotion—in the throes of drop-dead love, for instance. Good, let's do that. Making love with the sick. I had this job. Newly hired, I was to type. I took the job because it was close to home. Kept me available, reachable, a call away. Mothers do that. Martin, my husband, thought I was crazy. I didn't need the money—we didn't need the money.

Now, I could type. I had skills, after all. But my hands were surprising me—moving as they did from symptoms of one etiology to those of another. The paper ripped into the roller, flying fingers spun out words that the ribbon set free. New York, New Jersey, Pennsylvania. Addresses. Then the fingers flexed—into the "preacher's hand." Just one—the left remained quite itself, waiting for command. From that we went into the claw—*main-en-griffe*.

The company had specified breaks. That surprised me. Because the man who had hired me—he spoke about the family atmosphere. But you left your desk at your peril. So I pretended paroxysms of hiccups and took myself often into the ladies' room.

I don't know if the man had a first name. He was called Tiller—maybe that was his first name. He had hairs like thick black thread growing out of his nose. He wore pale gray jackets and a silvery, wet-looking watch, huge. You, he said to me, hey, you have a decent body. And I was flattered, the way pregnant women are when in the fourth month, before the bulge, they detect a man's approval—the analogy is to the years of my sickness. My body, I would have said, is currently camouflaged. Out of remission and into relapse.

The man, this Tiller, did something in the office. My sense of organization was blurred. We flirted, he and I. We joked, the way fellow workers can. And one day he stood behind me, I smelled his cherry Life Saver breath, one hand slid up my panty-hosed leg and swept the back. My body exploded that moment, I could have fallen into anyone's arms. In an office on brown Naugahyde, the lock easily forced. I was taken. Afterward, he told. I knew that. Married man getting it, father of three.

Those jackets of his were pale gray—the softest wool with gold buttons on each cuff—anchors aweigh. He hung up a jacket each day and slipped it on again in the evening, shrugged into it. I waited my chance to embrace that jacket—gently, tenderly, with ten fingers hugging the empty shell, the stains of carbon were blue-black on gray. He wore it home—my embrace.

Making Love

Madam, your son kissed me today.
My hand had clung just the moment before
To something like death. Madam, he made my
hand whole. He smoothed it out, he counted
away the lonely shudders. He opened my legs.
He thrust his hand, my hand in. Everything
tightened and grew wet. Madam, with the
physical touch I can forget. Here, he felt me,
here. I can delay, living in the time of
touch, nothing can happen until the sunset,
nothing until three o'clock, eat, swim, drown,
nothing until nightfall. Until snow. Madam,

he whispered love. It's a well-known refrain.
Madam, I believed it, but when the touch
was over, when fire—man-made or mine—had been
cleverly extinguished, I let him go. We parted
properly in formal fashion. Madam, do reclaim him.

How long have you lived with your illness? What in your life gives you the greatest satisfaction? (Use space 4.)

First answer: A million trillion years. Second answer: Poetry.

Do you understand the nature of your illness? (Use space 5.)

Leave me alone, Clive!

The turn

My suit jacket was hanging on the back of the chair. A redder-than-red pebbly wool. A Dior bought from the Back Room at Loehmann's. My hair had been trimmed on Tuesday at Reynald's. Make it wash-and-wear, I said. The girl who cut my hair—herself wore a plume of black macaroni curls that sadly framed her round face. Hairdressers rarely have suitable hairstyles—perhaps like the shoemaker's kids they grew weary of the same efforts, the same movements. They could not con themselves into believing hair that bounced would change your life. But wash-and-wear was plebeian. They charged too much for such a suggestion. Livable, the girl said firmly. I was tied into a smock of silver and maroon. In truth, my arms had spiders within them crawling and creeping from elbow to wrist—like itsy-bitsy spiders they wait until the rain has stopped. With livable hair I can avoid the comb. Up arm, down arm.

It was morning. The coffee was brewed, the orange juice

fresh, the toast crisp and well browned. Ruth liked hers with jam. Two kinds—strawberry and the bitterest of marmalades that I could find. Paul, who doesn't live here anymore, will eat his breakfast in the dormitory cafeteria. He will select scrambled eggs, one slice of toast, and a small glass of grapefruit juice. Every day he will eat that. Just as here, his sister will have her toast. Martin is still dressing. He sings in the last stages of dressing, pants up, belt being drawn through loops. A la-la-la rendition of the triumphal procession from *Aida*. Martin likes his toast with a thin coating of butter—unsalted butter. He especially likes a Swedish butter—the flavor of the cow's cud. He brings that butter home now and then from the gourmet food department at Macy's. He doesn't like the butter to melt on the bread—but rather to coat it.

The doorman buzzed on the intercom. It's the building party line—never use it for secrets. Violet Pensker and her mother are waiting for you, the doorman said.

"Bernadette," Clive said. The top of his head came to the middle of my forehead. When we stood face-to-face we did not make eye contact. He stared at my third button. An ovoid horn button, dangerously loose threads. What did I look at? Downward at the anomaly of his mustache—a glistening red, paste-on-style bristle. The man had generous black hair on his head. I wondered how that worked out genetically—the red mustache.

Clive squeezed my shoulder. "Bernadette, I guess we have to say that you have taken a turn."

I nodded.

But what did that mean? Clive and his folksy manner. The man graduated from Harvard Medical School, took his residency at P & S. And how are we today?

We have taken a turn.

Reflections from a tube-boosted quaverer

Now I had time to absorb this message as I sat in the Clivery waiting room waiting for Toby to pick me up. Dr. Clive's burrow was directly around the corner—off Park Avenue, he always said. He saved twenty-five hundred a month by that corner.

I told Toby to come for me at two-fifteen. Later, she swore I said four-fifteen. I would have sat in the waiting room for a half hour. You had to allow for traffic. Toby drove a blue BMW with acrobatic-looking wire rims banding the wheels. She parked that car anywhere. Nothing happened. After a half hour, I would have left.

It was the half hour that did me in. I sat in the Clivery waiting room, my examination over. Clive believed that the room gave comfort—he had finally reclaimed it from Amberson's spirit—and had modeled it after his honeymoon paradise. His words exactly: honeymoon paradise. The room simulated the lobby of a small English hotel—one located in the Cotswold region, I'd say. Quaint and with truly good china. Well, there are paradises and paradises. Anyway, the room gives you some idea of Clive's fees. Ready to read? The *Spectator,* the *Observer, Granta.* All the latest issues, nothing from Christmas 1982, Summer Travel 1975.

My disease was the type known as orphan. That meant just what you thought it meant. No one cared about it. My disease was identified, classified, and named by a German physician. He named it after himself. It was a kind of narcissistic response that you can understand. Immortality is hard to come by.

Remember that—because this is basically about immortality. I always used his first name. The first name of the dead German physician (1847–1902). Älois, I have your disease. It was a subtle disease that ate away at the core of being.

In the waiting room, I sat in a high-back chintz-covered chair with freshly plumped cushions and sitz bath feel. I began a trembling spasm, a certain amount of motor control slipping away. It was time to leave. The hell with you, Toby!

My hands gripped the arms of the chair, I would push myself upward. In a moment I would have been outside in gritty city air, trying not to sway, to stumble or skid off the curb—taxi drivers weren't keen on women in cloth coats who looked drunk at midday. Such women always wanted to go far away on unprofitable runs.

But what happened—my timing was off. Clive's Molly walked out of one of the inner offices.

She used to wear a white uniform, now she wore people clothes. That's what she said—not my words. Today, she wore people pink with people black shoes.

Clive inherited her, too. He changed her from nurse to a new category called patient adviser.

"Bernadette," she whispered to me, although the only other person in the room was a man whose lolling head proclaimed sleep, "the Doctor has noticed that you have refused all counseling."

"Right," I whispered back.

"Bernadette," Molly said, "it's right next door—through that door—a Mixed Meeting is starting. I really would like you to be there. I'm going in myself. Reception can watch out for your ride. The usual one? The skinny woman?"

I stared as Molly nibbled a nail, looked tense. Ambition scored high with her. And Mixed Meetings were her innovation. Was attendance low? I should have remembered that feeling sorry for people was the flaw that eventually got you.

"I'm really busy, Molly."

"Look, Bernadette—one meeting. Would that kill you? Could you do it as a favor to me?"

The point was—did I owe her a favor? Well, technically yes. Hadn't she sneaked me in once—before the fat man who farted regularly and filled the examining room with the fearsome odors of his life. All right—one favor.

This was a trick.

Molly opened the door. Her room was filled with people. Twenty-five at least. They didn't need me. What had she been looking for—the packed house? SRO? A Mixed Meeting was like A.A. You stood up. Hi, I'm Bob and I'm cerebral palsy. Hi, I'm Elaine and I'm Wilson's disease. I managed to skip my turn. I coughed into a handkerchief and they went right past me. Now, the principle behind a Mixed Meeting was that someone was always in a condition worse than yours—so I looked for someone rheumy-eyed, mummified, saliva balls at half-mast.

I was about to cough my way out the door, when this man crept to the podium. Tube-boosted quaverer. Still, sometimes you listen. "When I die," he said, "my house will be in order. Will yours? I have sorted through my belongings, I have prepared, I have thrown out. Don't be afraid—make your personal house orderly."

I stopped. My trembling body forgot itself. Did I imagine myself dead? Of course not. I never actually imagined myself dead. But I could visualize rooms without me in them. Not a presence hovering by the wall waiting to be exorcised. Just me not there. What else? Why, hands going through what was once mine. Out, out, out, someone says. Never mind who. All gone—swept clean. No room for clutter, no room for *that*. What was *that* anyway?

The realization made me cold—almost as cold as something that had to be exorcised. My God, that one-eyed, tracheotomied gentleman could have been the keeper of my soul!

Simple ideas. My theory always was that simple ideas were hard to acquire. My personal house was in trouble. And what had I thought? Had I thought? I was going to do it. *Pack. Sort. Throw out.* Hell, how could I not have done that!

The arrival of a friend

And that was why I was still in the office when Toby arrived at four-fifteen. "I'm not late," Toby said defensively. She said that when she saw me. "I wrote down what you said." She pulled out a small gold-colored notebook. "Here," she read, "four-thirty. Technically, I'm fifteen minutes early."

I should have complained. It was a great mistake, but I was thinking about other matters. "All right," I said. And that was what made her suspicious.

Toby was a celebrity by marriage, although she didn't expect to be recognized by sight. Her husband was Calvin Gordon Koeffner. You read about him in the newspapers. The biggest surprise was that Toby was thirty-seven. Koeffner never married anyone that old before.

She was my oldest geographic friend. That was a category, a perfectly usable type of category into which I clumped those people who at one time or another lived nearby. It was a passage, life's movement. My husband made money. Martin always swore that he would make money. We moved from Avenue B to Washington Heights to Twenty-fourth Street to Seventy-third to Fifty-fourth to Henry Hudson Parkway. The last move was hard on Martin. He had never lived in the Bronx before.

Whenever we moved, we acquired people. We dropped people. We can't imagine seeing them again. The people next door. Why not have a drink right there? Bitter cold outside, freeze your buttocks off. Exchange a few laughs over that blonde who was seen in the elevator. What kind of building did we live in anyway? Simple propinquity for cold nights.

Toby was Washington Heights. A time of tall, angular rooms—nice. An absurd plaster frieze over a doorway, the large toe of a cherub chipped. Toby was a long time ago. She stuck, though. She was married to Raymond in Washington Heights. They lived two doors down, fifth floor. Toby wondered once whether there had been a 6 in the address. I said no. Six, she swore, was lucky. Anyway, she said she hardly remembered Raymond. I told her he had wavy brown hair and he swallowed his laughter. When he was a child someone must have told him that he laughed badly.

Together, Toby and I went back to her car. I guess I got in. But she was lost to me. I was elsewhere—perhaps already planning the packing. My mind wedded to the idea. Was I supposed to respond? Yes, Toby. A nod would do.

I dreamed away. I am an artist. An American artist. Yes, another American artist. Still another American artist. Worse yet—an American poet. Not Hallmark's kind of woman poet. And I had been prepared to die and leave behind what? My life in whose hands? Stop tittering! You think the life of an American poet was easy to come by.

Still, when I am dead, you will love me.

Everyone loves a dead American artist.

Toby was talking. Calvin didn't satisfy her. Maybe it was the vasectomy. People said it couldn't be the vasectomy, but maybe it was. No one satisfied Toby. The odd thing was that it wasn't about money. It was never about money. Calvin's not inventive, she said. His sex technique was virginal. The bloody weight of his body.

Toby, suppose I died tomorrow?

"He needs more sleep," she said, "than any man I have ever known. God, look at the traffic!"

Yes, suppose I died tomorrow. Unlikely—all right, unlikely. I owned Älois' compendium. Symptom followed symptom. Turn to page 63. Was I atypical? Hell no. So I couldn't die tomorrow. But it was speeding up. My very own neurological degeneration—a body pulled until it snapped, nuked, dissolved. I always knew what was going to happen. Did I mention that Älois had illustrations in his compendium?

My life's work. Everything could go. I felt—yes, I was ashamed to admit, I felt a responsibility to society. How terrible, how cruel would be the passage of an artist who left no trace.

Now the implication is not that malice would be employed by my near and dear. What would they save? A valentine signed with love, Yours.

I would have liked to be born in 1950 (actual birthdate 1948). The evenness of a 1950—true poet of the last half of the twentieth century. Died at age thirty-seven—that gave me about eleven months. Cleared it with Älois's symptom chart. Give or take a month.

We didn't speak of death in my house—not any specific death or death in general. My husband, Martin, declared these conversations morbid. My son, Paul, said such dwelling was insensitive to the living. Daughter Ruth turned away.

But when I died—my life ended. And the artifacts—the leavings of the artist—remained. But who would put them in proper order? Who would know what to keep? Eleven months to recapture my life. It would be best if I spent these eleven months—this brief time—in total devotion to myself.

The other day I received this letter sent to me by the Best Wish Foundation. Where did they get my name? Insurance company, or maybe my doctor sold names. Anyway, the Foundation was having a drawing—no tickets to be bought from the likes of me. No, I was to be a potential beneficiary. All I had to do was enter my wish. So it came to me to wish for a kind of aloneness. Not the American ideal, is it? Selfish, they'd say. But then weren't artists that way? Selfish little bastards.

To be alone—sort of. I thought of celibacy. Don't snicker. Why not celibacy? I can't even recall the feeling. The Best Wish people—bless their collective heart—sent a form for me to enter my wish on. I should have filled it out.

> *I wish not to be horny anymore.*
> *Yours truly,*
> *Bernadette Amy Marrkey*

Would they have appreciated that? Would it have sat well in their philanthropic craw? They expected me to want a trip. Married woman and mother of two yearned for trip to the Disneyland of her choice or Wall's Drug Store or Old Faithful. If I said hang gliding—they would have hired an ambulette and happily hauled me out to a cliff.

I tell you that the training of women is a bitch. How selfish can you be? I mean even at the very end of your life? Anyway, I'm sorry, Martin. I love you, Martin. But this is it. I'll try celibacy. I'll try it. I love my husband—yes, I do. But we must march down different paths. My energies are limited. The object is to be ignored—to be allowed to just be. Packing, sorting, putting in order.

I hadn't thought it through—closing up your life was a much too loud death rattle. Therefore, the packing must be done in secret—although openly. What you did in front of people never truly interested them.

What was Toby's subject now? She arched her swan-true neck. "So I couldn't help myself," she said. "I finally asked him, Jerry, what the hell are you doing with your friggin' eyes?"

Toby was watching me. I must have missed an appropriate response. Nodded when I should have said no. Toby's mascara-thickened eyelids flapped in sideways glances. Her skimpy nostrils flared—she had caught the scent. She always knew when something was up. What would satisfy her? Turn her attention from the truth?

I gave her the probable approach of my celibacy.

"You all right?" Toby said. Her eyes glittered warmly. She could hardly believe what I had said. She was trying to figure out who to share it with.

I closed the car door. "Sure," I said.

With good control I reached my apartment. I steadied myself, one hand on the wall, one hand on the telephone. Packing. The thought came at me like a continual assault. I must obtain boxes, cartons, tape. Facing the problems of packing, sorting, throwing out.

Beginning of preparations

How many cartons? the man said. How did I know how many cartons? Lady, we have to know. How did they come? They came in dozens by size. They came twenty-five by thirty, and they came sixty-five by forty, and they came seventeen by twenty-seven.

How many would be needed? Stuff, possessions, coruscations everywhere. Hell, let them send me a lot. An assortment— twelve dozen. Yes, four dozen in each of the three sizes.

Okay, you got 'em.

I thought I heard retribution in his telephone voice. What

had I done? Suddenly I saw a Hoover Dam of boxes. I had paid extra for quick delivery, and the truck, rattling down the road, calling attention to itself, arrived—the boxes came flattened. So I bribed the morning doorman, Louie, and Joseph for the afternoons. Store them for me, I said. I knew they had places.

I'll sneak the boxes into the apartment two at a time in arklike fashion. Two in empty, two out stuffed.

This was where details counted—the plan. I made a plan. Written with a black felt-tip pen on a relic of an envelope—a misplaced treasure from New York Telephone. According to this plan, the boxes will be filled in an orderly fashion—a geometric progression.

But still, I knew something remained undone.

I had always read the lives of poets rather than the lives of saints. All those records for their followers to pore over, to extract from, to interpret. And me? Yes, I was finally thinking ahead.

I needed a journal. Never mind that I had never kept one. I must write one now, a true diary. Forget that it will have to be after the fact.

Entries could be made as I packed each box. That constituted order, didn't it? My life as told by me. Nothing left out. An artist's life must be whatever an artist's life was.

The entries in the journal will be backdated. Definitely a problem—but rules of honesty will still apply. No fabrications or elaborate strategies of evasion. Put in everything. The works—all those undesirable moments. Adultery. All right, adultery. Then somewhere, there was a death—not mine—not yet. No, honesty must be honesty. Call it what it was. A killing. A murder. Made you sit up, eh? A murder. One lost in the middle of my life. But you have to wait until the right box comes up— journal entries accompany each box.

Hey, confessional poet—why wasn't *all that* in your poetry?

No, I won't flee from the truth or imply secret meanings. Yes, my poetry had certain omissions. To be reflected now in the journal—and maybe that, all that should have been in the poems. If life were completely accurate.

The reasons of omission—were varied. Lies, vows, fears. Like a deathbed promise that you shan't or that you will. Secrets, though. Secrets come out in time. The journal will be witness.

Anyway, in a new act of cowardice, the ultimate responsibility must be left to my literary executors. I empower them—rip from the journal any pages that you must. Acting in my behalf—of course.

So everything will be recounted in the journal as it appeared in my life—those disturbing moments on my back on the sheetless Stearns & Foster mattress and Shifton's laughter, the nosebleed, the rooms, legs across the shoulders.

I was a confessional poet—my life—my poems. So much did appear in my poetry. Basically, the journal will exist as a supplement, an additional account of what happened and why. The birth of an American artist. Was the path predestined? A genetic fix? Could I have gone somewhere else?

This will be a great task—and only eleven months available for packing, sorting, throwing out—and the preparation of a journal. But I can visualize my literary executors throwing up their collective hands without that journal. Impossible! they shout.

I answer all expected protests with this guidebook through my life. The poetry is what is important. Pile up my poetry. Don't worry. I won't recite my poems out loud. Anyway, my poems were never lyrical. If I must be labeled, why then, say confessional poet. User of life. Written down on paper. You will be able to read the best of the poems in my *Collected Works*—as soon as I die.

But the life—they always wanted the life. This life or rather my life as compiled must be considered as unique—not an example of child of the last half of the century.

Not a metaphor or a symbol. Merely the life of an American Artist—one Bernadette Amy Marrkey, 1948–(probably) 1985.

The packing commences

I had Louie send up two flattened cartons on Friday afternoon. I pushed them into the hall closet behind the coats. No one noticed. With true prescience, I thought that Friday night might be a bad night, and I figured that Saturday would be a good time to get started on my packing.

Usually on Saturday mornings I woke up at eight-thirty. The righteousness of the first one up—that offered the same smug pleasure as perfect attendance or the star at Sunday school. Who was better than the first one up? Once awake, I moved like some damn burglar afraid to flush the toilet lest someone hear.

But the Saturday morning of My Big Pack, where was I? Me, that self-appointed guardian of the morning? Hey, Bernadette! Head on my pillow, hedgehog breathing. Did I hear the telephone? Not a bell—oh no, not for us—more of a synthesized skittering of flute and horn and distant pipe. A joy, strangers exclaimed. Neoclassical music.

Christ, was it truly the telephone, or was I still dreaming and lost in that period of sleep known as rapid eye movements? I dreamed about the telephone. The dream didn't bring on the telephone call—no preternatural wish.

I was in the middle of this dream that so possessed me that I forgot my intentions. In this dream, I was struggling with a woman on the uptown Lexington Avenue subway. The woman had wild corkscrew curls and deep burgundy lipstick. She was trying to snatch away my book. Idiot, she screamed. You know nothing about poetry. I am Dorothy Parker.

Was I grateful to be awakened? I heard that cursed thing— the flute, the pipe, the horn. I lurched from sleep and went from bedroom to telephone. Could I stop the noise before my children awoke? My bare feet slid on the silky surface of the rug, and balance was not fully restored until my knees bumped viciously into the edge of the coffee table. A crazy bone pain skittered through me. Damn all telephones! In particular, this one!

I lifted the receiver. No idea what time it was. The receiver, you must understand, was no light object. When I died, I would not miss this telephone. I thought I said, "What? What?" But perhaps I responded properly.

Toby calling from Rye. Her voice a mirror of where she was, and what was happening. She was at the despair end of her emotional cycle. Toby in her house in Rye drinking her coffee from a cup with at least three painted roses crawling up its side. Her lip print on the rim of the cup, a half-moon of fiery red.

In my nightgown I was chilled. I focused on the freshly painted white gleam of the room. I tried to listen. At the end of the room a window was open an inch as protection against the toxins of heat. I scratched beneath my arm and by my breast, and shifted my weight restlessly from foot to foot. That window muzzled by a sheer white batiste curtain. Can you see through that curtain? Of course not. Anyway, nine stories up. Nothing tall across the street. It was light outside, light inside.

"I'm doomed," Toby said. It was her Saturday blues. I knew all about her Saturday blues. They lived, she would say, in my jewelry box, in my closet, in the glove compartment of my Buick. Waiting to pop out on Saturday. The blues started the year she had trouble with her second husband. I found out everything on a Saturday, she always said. She received a letter on a Saturday—a dirty letter—photographs, a few strands of hair, a stained rubber.

"I'm stuck in this house," Toby said. "What the hell is a city person like me doing in the suburbs? How's by you? Streets like shit here—snow, snow, snow."

"Like that here, too."

"Listen—you do it?"

"What?"

"What? What do you mean, what?"

I heard a click then, as the timer went on for the coffee maker. Martin would have set it. That was kind of him. Gone to the office. That was right—snow or no snow. It approached tax time. Those were his seasons. Before tax time. Near tax time. After tax time.

"Yes," I said. "I did it."

"My God—just like that! I mean at the moment you're in perfect condition, aren't you?"

"Perfect," I said. It was remission time. So I had my seasons too. Before remission. During remission. After remission.

"Bernadette, are you sure you meant it?"

"Yes, I meant it. I gave up sex forever."

"What did he do? Did he try to force you?"

"No."

God, I must pack. It was time for the journal.

These were the steps that led me to this place—now, I must start my work. The truth of my life will be revealed—how an artist grows, how an artist lives, and perhaps, even how an artist dies. Thus, the necessity for the preservation of these records.

JOURNAL

———————◻—————————

These are the entries to accompany Boxes 1 to 6—ages four to eight. Items of interest to be included are all artifacts that will illuminate, i.e., drawings, notebooks, letters, newspapers, photographs, menus, souvenirs—anything that seems to belong to the artist's life.

This was the start of my life—a cunning and bleating life. And how I became a poet. It had to be always knocking around inside me—that was what I believed. One of those little horror dolls banging against my rib cage. Try to be something else, see what it gets you.

I went to hear Marianne Moore read her poetry at the 92nd Street Y. A boy named Lucien took me (I hoped his name wasn't *his* idea). He didn't want to take me—we were both age fourteen. He thought that I was a zombie, a hot-and-fast girl. I saw him as the jerk-off prince. But I heard he was planning to go, and the next moment I'm pressing up against him. I caught him near his locker, wrapped two fingers edged in Dragon Lady no-chip polish and kept the door from closing. Two, I whispered, get two tickets. He figured I didn't know what I was getting into. I knew. His hand rested on my knee as we sat side by side in the auditorium. Hush, I said.

This is how I became a poet. I dreamed it. Every thought I ever had shaped into a line. Spit backward into childhood. These were my earliest recollections, unpinned from the back of my mind.

Remember an actress named Dora Lindt? I bet you don't recall Barbara Eida, Sylvie Haerter, Connela Renquist? These women took their turn standing at the apron of the stage, armfuls of scentless roses, the bow, the applause, the deeper bow—show décolletage, ladies. Every last one of those women—an actress.

They made movies—although not Connela. They had followers, scrapbooks, programs. Where are the women now? I see them rocketed into eternity. Gone, blown away, the press of time—too heavy. See it this way—even their scandals disappeared. The party at Zazu's when Connela appeared in diaphanous trousers, and then what happened before dessert.

Still, look up their names—you might find one or another in the indexes of those truly inclusive histories of the theater.

But the poet's focus, oh the poet's eye fell on Ursula Marilyn Berne. Don't rack your memory—if you never heard of the others, you certainly never heard of her. But she was pretty. A woman partial to clothes that outlined, profiled, unimagined the body. Shoes with heels that tilted the hips and pushed the rump up and out. Capture her at the height of her powers—slight and short though they were. Ten minutes of pretty—she had them. Long black hair, Gypsy curls, a valley of a dimple, sable-colored eyes. Blemished only by a tiny scar, curved like the moon in its last quarter, beneath the left earlobe. Her manner was copied from movies but nicely incorporated into her style. She was age twenty when she had her baby. She considered leaving the child in the hospital, not signing papers. No, just the silent good-bye and so long. She remembered movies where a baby was abandoned at the door of a church, usually in a snowstorm. She had thought about not having the baby—but that thought came too late. She failed to plan fast enough.

Then before alternatives appeared, she was out the hospital door, baby in hand and a bagful of samples of babyland's best.

Boy, was that baby lucky someone came along not to take

responsibility but to give a helping hand to Ursula Marilyn Berne. Ursula told the man she really wanted to become an actress. Anyway, she was going to be an actress.

The story Ursula later told her mother was that a man traveling through Rochester had told her that she was movie material. He gave her his card and didn't do more than put his arm around her shoulders, squeezing tight. See me in Hollywood, he said. Ursula was impressed. Perhaps the man left quickly, because he had to catch a train. She put his card in her wallet behind the paper picture of Susan Hayward that had come with the fan of plastic windows. Unlikely her mother believed a word of that tale. Her mother was nobody's fool.

I want you to know right from the start that all of this was hearsay, speculation, improvisation.

Now, here is where memory—that chamber of leftovers—actually started. In a room—the room was of no importance, ignore the room.

Ursula was humming, background music to a movie just before the big scene. She was movie material. It was 1952, and when questioned she sometimes said that her husband was in the army. Just another enlisted man stationed at Fort Dix. Another time she said he was in San Diego. But mostly he wasn't around.

That morning—the morning trapped in memory—she sat on the edge of the bed and slowly dressed. Her stockings were a shade called "Champagne Night." She liked names like that. "Tiffany Blue." "Palm Beach Pink." She raised one leg, slipped the stocking on—no one around—she caressed the length of the leg, kissed the knee.

Movie material. Purpose, she believed, was seventy-five percent of anything. That and energy. She was a bundle of energy. Hell, just look at her. Right then she stopped dressing, stood up, unzipped her robe, stepped right out of it. She was due at

Jipson's Restaurant at four, where she was the hostess and said "Follow me, please," and "Your waitress will be right with you." She practiced those phrases. You could be discovered in a restaurant, found, admired.

She calculated that she had at least ten minutes to spare. She unhooked the Sweetheart True Uplift Bra and was ready for the mirror. The front view was great, then side views. She cupped her breasts tenderly, the nipples bounced outward. God, I have it, she said. I could be an actress. I could be a goddamn good actress. Her breasts were small and high. Body styles change. Hers was popular. No sign on that smooth belly, those apple-cheek thighs of the birth of a baby. The kid slipped right through the hole, she used to joke. Sometimes a man laughed and said show me where.

Clad now only in her Summertime All Favorite Lace Panty in "Peekaboo Blue," she smiled lovingly at the mirror. She saw the child reflected in the background. An audience—an attentive, approving audience. That's right, she remembered, the kid was going to the woman next door or around the corner or over the pizzeria or across from the candy store.

"Are you hungry, baby? Want an apple?"

I shook my head. (This is me now—totally present.)

"If I took half—you take the other half?"

"Yes."

If that was what she wanted, that was what I wanted. I was willing to be agreeable.

"What do you think, baby? Am I going to be an actress or am I not? One day soon—out of this hot-plate heaven forever."

She rehooked the Sweetheart True Uplift Bra. The mirror caught her attention again. Maybe she meant to put on different clothes.

It was a rented-room mirror—pockmarked by the plagues of life, fastened to the back of a closet door with plastic-tipped screws in a starburst pattern. Sooty in appearance, that reflecting glass. Lipstick streaks—guess how they got there?

Quick-change artist Ursula Marilyn Berne stood in front of the mirror dressed now as if for a party or a masquerade. Where in the world had she found that flow of a black velvet skirt and shawl the color of marmalade? Who could look at her and not wonder about other shores?

"I am an actress," she said, beaming at the face. "An actress! Most certainly an actress."

She tried breathing hard, tried pouting lips. She could do a love scene. She knew that. The audience would be crawlingly orgiastic.

Poet that I was to be—I had a problem with the word. Did *actress* mean *mirror*? Why not? Watch Marilyn Ursula Berne closely. She will soon depart. But right now she brushed and twirled that ebony hair. Gypsy hair, the man said. A gorgeous Gypsy.

We all had our idols. Didn't I just mention Marianne Moore? I also think of Louise Bogan. So it was true of Ursula—the need for mentors, for models. Taped around the mirror were pictures of movie stars savagely ripped from magazines in beauty salons, waiting rooms, from the shelves of unattended newsstands. Rita Hayworth, Hedy Lamarr, Linda Darnell. Didn't *she* look as good? Ursula studied the pictures, she copied the movie star expressions, she added more makeup. Such twisting and turning, small pirouettes, arms akimbo, hands on hips. Clichés of the movies—she loved them all.

I waved at that body, but no response. My tears—experienced as I was—I knew would have brought forth no notice. How to capture her attention? The secret was mine. Forget any sobs for the maternal touch, whines for possessions, pulls at her flesh. You want her? Why then, play mirror. Mimicry was the key. Little girl, aged four, with black baby Gypsy hair.

Slyly, I moved to the mirror, knew my position—two steps back and one to the left (the right side was her best). She turned, I turned, she twisted, I twisted. Tiny child playing seductress beside her in the mirror. She giggled. "Look at you! My little bird. My bitsy actress. Let's bow, sugar." Together we bent over, but heads raised—her bow offered to an unseen crowd and mine to her. Then she dropped to her knees, momentarily careless of the pressure upon those "Champagne Night" nylon sheaths, and hugged me. I saw her smile reflected in the mirror.

Now, in order for me to have seen her smile that way, she had to be smiling at herself and not at me. Since that time I have noticed that people when faced with a mirror generally smile at themselves and not at you.

My mother was not responsible for my being a poet—just for my being. Her time had arrived. Oh fame, oh bigger-than-life celluloid fame. Ursula packed everything—two suitcases, one trunk. Could I be dropped off at a neighbor's? Sent forever to buy six cents' worth of Red Devils? No, I would tell. Sure as hell, I would tell. Announce my real name, *her* name—so forget that. Then she had an idea.

Actress, actress, actress. That was what the wheels of the car sang. The rhythm put me in a trance as I sprawled alone in the back seat, baby legs immodestly spread. The ride was long enough to be significant. I fidgeted recklessly. Sometimes, she yelled. Be still! The upholstery in the car felt like tiny brushes coming through my underpants. I jerked, sizzled, danced.

"George Washington Bridge, George Washington, Washington Bridge," Ursula sang. Truly, in voice no better than mine. She said that we were going to the Bronx to a lovely, lovely lady.

There was a man driving the car. Possibly this was Daddy. A

Daddy? The Daddy? Throughout this ride I heard her voice—
Ursula's voice. The man never spoke. On the other hand, he
could have been angry. "Just you wait," Ursula said to me. "You'll
have a grand time."

The car stopped. Ursula took me into a bathroom where my
face was scrubbed with wet paper. I was stripped of my traveling
garments—red slacks with a hole in the pocket where my
fingers had dug one—and peeled from my shoulders my white
blouse with its trails of chocolate from button to button.

Ursula had bought me a new dress—stiff green cotton with
yellow embroidered flowers, tendrils across the waistband. My
hands pulled at the yarn with its satisfying bumps and knots.

The man who never spoke—I had forgotten about his reaction to the dress.

"Waste of money," he said.

"That's what you think," Ursula said. "First impressions are
last impressions. Anyway, *she* likes kids looking good."

Ursula Marilyn Berne left me yearning to be an actress—slowed
my life down. I examined this obsession in several poems—
"Legacy," "Kinship Two," and "Stage Fright." In these poems I
evaluated and assessed the mother figure as obsession.

I have never wondered whether Ursula really meant to dump
me. Of course she meant to dump me. In the Bronx. An apartment house, two blocks off the Grand Concourse. It is not the
Bronx as you know it today—or even as it will be tomorrow. I
was headed for two and a half rooms facing the street—that
was the cachet. Facing the front. They smelled. God, those
rooms smelled of cleaning solutions, veils of disinfectant, songs
of bleach.

Who was there? Florence. "You didn't call me," she complained to Ursula whose coat was still buttoned. Of course they

didn't call her. She would have been prepared. Her no would have been firmly ready.

She was taken by surprise. Ursula knew that surprise was the way. She had told that to the man. Florence's Achilles' heel. A Florence surprised was a Florence confused. A woman who stood blinking in the low wattage—perhaps she had been dozing on the couch in her yellow and blue striped robe, a roadmap of seersucker, and her head a glittering marquee of tiny pins.

"What?" she kept saying. "What?"

Ursula sat me down on a couch that had a strange covering. A towel, I thought. Some words were whispered; later, voices grew louder.

"Listen," Ursula said to Florence, "give me a chance. A few months—what's a few lousy months? You can leave her with some neighbor during the day."

Ursula was on her way to Hollywood to be discovered. She didn't have time to sit down. She and the man were in a hurry. Did I guess that I wasn't going?

They overwhelmed Florence. They gave her a bottle of Evening in Paris cologne, they gave her a box of pale Fanny Farmer caramels—and me.

"Mine?" she said.

"We'll be back in two shakes," Ursula said, and knelt gracefully beside my chair. She unrolled a small calendar. "For you, honey," she said. "See, here are the doggies, Bernie. We're in the doggies month. Now flip the pages—each picture is like four weeks. Now see—here are the polar bears. We'll be back when the polar bears are on top. The calendar is yours, Bernie."

"You think she knows what the hell you're talking about?" the man said.

"Shut up!" Ursula said.

*   *   *

Was I made a mourner before my time? Were there no tears, no screams, no pulling at my mother? Take me, take me! Did my heart drizzle a confetti of pain? Perhaps I thought it all more playacting.

Florence never said that I yelled. I could have been reassured by the physical resemblance between Florence and Ursula—their nasal-harrumphing voices, their slouching stance, stick fingers drumming rat-a-tat, sharp gasps of coughing breath. Up close, though, Florence smelled like old potpourri. Ursula Marilyn Berne smelled of something in color.

We were alone. The woman stared at me, hopefully rubbed her eyes.

"What do I call you?" I asked.

She sighed—we were strangers to each other bound by blood. "Not Grandma. Nothing ages you like names. Call me Florence—you're too young for Flo. You want to eat?"

I shook my head. "I can do imitations," I said.

"Yeah? Who of?"

"Mae West," I said. Hand angled on my right hip, lips licked, I shrugged into character. "Why don't you come up and see me sometime!"

"That's not half bad. Who else?"

"Groucho Marx."

"Don't like him," Florence said. "Smelly cigars. Anyway, don't expect privileges. I got one bedroom—mine. You'll use the fold-up—you don't weigh enough to indent it. Do you roll around much?"

I shook my head.

"No sense in taking chances." Florence pulled a fold-up cot from a closet, past clanging hangers, and shoved it halfway into the kitchen alcove, where she ringed the bed with chairs—in case I rolled.

I had been left with a small gray suitcase—colorless nail

polish dabbed over its labels: *Paris, France* and *Rome, Italy.* Florence rummaged through the contents. "No pajamas! Christ, was I supposed to clothe and feed you too? Well—we'll go shopping Thursday—stores open late. I'll buy you one set—I'm not made of money. Till then—you'll sleep in your underwear."

Immediately afterward she spent a long time on the telephone. These were calls I knew about—arrangement calls. Ursula made such calls. It was arranged that I would spend the following day with a Mrs. Ludovic.

The next morning I was up early. Florence approved. I put on my traveling clothes—I figured it wasn't a green dress day. Still, Florence mumbled that the blouse was dirty, that the slacks were a disgrace. We had toast. She would have to buy milk. She took coffee black. So I had toast and apple juice.

Florence dressed, frowned at the mirror hanging on the back of the door. It was a small mirror—I didn't know they came that small.

"Anyway, you might as well learn from me," she said. "Fashion is my middle name, Bernadette. Pay attention to the way I dress. For instance, everyone this season is wearing white dots on navy. Now me—look at this. What color is this? . . . All right— so you don't know your colors. This is chartreuse dots on white. This is fashion."

The life of a poet begins in different ways. Florence was only forty years old when I arrived. I figured that out later. Forty years old and saddled with this kid. Blood was thick, she would say. Or, For God's sake, be still!

Two and a half rooms—we crowded them. When we were alone, Florence lived in Pond's Cold Cream and pin curlers. It was a case of saving both face and hair for important occasions. I learned from Florence the value of not wasting life.

Straight up front I say that I don't think Florence loved me—this is not to imply abuse. I wasn't her choice. Maybe if someone had told her for certain that she was never going to be free of me, she would have palmed me off fast before I settled in. But what happened, I think, was that I acquired after a time her smell—like a littermate. I became a member of her tribe, and she bossed me around, scrubbed me clean, disinfected me everywhere.

"Big ears," she said, "you mind your business—and when I say stay where you are—stay where you are." Where you are was behind a curtain. A curtain run up on a string. I slept behind it, graduated from the kitchen alcove to a corner of the living room.

The first curtain that separated me from other activities had purple stripes with rippling edges on a cerulean-blue background; later that cloth was replaced by one with outsize green roses printed on a trellis of yellow rayon. Once, a man from the other side of the curtain said, Flo, the kid is an albatross. And Flo said, Yeah. But I didn't hear any confidence in her voice. Perhaps she didn't know what that was. I liked the word—*albatross*. And years later, when I told Florence that one day I would no longer be an albatross around her neck, she stared at me like I was crazy. I don't know what happened to that man.

I am not going to say that behind that curtain was the place where I learned about life, because it wasn't. Forget sounds. I wasn't interested. My routine was different. My routine was based on experience. What I did at night was to visualize a mirror, and around the mirror a sulphur-yellow-colored dust that obscured everything. I stood in front of the mirror clad in Fruit of the Loom Cotton Underpants in "Plain Pink" and did my latest Mae West recitation. It was not quite counting sheep—but it worked.

*   *   *

The power of words came to me young, although my early life was neither dreamy nor full of reflection. But before I realized that I was a poet—there were other stages. Not to deny that the poet was always there.

Look, if I must live with Florence, I had to make the woman like me. So I went into my act. I observed, I watched. I went for the neighbors. I tried the poses learned at Ursula's side—a few innovations on her pas de deux. I did my Groucho Marx— outdoors you didn't have to consider cigar smoke. I was amusement for the women in Florence's building as they sat on canvas-covered folding chairs on the sidewalk in front of the entrance and monitored the traffic. They laughed. *Schöne Mädchen!* A regular little actress, the women said. I flirted, I giggled. My movements under control. Not a pretty kid—but perky. Like what's her name—yes, remember Fanny Brice? I hitched up my waistband, tucked sweat-dampened hair behind my ears, and tried a shuffle, tap, tap on the Bronx concrete. It was very tiring—out in the sun.

Florence was not displeased. "Well," she said, coming close to approval, "blood will tell."

My soul bloomed, and I readily accepted green blouses and maroon skirts.

My earliest entertainment was the movies. Florence preferred movies to television. And, of course, these excursions were important to a poet, surrounding me as they did with life.

The movies I saw with Florence were films in which actresses were wretched and betrayed. Barbara Stanwyck in trouble, Joan Crawford abandoned, Bette Davis adrift. I learned the value of tears and their possible use. I practiced the art of useful crying, which was different from the loud sobs that followed a scrape on the knee.

These were my favorite movies: *Home Is the Hero, Love in the Afternoon, Imitation of Life, A Certain Smile, The Cool and Crazy.*

Pads of paper were readily supplied to me. They were cheap. Paper kept me quiet. I started writing poetry when I was six years old. I say that so the inclination to believe I was some sort of thwarted actress is obliterated. I had simply publicly declared myself to be an actress, and I was embarrassed to admit that I had never meant it.

In high school, I joined the Drama Club. Those girls wore long, full wool skirts and hose. Others wore pleated skirts and white ankle socks. It set you apart. My friends were Myra Davies, Ellen Kealer, and Louanne Smith. We had all declared for Drama.

"Guess what?" Ellen Kealer said one afternoon. If the group had a leader, that was Ellen—she came from a line of matriarchal rulers. "My uncle does business with Ida Lamprey's nephew. And he said that he could get me in to see her. Me and maybe two, three others. You want to go?"

We nodded.

There was a conscious pause, and I asked the question. "Who is Ida Lamprey?"

Everyone stared at me with scorn.

"An actress—for God's sake," Ellen said. "My uncle says she was in everything. Her nephew told my uncle that Maxwell Anderson was supposed to have adored her acting. She was in *Awake and Sing.* She was in *Our Town.* She was in *The Little Foxes.* He even thinks she studied with Stanislavski."

"What about movies?" Myra asked.

"She didn't like them."

"That says plenty," Louanne said.

We exchanged glances.

"They put her in Westerns with Randolph Scott."

"To puke," Myra said.

On Saturday, we assembled outside Ellen's building. We were headed for Broadway—actually one block off Broadway, to the west. The sunlight flashed a rusty glow. The air was rich with urban fragrances. It was February. We all wore long black skirts, short jackets, and dangling from our necks were bright scarves with fringed ends. Mine was the most colorful—chartreuse, black, and white. And once safely away, I put on Florence's mother-of-pearl earrings—borrowed.

We felt almost too good to be grown-up. So we laughed, mooned, and shoved each other, anticipating the event, the day. It was too exciting for dignity. An actress up close. The real thing!

We rode the subway downtown, shuddering together, ignoring the seasick motion. The ride seemed long. "Should we eat first?" Louanne asked when we reached our stop.

"Don't be stupid," Ellen said.

"How old is Ida Lamprey?" I asked.

Ellen shrugged. "Retired. My uncle said she's retired." Ellen had spent the entire ride pulling again and again a piece of paper from her pocket and squinting at the address slowly fading into the folds. In truth, we were nervous, our hearts gyrated, our voices pealed from a distance into our dazed ears.

There, there. We pointed. The address was right, but it was no castle. Ida Lamprey lived in an ordinary gray stone building. A gray stone building—home to a thousand aunts. A chipped gargoyle slavered over the doorway, a sightless lantern swung above that carved symbol of teratology.

Our timing was off. It was a quarter to eleven—we were

expected at eleven. We didn't have the nerve to ring the bell early. I saw our reflection in a window. I thought we looked exotic—even older.

We stood outside, stamping our feet in the cold, and spoke about absent comrades.

"Marilyn Rose got the role of Cassandra."

"What did you expect?"

"She stinks."

"Yeah, but she rubs up against good old Coach Kelly. Oh Mr. Kelly, sir-rah, is mah interpretation right? Ah mean do ah have it?"

We pushed each other with glee. Never you mind, Marilyn Rose. We were going somewhere. We are tomorrow.

"It's time," Ellen said.

We sobered. Our manner grew rapt and formal. Ellen rang the bell, another bell responded. Ellen's silhouette firmed into dowager lines. She pulled open the lobby door, and like the chorus in a musical comedy, we tumbled after her. I sniffed the air. Why, this building smelled like *our* buildings. Salami, a harvest of garlic, time-coarsened flavors. The very air blotted with oily stillness. Cracked tiles under our feet. Blue and white shaping hexagon designs—floor to a million bathrooms. A tricycle rested on an unraveling hemp doormat.

Still, when the elevator came, an old man pulled back the gate. We had to operate our own elevators. "Five," Ellen said. Would he ask where we were going?

"Five."

For my friends—this was their first actress. It was my second. The first, of course, being Ursula Marilyn Berne. But I assumed no air of superiority.

On five, in the narrow darkened hallway, a door, as if sha-zamed, flew open. The woman in front of us was wrapped in soft, pink flesh. She allowed a moment of silence. Temperament

and breeding wandered across her face. I almost backed away—
but Louanne's bulk blocked escape. The presence wore a long
dress of ecru lace over watery taffeta—or was it a robe? It was
clean, in good shape—this wasn't any Miss Havisham. The
silvery hair lacquered into a cornucopia of pinned curls and
rolls. She wore a map of beige powder, mandarin-red lipstick,
cunning mauve rouge. The very sight of her silenced us. She
had the walk, the carriage, the movements—the woman was an
actress.

"Girls," she said. "Come in."

The apartment resembled whose? Silvzunski, who lived
downstairs in rooms that faced the back courtyard? I used to go
there when Florence played cards. Or perhaps the fat balding
woman with the tufts of straw-white hair—what was her name?
Lusha. Mrs. Bergmann's apartment? Ellen's apartment? I took a
deep breath—surely it was only a first impression—this ordi-
nariness.

The tunnel-shaped living room was seedy, especially with all
the shades up. Papers piled upon notebooks piled upon pictures.
Already it was better. Look at that clutter. What aunt or named
cousin tolerated that? See the single shoe beneath the chair. Yes,
this was the aftermath of a life in the theater. The piano covered
with a velvet throw embossed to resemble the mysteries of an
Oriental rug.

"My dears," Ida Lamprey sang robustly. "Sit—no, no. All of
you on the couch—it's a big couch. That way I can see you."
She gestured at the couch, and we sank into the cushions, felt
the rising springs.

"Tea?"

Tea? We wanted Cokes and cold beer. She would have immediately won our hearts with the offer of a cocktail—never mind
the hour. A drink with a debonair sound—Pink Lady.

We would have refused the tea—our hands, our legs, our

hearts trembled. Thank you, but no. But how? She was going to serve us tea, she had planned to serve us tea. In front of her chair on a small table was a green glazed teapot with dragon-shaped handle and a row of matching cups. So we must nod, and murmur acquiescence, and china warred lustily against china.

"I have been told that you are all aspiring actresses. *N'est-ce pas?*" She stared at us, eyed us, evaluated us. "My life," she began, "was only the stage." She plunged us through a repertoire of plays we had never heard about with plots that turned on maimed soldier heroes, amnesiac heroines, and lovers mistaken. Directors named Mario or Tomas or Bojack, cheating publicity men, vanishing agents. Ida's roles were fat, her suitors multitudinous. Had we heard of her Grand Tour of the West? The ardent imprecations of the press? We numbed to the voice.

"Movies?"

Louanne, how did you find the courage?

"Avoid them," said Ida Lamprey. "Movies are death to the actress. The theater in the thirties—that was theater. Look here, see this."

She reached beneath her chair where scrapbooks were piled. She opened a red-bound book—tiny bits of browned newsprint fluttered and arabesqued mothlike into the air. She showed us programs of plays that had lived in vanished theaters. Glossy pictures veined with cracks. Ida Lamprey smiling and regal in *Summer of the Aristocrat*. Ida in gingham and apron in *Kansas Summer*. Ida dressed like a streetwalker in *Sea*.

She warmed to the audience. Where we sat—the four of us imprisoned side by side on the couch, our shoulders grown plump from the curve of the feather-filled velvet cushions, with the descending sun casting a mist of light into our eyes. We blinked, looked away, lost our concentration.

Was it something in a scrapbook that set her off? Perhaps a disintegrating clipping made her want to tell the story before it vanished. Or was she lonely? Yes, lonely for someone to carry forward the secrets of her past.

"Girls," she said, "shall I give you a little *soupçon* of life? Why not? Look at you—I can see that none of you is too young to know about love. And, of course, love is what life is for an actress.

"What shall tell you? It was not the love of my life. For an actress—and don't forget—the love of her life is theater.

"But this was an event. Yes, an event that happened the year—the first year—I was in London and playing a West End theater called Sheridan's. A little comedy called *Simply Sally*. The ingenue was quite terrible. A matinee performance—that stupid girl was delayed somewhere or planned to be. Nevertheless, someone else was to play my role, and I was told to prepare to play Sally. It meant nothing to me—not at a matinee. I was simply annoyed. They had to pin the costumes—I was thinner.

"Listen, girls, pay close attention. Life, you see, is making the best of coincidences. Do remember that. I could have gone on and given a lackluster performance that afternoon—been careless. But no—I went on as if that performance mattered. Now, no one had told me in advance—basically unforgivable—that His Royal Highness was present in the audience. I never knew.

"Yes, exactly what you are thinking. Edward, the Prince of Wales. Well, immediately the curtain went down, I was all for slipping out of those too loose clothes and going out for a pot of tea—that was when they told me. He was coming backstage. I didn't even have time to change, and up close you could see the safety pins in the dress. Then there he was.

"Oh girls, imagine! A prince—no matter what. Truly a prince. Though what a thin, pale, and unhappy young man, who kept plucking at his sleeve. Still, his eyes were mysterious. Silvery-gray cages—those eyes. I tell you right off that yes, I was older—not that much—but some.

"I curtsied, a skill of acting. His Royal Highness offered compliments, and then, although I was terribly pleased, I assumed that was that. But the very next day a messenger arrived, and I was handed an envelope. Such stationery—creamy and opulent and scented with an entire grove of lime trees. I was invited to dine with His Royal Highness! I nearly fainted in the dressing room. The invitation was for Saturday. Three days to go! My heart was exploding.

"To whom could I turn for advice? Envious people could not be chosen. How to behave? What to wear? There was certainly no time to find a dressmaker. I cadged the key to the storage locker at the theater. Among a million bits of silk I found the dress—a costume used for the role of Queen Christiana in *Forgiven*. It was peach satin, thick as a carpet. It was superb.

"Now in truth, Wallis Simpson was already on the scene. Simping Simpson, I called her. If she couldn't hold him—none of my business. The Prince sent a car to the theater to carry me to a house borrowed for the evening.

"The dinner I scarcely remember—cold boned trout, the creamiest of vichyssoise, goose Esterházy, sweetbreads velouté, puree of broccoli, pomme de terre Richelieu, macédoine of fruit, Grand Marnier soufflé, a Château Lagrade, 1882, and an 1894 Rothschild.

"Afterward, we took our coffee in a small drawing room, where we sat side by side on a couch. Empire couch. Suddenly, that royal hand was on my peach-colored knee—a hold incredibly firm. Then what happened—was a marvel.

"Soon I saw him every Saturday in one house or another. I thought the girl who had the role of Sally would kill me. Another bloody American! she was heard to say.

"The Prince was a man made for sorrows. Else that divorcée would never have hooked him. He liked to sit in the evening after his brandy and embroider—he did skilled needlework.

Used beautiful thimbles—like jewels. I can't even put up a hem.
I remember to this day that he was working on a garland of pea-
green flowers—heartrending flowers, I thought. So unreal. The
background was cream-colored linen.

"What shall I say? The world overflows with some details. I
will simply say that he was not an experienced lover. Then
too—what they never speak about. He was troubled with common warts—verruca vulgaris—on his chest and back. Tiny
nubs in a random pattern. I actually went to the chemist's—
nervy girl—and bought him a tube of William's Wart Remover
in a tar base. He thanked me. I wasn't squeamish, but I gave
myself a good look-over after our Saturdays.

"Of course, *she* had to hear about us. I could have fought
Wallis Simpson—perhaps even come out the victor. Ah, but
the poor man. Can't you see the headlines? Prince as prize in
fight between Americans—the divorcée and the actress. I
could not do that to him. I decided that the Prince was not to
be my fate. I had my career and a good role waiting for me in
New York."

Ida Lamprey bowed her head, took a breath, and reached for
her cup of tea. Ellen grabbed the chance. It was two-thirty.
"Excuse me," she said, "but I promised my mother that I would
be home by three." It was the same artificially sweet voice that I
remembered Ellen had used in *The Importance of Being Earnest*. An
upbeat inflection at the end of each sentence convinces the
listener that what you said was true. Our drama coach told us
that.

Ida Lamprey rose unsteadily, legs numbed by sitting too long.
Or perhaps it was only the intrusion of the present. "Of course,"
she said.

There was the struggle into jackets, the polite thank-yous,
then we were outside. It was colder.

"Look at this," Ellen said, and pulled paper from beneath her jacket. "I lifted it when the old bag was pushing away ye ancient tea cart. Cuckoo will never miss it."

We stared. It was a program from *Affairs of Anatol* starring John Barrymore. His photograph on the cover. A profile staring east.

"Christ!" Louanne said.

"She didn't show us this one, did she? And," Ellen said triumphantly, and pointed, "look how far down Ida Lamprey is in the listing for something really important—she's among the flotsam."

We stopped for hot dogs and then went on to the subway. We were tired now, almost sleepy. We grumbled, complained. The ride dragged on. We hadn't learned what we wanted to know. What was that? The secrets of life as an actress.

I clung to a pole on the subway. Peach-colored satin just a blush past virginal. The actress sitting so still, and his hand. The intensity behind the long, cool fingers resting on her knee—and she hardly feeling the pressure because the material was so thick. But her speckless breasts were half exposed by Queen Christiana's dress. Then later—a zipper?—no, hooks. His hands were skilled—the precision of needlework. Slowly, he undid each hook. The satin dropped—she was ankle-deep in cloth. He loved her. He made love to her. She took him—the strange man whose chest and back bore tiny fleshly pegs. I saw them—his legs, her legs.

I was poked sharply.

"All that garbage about the movies," Myra said. "Just because she didn't make it in Hollywood."

"You bet!"

"And," Ellen said, "did any of you believe that shit about her and His Royal Pain in the Ass—Prince Warty Needlework?"

"No."

Then she looked at me.

It was the pull of that group to which I belonged. How could I resist those faces—tiny, mean eyes.

"No," I said.

The assent was unanimous. Why had we done that? Was it in a revelry of envy?

The woman faded, of course. I had killed the vision. Oh, what had become of that peach satin? That hand upon the knee? I had denied Ida Lamprey's life. Too late to recall my word. I made the truth go away. Peach-colored satin that could have danced in my words. I had believed her. And having believed her—it was betrayal. My heart, you understand, had carried me right with them into the bedroom, the naked Prince and Ida, the borrowed gown in carnage. I could have done it in words. And now what was left to me? I could not write the poem. The poem that was almost complete within me.

What a loss!

By age six, I had written not entire poems but rather single lines that pleased me. These lines contained only pictures of the world as I knew it. A young poet's world. Babushkas, chairs, candles, rag rugs. Those symbols I saw—their meaning I put into my words. In a way I wrote directly into history.

Some symbols in life you cannot trace. Show me an armor-gray cat with stripes and I jump, my skin chills, and some ancient aversion engulfs me. And if I cannot avoid the cat—my nerves become a fretwork of wires. Yet why? I must leave that to another life.

On the other hand, I have been obsessed—yes, and harassed—by a pattern of white feathers looping and entwining on a beige background—a clever creation of two-dimensional feathers achieved through shadings of chalk white to clotted cream to parrot gray—building a puffiness. Now, the effect of that pattern that waved its countryless flag in front of me was always traceable—no costly analysis needed.

I admit that no poem exists that carries this burden. A dozen times I tried to write about feathers of white. Each time, my fingers curled around the pencil and stopped as if the words could not exist, or no one would want them. Or as if they were taboo—as if it were a charmless conspiracy, a poet's block—in chill, I could not.

I have started backward for no reason more persuasive than that this very morning I read in the newspaper a rave review for a famous Shakespearean actress, Dorthea Minders, whose portrayal of Portia was declared a triumph. She carried the play, her every gesture a campaign of skill, her pouting mouth a beatitude. Who was this Dorthea-Portia to me? She and her husband had been Martin's clients for a long time. The connection to them was through my marriage.

That review bounced me back to 1980, which was the first year of my illness. How severe was the prognosis? No one knew. Let me state that I did not date events as before my illness or during my illness or after my illness. I simply remembered that was the year.

It was an invitation extended by Dorthea Minders and husband. An afternoon party in their new house in Southampton. I was hardly dazzled by the idea. Consider that it was August. Forget that I was in the middle of the series of poems entitled "Basic Knowledge"—take into account what a summer ride from the city meant. What was at the end of this ride? A two-hour party. That thought plunged me to the fulcrum of dissent.

"I don't want to go."

We were in the bedroom on either side of the bed, on which had been thrown a summer coverlet of cotton with its bas relief design of seasonless peonies. Martin wore only his Jockey shorts, I wore nameless white cotton underpants. My knees bumped the bed and it swayed as if beaching were ahead. It was a sexless scene, as are most scenes of marital war. Nude, we would not have appealed to each other.

"I don't understand," Martin said in a husband's voice of muted violence. "What is so terrible? Tell me, what is so terrible? All you have to do is sit in the car—in the damn air-conditioned car. I'm driving."

"I don't want to go."

"They pay me—you know that? They are my fucking clients. The source—I might add—of your support. The invitation was for the two of us. Do I ask you to do this every day? And what the hell do you have to do that is so important anyway? The kids are at camp. It's a goddamn Sunday."

"I am in the middle of a poem—I am writing, planning to write, writing the entire afternoon."

There was a pause. He was changing tactics, one hairy finger went to his mouth, and he crunched a nail. "Listen, Bernie," he said, "they always have theater people, movie people—almost no one else. You'll love it. You know how you feel about the theater."

"What?"

"The theater."

"I feel nothing about the theater."

"Come on, Bernie, don't get on your high horse. You're as stagestruck as anybody. You were acting in that off-Broadway workshop when we met the second time. You were a drama major. You just knew when to pull out. Now—I am asking you to come with me this afternoon. Write your poems tomorrow. You have Monday through Friday to write your poems."

*   *   *

Stagestruck—God, he didn't know me! I got dressed swiftly, carelessly. For now the urge to write—at best a frail entity— passed. I can never write in a spirit of anger—it dulls my receipt of visions.

We had a two-and-a-half-hour ride. We rode in hostility. I would have whistled my approval at the sun-bronzed backs of cars forming the camel train in front of us. I yearned for break- downs, traffic cops snarling in victory, the furious blare of radios gone mad.

But when we arrived, I was amazed at the beauty of the new house. I felt joy, and the fence guarding my emotions lowered. Never mind how I had arrived. Or that my lips had tasted submission.

What I saw was a fabled tower made of cedar ringed by cathedral-like windows. I felt that design. I was trapped in that interior coolness, laced with green, curious corridors. The long trip forgotten.

I understood that I was not important to the afternoon's function—merely that I be there. We parted. Martin went in the other direction. That allowed me freedom to wander among the invited—Geraldine Fitzgerald, Bill and Susie Flynn, Julie Harris, Basil Humbolt, Jason Robards, Dominic Rutkin, Win- ston Xavier.

Dora's husband squeezed my arm and gave me a drink popu- lar that season—a healthy-looking fruit juice pink with gin. I wandered uncontrolled through the rooms. Dora, I knew, bought many paintings. She had a Collection. She referred to it as *the* Collection. Now some were granted space here. Large canvases awesomely blotchy.

Back and forth I roamed until I followed a group of new arrivals out onto the terrace. William Inge, Alexis Smith, Max- well Titsch, Bradford and Lou Pillard.

It cannot be explained why I looked down. One moved in certain ways, here the glance, then the head thrown back. Or downward. Perhaps the sunlight was too intense. Nevertheless, I looked down, my feet already planted on the terrace—I wore sandals that day—flat and fashionable sandals. Yet with excruciating exactness I slipped on the grooved floor. My legs neatly folded. Glass, splatters of pink, ice cubes, flung everywhere. People were at my side in an instant.

"Are you hurt?" two, three voices queried.

"No, no," I said, pained by the embarrassment of being seen, and took someone's arm for support and stood up. "It's nothing—I am not hurt."

Martin wanted me to lie down. Had I tired myself? No, I had not. This occurred in the early stages of my illness—its course as yet not fully known to us. But the fall—I knew what had caused it. Could I admit it? Could I say I fell at the sight of the tiles on that terrace? Only at the sight of them. Tiles that had printed feathers of white on beige. I could not, no one could have.

So I stayed in the house for the rest of the afternoon.

Life must be a series of pleats or wrinkles—and endless. So certain things created to oppress—and not to let go—must occur again. Things as well as events are cyclical—the tiles reappeared. Now, much of this type of experience I dealt with in a series of poems entitled "Backwards, Forwards, Again"— although those poems were written in 1969, they expressed the emotions of how this felt. Not that I ever wrote the words "feathers of white on a beige background." No, but the sense of doom, of approaching annihilation, of coming apocalyptic events, was in that poem—pared down to twenty-seven lines.

At any rate, the tiles reappeared many years later. In 1983 to be exact. Because of the remodeling. The kitchen. We had planned to make some changes in the kitchen before we moved into our new apartment—purchased less than a year earlier. Forties patterns had emerged again. By now, shopping tired me. Martin made all the initial shopping forays and took me whenever possible to see his finds.

It was obvious what he had found for the new flooring. Beige tiles with a white feathery pattern—a copy of a popular linoleum circa 1940.

And once again at the sight of the hated design—intense nausea and sour taste and yes, even a sharp pain in my back. I staggered, and Martin's arm was around me at once. He thought what happened was caused by my illness and looked grief-stricken. I took my trepidation in hand—could I go through life such a prisoner? We must buy that tile, I insisted, before collapsing.

Yet to trace this mindless distaste for a mere tile was never difficult. Even so, a spell of coughing paroxysms seemed imminent, controlled only by pushing my nails into my palms. My bladder shuddered and my body threatened herniation.

The tiles? Oh yes, the source for this dislike can be absolutely pinpointed to the day when I was six years old and Ursula Marilyn Berne returned to New York. Can't you see it? An August afternoon, the enameled sun, a child's Saturday, and I, sweaty from a successful street game of tag, ran upstairs. Sometimes Florence didn't work on Saturdays in summer when things grew slow in the cleaning supply business. Yes, that day she sat in the living room with Ursula and a man. A fan in the window briskly stirred the unfiltered detritus of the city. You must understand, I was not prepared for the reappearance of the actress with her pale oval face and her black curls.

"My sugar pie," Ursula said.

It must have been caused by the heat—a child's disposition toward the dramatic. I threw myself down on the linoleum, and my voice became the crackle of an animal that keened and wailed. *Yah-wee, yah-wee.* I lay on my back and flung my legs first up then down like scissors slicing up the floor. My body writhed as if into a fit. I don't believe the pattern on that linoleum was raised, and the sensation of crushing feathery curves beneath my body as I rolled down beige hills was probably not real. The scent of true city air was powerful although untrustworthy.

The screams—blood must have poured into my head—else how could I have had the strength to support such frenzied sound. No doubt I would soon have rent my shirt, pounded my head against the wall, and retched.

Of course, they yelled back. Stop! they shouted. Catch her, for God's sake catch her. Ursula bent over, but quickly jumped back to dodge my flying feet shod in Buster Brown oxfords. The scene was mine. I could not be stopped.

"A basket case. She's off her rocker," the strange man said.

"Christ—you better get out," Florence said.

After they left, my internal storm subsided. Florence trapped me in her arms, I could no longer resist. She stripped off my clothes and sponged my body with a rag dipped in a mixture of water and some sweet-smelling cologne.

"Baby," she said.

Dinner was an unannounced series of favorites—hot dogs, beans simmered with catsup and molasses, dill pickles. Chocolate pudding. And glasses of Florence's special lemonade—made the way I liked it with just a touch of sugar.

Later that night, I thought about the reappearance of Ursula. She looked the same—absolutely the same. Whereas I knew that I had grown taller and now wore my hair in a thick braid. I came to a child's conclusion that some people changed and others did not.

Did she march past me again? Never. Although Ursula Marilyn Berne sometimes sent postcards to Florence. The last one arrived when I was age twelve. Afterward, whenever I thought of Ursula, I thought of her as dead. That shows how far the anger of a child carried. My friend Toby once suggested that I ought to try and find Ursula—she's your mother after all, she said—but I decided that was only Toby's curiosity and not mine.

Although I believed that Ursula's whereabouts were known to Florence, all I knew was that Ursula actually did go to Hollywood. That was because of the movie—a real movie.

It was 1956, my teacher's name was Lawrence, I was a member of the stage crew for *The Boy Lincoln*, and was in the middle of a long narrative poem about subway sounds. And Ursula Marilyn Berne appeared in a film called *Crowded Nights*. Forget looking for the movie. Who would have saved it? Who told us about *Crowded Nights*? Ursula sent Florence a postcard announcing her coming triumph.

"Wait until you hear this, Bernadette," Florence said. You'll never believe it." She read the postcard out loud. "Can you believe this?"

"No," I said.

Still, we began to read movie advertisements regularly. I was the one who saw the announcement. "It's hit the papers," I said.

Ursula Marilyn Berne wasn't actually listed in the screen credits, but she could be recognized in three separate scenes. Twice, she sat on a train—they put a hat trimmed with flowers on her once, and the other time she held a magazine. The best shot was when she was dancing—a flamenco dance in the background—while at a small table in a restaurant a man and woman plotted the murder of the woman's husband. Florence took me to the Paradise on the Grand Concourse to see the movie. Great theater—I loved the clouds on the ceiling. We hid out in the ladies' room after each showing when the ushers were trying to get rid of people. In all, we saw the movie five times, each screening with a fresh Hershey bar.

Although I began to write poetry at age six, I considered that as a secret vice or a hobby. My energies, my thoughts, and my dreams had for so long been concentrated on becoming an actress.

However, with the egotism and self-concern of youth, it had never occurred to me that others around me might have pursued such an ambition. On a Sunday afternoon, I sprawled on the couch reading about the life of Lillian Gish. Were such lives still possible? I stretched, looked up, and saw Florence sitting at the table drinking coffee. Her gaze was uncharacteristically introspective and even remote—neither smiling nor even aware of me. Florence was always someone I saw entirely in the present, as if her past had dropped into some forgotten hole, her spirits constantly in neutral. It was the first time I wondered about Florence. So I asked a question—a start-up question— certain that it would bring a denial.

"Did you ever want to be an actress, Florence?" After all, almost everyone had imagined themselves in a movie at some time.

Did Florence look at me? Past me? Had I caught her off guard?

"Actress? I was a kind of show girl once," Florence said, and then, realizing the extent of the admission, blushed, rosy streaks showing through cold cream.

What had I thought? That Florence always did what she did. And even that was a kind of acting—Florence was a demonstrator of cleaning products in department stores. Spots gone before your eyes.

I gave her no time to retreat from her confession. Florence as show girl!

"That's great," I said, and dropped my book. I sat up and firmly planted my feet on the ground. "Why didn't you ever tell me before?" If that was true—was there then genetic predisposition? "When?" I asked. "Where?"

"Now I started something," Florence said. She had regained control. "It was nothing."

"Something!" I watched her—possibly she wanted to tell—a shimmer of saliva at the corner of her mouth, the flutter of a shoulder. Did she want to retrieve the tale from memory storage?

"Christ—you don't let up," she said. "Before you were born— I was up in Buffalo."

"Buffalo? How did you get there?"

"Oh, one thing and another. Anyway, I needed a job—money to get back home. I can't sing and I can't dance. Let's not pretend—I know what I hear. But—oh well—I was young. Young goes a long way." Her fingers made a melancholy passage through her hair from pin to pin. "Life is luck and a lot of coincidences. Go and try the Chester Club, I was told. Some girl got fired or walked off. It wasn't much of a club—but they had a show and a chorus of six girls. I auditioned and believe me, that was nothing to shout about. But the man said I was cute enough—and the noise of the other girls would cover up my voice.

"Look—nothing happened—I knew how to take care of myself. But this man had an eye for me. Never mind that he had a wife. Strange things happen in this world, Bernadette. This wife was like a dwarf—almost. She wasn't ugly, but he was maybe five feet seven or so, and she, barely four feet. She had an odor about her, a milky sour odor, and a way of wheezing when she spoke— which wasn't often. The man was always asking me out for a drink and I was always saying no. All right, once or twice we had a drink together. A couple of the girls were jealous, because he wasn't bad-looking. Then one day his wife isn't around. God, that gave me the chill, just recalling that. I mean one day she was there—the next, gone. It was all we could talk about, whispering in the dressing room. Five days since she'd been seen. Five whole days. Someone said that he probably killed her. To tell you the truth, I half believed it and was scared.

"One of the girls—Rosemary—pointed out a suitcase. A thick one—what we used to call a Pullman case. It had sort of suddenly appeared on a high shelf above where the keys were hung. That wife could have fitted in the suitcase.

"I had to know—so I got Rosemary, and the two of us stood on a chair and pulled the suitcase down. It was locked, so I used a nail file on it. There was something inside—soft and small and wrapped in a white towel that was pinned together with a safety pin.

"We were too frightened to yell. We closed that suitcase, and how the hell we got it back up on the shelf I never knew. That evening just before we went onstage, the wife suddenly showed up—looking kind of pale. Anyway, that night I packed up and bought a ticket home. I never sang or danced again. Enough was enough."

"Florence," I said, "what did your dressing room look like?"

"You forget everything you just heard—or you'll be sorry, young lady!"

Florence was never given to compliments. But one evening when I was brushing my hair, she said, almost in amazement, "I really think you could be an actress. You've got your looks—it happens that way sometimes."

Did I? Had my looks finally arrived? I pushed my face close to the mirror. I looked the same. Still, if Florence was right—

could I be destined—yes, even forced—into a life of acting? The next day, I went to a barbershop.

"Cut it," I ordered.

"Your mother know?" he said.

"Yes."

My best role in school came when I played Petra in *An Enemy of the People*. I wasn't terribly good. I had the family voice—Florence's voice. No competition for the blonde who played Mrs. Stockmann. When she spoke, you listened.

I had to work to memorize the lines. Couldn't keep my mind on them. Even Florence coached me. The crew that painted scenery had its usual good time—that's where I wanted to be—I wanted to rejoin them, but someone had whispered star in my ear.

It was a feeble talent that I possessed. If I had greater courage, I would never have walked on any stage. The extent of my inability to risk embarrassment can be seen in what I had printed beneath my picture in my high school yearbook—*Ambition: To be a great actress*. There was an explication of this in my four short verses entitled "Part Two: Stage Fright Came and Went."

I was grateful that I eventually understood what an actress was—and that I wasted no further time on that charade. Martin always had many clients who were actresses. I met them, but we hardly did more than exchange a greeting. Martin tended to their business—and I was the wife. It never mattered. You might say that I had my fill of actresses.

On the other hand, there was a last actress. One dreadful summer—a summer of endless heat. Historic scorcher, the newspapers said. I have often wondered about the truth of such observations. Don't we set events in that way, swearing they occurred in the fiercest snowstorm—the world a whiteout. Or the wind bore down like a locomotive pulling the city's debris. And the sun, surely the sun was a livid crescent. Perhaps the magical powers of weather were necessary for some memories to be real.

Nevertheless, it started off as a good summer. We had moved again. Things are rolling, baby, Martin said. He felt good. He had huge air conditioners installed in our new windows. We made love on chilly sheets. My sweetheart, Martin said. Just look where we are now!

I could have stayed home—we had the new air conditioners. Martin would have nothing to do with that. We'll take a house, he said. On the Cape. Actually, it turned out that he had already done that.

The hottest summer in many years. Fry on a stone, fry on a wall—each exposed surface a griddle. Martin found a girl. Her name was Naomi, the niece of someone in Martin's firm. She was to take care of the children. At first I protested, but then it sounded good. I began to think of this as *my* summer. A poetry summer.

That lasted less than a week. Naomi abandoned our house. It was a boy. He had betrayed her. I thought it happened too soon. Naomi said no. I must understand, she begged. How could she look at that particular ocean. Or that wave. That one over there that flung itself to mindless dissolution on the shore. No, she could not. There was nothing for it. She could not.

"Shit," Martin said over the telephone from the city. "Why did you let her go?"

"How could I stop her?"

"You could have. What are we to do now?"

"I'll take care of the children—who else?"

*   *   *

From a penciled note on the local supermarket bulletin board, I found a day worker to piddle through the rooms with a dust-cloth and weep over the refrigerator.

Martin was pleased with the house he had rented. It was near Wellfleet. It was on the water. Prescience, he declared, our taking that house for July instead of August. For July was that month, that scorcher month of which I have spoken.

A tiny house—but a well-sited terrace that made the most of the ocean view. There I sat—Queen of the View. Princess of the Shore. Me and my babies faced each red dawn with blazing optimism. Oh, I loved it. Martin was in the city, and he came out like good husbands did on Fridays and left again each Monday morning.

We made love Friday nights and Saturday nights and Sundays after lunch. "There are advantages," Martin said, "to not having a strange girl around."

"Definitely," I murmured.

My babies. I was ashamed how at the start of that summer I concentrated on myself—except for weekends. The house silence echoed with extravagant visions. I exploded with energy—my poetry never meant more to me. That was the summer I wrote "The Eccologues—My Sturdy Years."

But where was my mothering soul? My mothering soul must have been asleep. My own, my blessed Paul was five, and Ruth, barely one. Then one afternoon, Paul—that fair-skinned child—sizzled. His baby body turned a soft pumpkin red, hills of blisters predicted a mountain range on his back. Painstakingly, the doctor sterilized needles and opened the blisters. Watch this kid, he said. Almost second-degree.

How had I permitted that pain? Made the sun an enemy? It was my concentration and my devotion to a poem as we sat on the terrace. A poem that began "On a concrete street . . ." I never looked up to see the small boy pull off his shirt. My fault! I

promised God anything—if I could absorb his pain. I won't lie—
I promised anything—but I didn't promise to give up poetry.

My baby wept endlessly with his head on my lap—but
otherwise he could not bear my touch. Ruth offered compan-
ionable sobs, fretted by the heat and away from familiar paths. I
tended to their sorrows.

I thought I grew thin and shadowy. People came. Toby spent
a week nearby. She and her husband stayed with someone
named Loud whom she swore I knew. Things had gone sour and
Toby's husband wasn't able to afford a place for the summer, so
they had become guests. She felt the strain. Everyone was
prospering.

Toby brought me a large jar of Pond's Cold Cream. For Paul's
burns, she said. Slather it on.

"God, honey," Martin said, calling from the city. "How is the
poor kid?"

"He hurts."

"Tell him that Daddy will bring him something from the
city—let him look forward to a surprise. But Bernie, we will still
have to have the party."

"What?"

"There's no way out—remember that it's part business. Now, I
will bring everything with me in the car—I swear. I'm ordering
trays of stuff. Not to worry. Bernie? Bernie?"

"Yes," I said.

Our cocktail party had been planned two weeks earlier. I
cleaned the cottage, ordered supplies, glasses, tables. The
babies cried and cried. Still, the party would go on.

Then on the expected evening, people filled our terrace.
Twenty people dressed in summer colors, bright and fiercely
smart-looking, arrived almost at once. I moved between guests

and the babies' bedroom. Perhaps more people came and others left when I was inside the house.

The weather had improved—ripe for a party, a touch of breeze to blow away bugs. Some pretty outdoor lights that had come with the house glowed like the palest violet. Citronella candles balanced on the wooden railings that outlined the terrace.

Rented tables covered with rented cloths clung to a wall. That was where the cheeses put out feelers on the wooden trays, casting shadows of oil. Each wheel deftly splintered and surrounded by purple grapes. Small puffs to drink up the salsa. Liquor and wine and mineral water. I ripped off amber-colored cellophane tents in the kitchen before carrying the trays outdoors—each a spangle of commercial catering and crammed with the city's bounty.

I saw a basket of silk flowers in the middle of a table. They had just appeared. A house gift? They were large, swollen blossoms, colors drawn from some jungle picture.

Toby was there. "You look terrible, Bernadette—you should go lie down."

"Don't be ridiculous," I said, and laughed. "I'm the hostess."

"Nevertheless," she said.

Martin beckoned and I left Toby. "Sweetheart," Martin said, "look who's here."

Martin's arm curved around my shoulder, drew me close. The woman in front of him was familiar—certainly someone I had seen before. Like an odalisque—a face from a museum, a face from a calendar, a face that sold.

I knew that next to the woman I grew haggard and pale. Still, the woman smiled kindly. She took my hand in her cool, firm grip. Her fingers a dazzlement of stones and gold. More rings than most people wore on the Cape in July. "My pleasure," she said warmly. The actress voice bonged sharply and then softened.

She must have sensed my hesitation—I didn't actually recognize her.

"Call me Nita—that is my real name," she said.

"So pleased," I said. "Nita."

I heard a wail. They had no pride—they called in full strength. I excused myself. The babies, I would have said. Martin and Nita had turned away already or perhaps been swept up by exclamations of joy.

I soothed the babies. Patted Ruth's back until she burped, a froth of milk bubbled at the corners of her mouth. Offered the prescribed doses of baby aspirins. Massaged their backs until they slept. Fifteen minutes later, I returned to the party.

Toby, glowering, sipping her drink, searched me out and found me at once. "Look at that!" she said.

I followed her gesture. That was Nita.

"She looks like she's dressed for a party."

"This is a party."

"It's not that kind of party, Bernadette. This is a Cape party." Toby wore jeans and a red chiffon blouse.

"Listen, she seemed perfectly decent to me," I said. "Told me to call her Nita—the real name."

Toby frowned, then shrugged—but not true assent. "All right—maybe it is me, Bernadette. Maybe I'm just being sour. My life is in an uproar. Sometimes I think I'm going to leave *him*."

"You don't?"

"It's not just the money—the man flounders even when he moves ahead. I don't know."

"This is hardly the night to make a decision. Listen, I must go and open another bag of ice cubes."

"I can't imagine why you didn't hire help."

"Everyone was taken."

The party went on. My chores seemed endless, trays of food

to replace, bottles to open. It was quite late—yet people showed no inclination to leave. Was that success?

If it weren't for the children, I could have abandoned the party and walked on the beach. I was hot and sticky, my hair gone to frizz, my skin shiny. The dress. Oh my poor dress! A foolishly chosen white piqué sundress with its tight skirt and bodice wrinkled from bending, from children, from effort. A drizzle of berry juice across the hem. I looked like the classical portrait of an upstairs parlormaid.

I stood by the window, held Ruth tightly in my arms, smelled her richness, and pulled back a curtain. The scene had thinned a bit. I couldn't locate Martin. Strangers waved at each other—bidding themselves good-bye. Plans for tomorrow rang out. My duties were suddenly basically over. I settled the baby back in her crib. Paul slept fretfully, his tiny fists pushing into the mattress.

I crept from their room, silently crossed the hall into the bedroom I shared on weekends with Martin. Under my side of the bed I had placed my most recent notebook. I had within me a poem. I felt a need to relate the evening in a form that I could see. "The red chiffon moved . . ." I wrote.

Afterward, I didn't mind returning to the terrace—I was relaxed, I moved with pleasure, the first line was finished. The air around the house seemed caged—smelled of alcohol, of women's scents, of softened wax. A few men, Toby's husband among them, had settled in one corner to talk in hushed tones. Wives or friends laughing in another corner. Toby leaned against a railing.

She came over to me.

"It feels warmer," I said to her. "Isn't it warmer? It's late, the air should have cooled—but suddenly it feels warmer."

"Warmer—it's hot," she said. "Listen, I'm normally never one to say this—but when did you last see Martin?"

"Martin? I don't know. Why?"

"Christ, you have no eyes. He went off with her—the actress. They left the terrace more than thirty minutes ago."

"She's a client," I said. "They must have had business to discuss."

"My God—are you going to tell me that he needed privacy?"

"Probably." I looked at Toby. Twilight had deepened into a dark sweetness. Nothing was quite clear even in the illumination from those pretty outdoor lights.

Toby stared at me. Her nature required confession—what she saw, what she imagined, what she thought. She chewed her lower lip, she tucked in her blouse, she pushed back strands of hair.

"Well," she said, "the bugs are coming in now. They'll get bitten up talking away from the citronella."

I nodded. How brave of Toby, I thought. How close to perfect friendship we were at that moment.

Reflections on the joy of packing, sorting, throwing out

I've done it. Amazing, isn't it? I have truly begun, and that very action has renewed me. I felt warm and strong—a noisy crowd of one. Hooray for me! Such a rush of joy.

What have I done? I have recreated my life—ages four through eight. Packed away all those meaningful scraps. The papers. The first poems. The paisley scarf. But more than that, I have also made the necessary journal entries—an explication of years four through eight. That was her life, someone will say. Within me lives a scribbler's obstinacy, a sense of symmetry, of tit for tat.

God, what an exhilaration of intaken air. I felt like bounding across the room, my balance restored. Certainly something to facing the truth, a kind of primal clarity, a pervasive suasion, a monastic ardor.

What I have is truly something solid. I have completed the first six boxes—taped, labeled, codified, solidified—done. Such an amazing amount of material to put into those boxes. However, I have been selective. What's there—belongs.

How many can say that they have looked backward into their childhood with such completeness? Never mind that there were no diaries filled at the time. Memory is a kind of diary—lock and key and total privacy.

I see this as a start. After all, it's my life that I am leaving behind. The boxes bulge silently in the doorway and fatten the wall, internal cornerstones. Paul has gone back to his dormitory. Good. He would have been suspicious. He studied the literature of the past, I was not in there. What's that? he would have said and picked and pried and looked.

Ruth was not sanguine about what she saw, but the curiosity was less sharp. Mess, she declared and glared at me. I understood. Ruth was distancing herself—I have seen that beginning. She was not convinced of the surety of mortality. Maybe she had the thought—not unusual—that if I was to die, better that I should be already dead. I loved her, don't doubt that. But ever since Clive told me about my taking a turn, I have tried to truly see her.

From her ancestor surely came that long black hair, that gliding walk, and the girl declared herself for something amorphous called Arts. I believed that her interests lived elsewhere—perhaps they were secret. Unfortunately, her physical resemblance to Martin grew stronger every day. I was not being hard on her. She was twelve but already she was losing her looks.

*   *   *

We lived in this apartment. Can you have boxes stacked in the hall? Maybe for a day or two, but no longer. I called a storage company in Brooklyn. Aladdin & Sons. I chose the company because of the name. The genies of storage—fitting.

I have boxes to be picked up, I said on the telephone. Come and pick up these boxes. There will be more—some every week. Lady, the man said, it's cheaper if we make one pickup. No, I said, I'll pay. You must come and get these boxes a few at a time. I imagined that the man shrugged. It's your money, he said.

He left me heroine of the purse.

The boxes and me. Ruth will be all right. I have reduced the demands upon me. I no longer slept with my husband. And he was not forgiving. "How much," he said, staring at me, "can I take? How much?"

There was, of course, no answer to that.

First he decided I didn't really mean it, then he grew angry, and then he watched me for signs of disintegration—was I hiding them? At last he lapsed into silence.

At night I filled the space beside Martin but we did not touch. Once, twice, I felt his hand wave and form an importunate arc above my shoulder, my back—the air trembled. I was tempted, my hips arched, my legs yearned—I would have stumbled behind him. But the need to disclose my life had an impatient grip. So I was forced to confine all movements, all stirrings, and to avoid warm folds of the sheet.

Martin got out of bed.

"Damn you," he whispered. "Damn you, anyway."

As I suspected, my packing was taken as a sign of straightening up. Evenings, I sat up and waited. I thought it best to go to our bedroom after Martin fell asleep. Anyway, my need for sleep had declined. Perhaps I made that happen.

I sat alone in the living room reading and reviewing my journal. Usually I drank a glass of chilled and very dry vermouth. The actual reading of the journal after the day's entries was not all that reassuring. It was more disturbing.

When I wrote those words I had believed they were complete—all right, as complete as anything recalled from a distance could be. I had constantly aimed for completeness and depth—but perhaps I hadn't stirred my memory in the right places? Had I acted the censor? I had left out, deleted, denied— not to avoid honesty. But who will believe an explanation of a thoughtless omission of events that should have appeared?

Twice, I almost started the journal again—thought about footnotes, addenda. But I cannot go back—or I shall annotate and remove and add forever. Consider the time left to me. Alois and his symptoms at my shoulder. No, what I hadn't thought to write—for whatever reason—I must omit. What wasn't there—wasn't there.

Ah, but afterward, will it be said that I promised my life—and didn't deliver?

What had I forgotten? Should I have mentioned that twice I received autographed photographs of movie stars sent to me from Hollywood by Ursula Marilyn Berne? Glossy eight-by-ten prints. The photographs were inscribed "To Bernadette." Rory Calhoun and Piper Laurie and Troy Donahue. Later, I learned that anyone could write away and get these pictures, and two of my friends to annoy me did just that. "To Marsha" and "To Lea" was written on *their* pictures. Suck on these, the girls said, and pushed the photographs in my face. I stared coldly back. You'll never be anything, I said. You have no style.

My first published poem—written for the school newspaper. By Bernadette Amy Berne, age eight. (Inserted here, because this copy of the newspaper [volume 12, issue 14] seems to be disintegrating.)

> There is a pumpkin near a tree
> That pumpkin doesn't look like me
> That pumpkin wears a ghostly face
> That pumpkin comes from another place.

Florence took the newspaper with her to work. Talent, she said, is in the blood. And I was pleased. The truth was that my love of poetry had begun. But people gave approval if you said you wanted to become an actress. To admit to wanting to become a poet—or even to know that you were a poet—impossible.

Someone in the school office called Florence. It was junior high. She's difficult, they said, meaning me. Arrogant and a teller of stories. That's what the school said. Busybodies, Florence said, but only when we were alone. Mind their own business.

But I told lies. I said that my mother was married to Tyrone Power. I said that my other grandmother had a connection to the Czar. Also, I added that my father had won the Purple Heart for extreme bravery.

Sometimes I was believed. I realized that the more impossible the tale, the more it was apt to be accepted. So my stories grew more involved. Still, there was always the bit of truth. For instance, I told everyone that I had been named after Jennifer Jones in *The Song of Bernadette*. After all, in a postcard from L.A., Ursula had written that even if my name weren't Bernadette— after seeing Jennifer Jones in that movie—I would have been renamed, even legally.

But perhaps I needn't have recorded that. Read my poems: "Simply Jennifer" and "Liar to the Bone." Those were clean, fearsome poems that prodded the skull. There's even "Broadway That Grayway," which took into account my brief assignations with the MacLanes.

The MacLanes—I can see them both quite clearly. Not good-looking boys, not interesting boys. Roy and Arthur MacLane were brothers with very white skin—that's all they seemed to be—just a barrier of skin. The whiteness gave them a subhuman cast, an albino alienness. Their mother was Catholic and she told them to stay away from me. They smirked at her advice. They had an uncle who got free tickets just before a show closed. He ran some kind of scam. My friend Myra warned me. You pay for them, she said. Arthur took me to a revival of *Long Day's Journey into Night*. No one famous was still in the cast. Nevertheless, these second-stringers could act. Almost poetry, I thought, their words. I sat on the edge of my seat and hushed that boy when he got too near. I could never act like those people on the stage. Maybe I didn't even want to. Did Arthur move to action with a warm tongue? I honestly cannot say. Later, his brother Roy took me to a production of *Cat on a Hot Tin Roof*.

Martin was proud that I was a poet. I love that in you, he said sometimes at night, his arm beneath my head. My sweet, sweet poet.

I believed him. That he was proud that I was a poet. I don't see why you can't be a poet, if you want to, he said once, we can afford it. If he wanted to, Martin could read my poems. My poems were intended to be read. Secrets were something else.

*   *   *

One of my most productive periods was the last week of that July spent in the house at Wellfleet. I wrote fiendishly. Some of my best work came that summer. "The Eccologues," "Sponges," "Houselights," "Imputation."

I dreaded all interruptions, anything that interfered with my receiving images, thoughts, reflections. And interruptions are what people bring you. Certain as they are that interruptions are truly welcome. Work being the burden.

I sat on the terrace in back of that tiny house one weekday afternoon bent over my pad, when someone called out, "Hello!"

Damn.

I looked up.

A man stood at the edge of the terrace, teetering on worn railroad-tie steps. A stocky man, his silhouette outlined on a pastel horizon. He had a curly nest of blond hair on his chest, the keys worn on a chain around his neck clucked at each other as he moved, his khaki shorts pouched beneath an inverted navel. Still, with a courtly flourish the man took off his summer cap with its green celluloid visor. "Didn't want to startle you," he said, "but Toby told me that if no one answered the front door—this was where you would be. I'm Arthur Loud."

Toby! I should have known Toby would do this. Visit my friend, she would have said. She won't mind.

I mind.

"Yes?"

"Look," he said, and squatted down beside me. "I told Toby that I was certain I knew you—of course, I don't. We'd met before, I said. So she told me which was your house. I am here basically on a lie—to meet you. I admire your work. I am an admirer."

"What?"

"I read 'Dazzlement.' "

Some words you absolutely cannot believe. "Dazzlement" was published in an obscure journal, *little feet*—after volume 1, issues 1 and 2, it reached its own epiphany and vanished.

"What?"

"In *little feet.*"

I was truly surprised.

"You really read the poem?"

He smiled a wide octave, sank to the terrace stones, damp with ocean sand.

Each morning, as soon as I was alone, I checked the calendar. I must keep to my schedule. I whispered to Louie the doorman. Tomorrow, more boxes. The whisper was accompanied by a folded five-dollar bill. I was already planning the packing for ages nine through eleven. How many boxes? the doorman wanted to know. It was hard to estimate what I would need. Every time we moved, I stored—forgotten possessions, ripe treasures. Items of trend and fashion were put away to wait.

I hunted for storage receipts. Found the two I wanted in an old brown travel kit—its plastic sides a sarcophagus sealed by time—carbon-smudged paper stuffed between a toothbrush case and a whisk broom.

The receipts were from Livingston & Sons—an old storage building down by the river where piers sunk deep into the mud slowly dissolved. I am almost certain that was where I had placed material needed for the next set of boxes. Thank God we always paid these storage bills—although Martin did inquire about what was there. No one knew for sure.

I ordered the return of stored material from Livingston & Sons.

The man said all right, lady.

Tomorrow, I said. I'll pay to get them tomorrow.

You got them tomorrow, lady.

I fell in the afternoon—actually sort of slid along the wall, my nails made prisoner scratches along the plaster. The path of desperation. Probably just as well that I slept now with no one—hard to hide my tattoos of black to blue to purple to yellow.

Anyway, the sense of movement to a desired goal was overwhelming. I cooked a real dinner to celebrate. Favorites. Chicken with olives and a side dish of angel hair with pesto.

"Where's Daddy?"

"Working," I said.

"Again?"

"It's tax time."

"Shit."

I never comment on these verbal vents—profanity, after all, has its uses. Ruth slouched in her chair; she wore a gray sweatshirt, jeans, and her hair was held back with a gray rubberband. I never imagine Ruth older. There is a school of therapy that says you should do that. A know-from-nothing school. Visualize your child's graduations, your child's wedding, your child's children. What a crock!

I want to see my children as they are—of what value am I if I see them as they will be. Considering that I won't be there. How can I imagine the truth.

"I want to spend the weekend with Helen," Ruth said. The irises of her eyes—green-blue—tightened like one of those scopes that you turn for tighter focus on the distance. She didn't pluck her eyebrows, they grew nevertheless in the shape of slender wings. This was a test.

"All right," I said. I didn't pass.

She stared at me, hostility escaped, her wings fluttered.

"What? You don't like her! I thought you didn't like her."

"No, I don't like her. I think she loads guns for others to fire, I think she's unpleasant, I think she's a liar, I think her personality resembles Howdy Doody on a bad day, I think her mother is an android, and I fully understand why her husband skipped town. And—I think Helen should not be your friend."

"But you don't give a shit if I spend an entire weekend with her?"

"False—but I don't believe that I should decide your friends. Your responsibility."

Ruth stabbed a piece of chicken; a rich goo splattered the cloth, the glasses, but didn't quite reach me.

The delicate tissue of our relationship shimmered on the plate. I figured there was a fifty percent chance that Helen was dead meat.

JOURNAL

These are the journal entries for
Boxes 7 to 16. The culling, the
selecting, the discarding—call it
by any name. What goes? What
stays? This belt buckle? That note
from the man? I strengthen my
soul—and my resolutions. The
life!

"Guess who came into Jeffer's while I was demonstrating the Odorima method for removing food smells from everything?"

"Charles Van Doren."

"Don't be a smart aleck—see what that gets you. My cousin Barbie—I think her married name is Shaw or maybe Sherman."

"I didn't know you had a cousin," I said.

"Cousins, my friend, cousins. You think we crawled from under a rock? And if I got cousins, then you have cousins— maybe once or twice removed but cousins nevertheless. So there I was on my little platform—now I don't really see faces, you know. Clothes—I sometimes see a good dresser. But a blur, that's what they are. Then suddenly this face pushes forward. Florence? she says.

"Anyway, I hadn't seen this one for God knows—six, eight years. But I knew her—there's that family resemblance. Forget that she's a kind of a weak Winnie. It's physical resemblance that I mean. So I knew who she was.

"Well, I cut short the demo, and went right over to her—she was surprised to see me. The cousins—my cousins—get together now and then. A club—yes, a kind of club. A Cousins Club. Well, they send notices—I'm doing them this year, Barbie said. So put us on the mailing list, I said."

"Your cousins have a mailing list?"

"A newspaper—a newsletter."

"God!"

"I'm warning you, Bernadette. Anyway, I found out that the next meeting is a picnic. A Cousins picnic. I got the address. I haven't kept up with those people for years, I was busy. Well, the next Cousins is this picnic out in Bellport. We are going."

"You go," I said. "I'll stay home."

"You'll go," Florence said. "Believe me, you'll go. Anyway, family is a wonderful thing."

And that was the first line of my poem "Past the Country Road." I suppose in fairness I should have attributed the line "Family is a wonderful thing . . ." to Florence before—but here it is now. Florence's line.

I chewed upon the idea of family for a while. As far as I had ever known, there was Florence and me—I discounted Ursula. Now, quite suddenly—cousins. Everyone I knew had relatives. Everyone except orphans. It was reasonable to assume that basically I was an orphan.

It didn't even pay to pray for rain since according to Florence there was an alternate rain date. This was a no-matter-what picnic. No chance that it would not occur. The picnic was set for August 16—a Sunday afternoon.

I was surprised that this made Florence nervous. But she didn't have to go. If I didn't have to go to something that made me nervous—you would never catch me going.

Clothes became an issue. She went through the closet. Wear slacks, I suggested. Shut up, she said. In the end Florence settled on a Bemberg sheer dress, white background printed with a sea of flowers.

"Flowers go with picnics," Florence said. "Now you."

"I'm going to wear slacks."

There was a momentary hesitation. "For a kid—that's all right."

We had a train schedule for the Long Island Railroad. It seemed like a waste of a good Sunday—I could have written some poems, we could have gone to a movie. I had checked off in the newspaper a revival showing of *How Green Was My Valley*.

Then I became, I suppose, a little curious.

We headed for the train. Florence in her dress. Me in a yellow and green striped skirt with almost matching yellow blouse. Florence lugged a shopping bag with what she called the "offering." It appeared that you could not go to a Cousins' picnic with empty hands. The shopping bag contained our largest mixing bowl filled with two quarts of potato salad. Florence bought the potato salad from the deli and dumped the contents of these cardboard containers into the bowl. "If anyone asks," she warned, "I made it."

I nodded. We had never been much in the way of eaters. Florence said that food was something you had to put into your stomach. She had regular meals. Monday was tuna fish salad; Tuesday, franks and beans; Wednesday, grilled cheese sandwiches and Campbell's tomato soup; Thursday, meatloaf; and Saturday, the leftovers of everything. Sunday, after the movies, we went to the deli or more rarely to the Oriental Palace. Florence had one company meal—baked chicken. Every morning she made the coffee, strong and bitter. We never gained weight.

Florence had no sweet tooth, and she thought that a lot of things killed you sooner or later. French fries, soda, anything sticky. Fruit was all right. You bought whatever was in season from a peddler. Only idiots or the pregnant with excusable cravings ever bought out of desire.

Once we were on the train, Florence acquired a calm, almost relaxed manner, and I grew nervous. I tried to consider what was about to happen as a life experience. Something to live through. And indeed I might say in advance that this day became "Picnic, Bellport, 1960," the final version of the poem written in October of that year.

Impatient with the sameness of the view framed in cloudless sunlight crawling past the window, I pumped Florence for information. How did it happen that we had cousins? And whose were they? Florence was not generally giving of such facts, but today a tranquillity sang in her.

"This side of the family—my mother's side. Old family." She took a breath. "Edgar, Hamish, and Simon," she said, like a recitation, "founded the family in 1901. Came right out to Long Island before it was anything to speak of. Those boys had one sister—Bertha. She stayed in New York City. Bertha had two sons—one was named William. He married twice, once to my mother and then to someone else. I'm the daughter from that first marriage. That's how I'm a cousin. And if I'm a cousin, then you are a cousin."

"Who told you all this stuff?"

Florence sniffed, sharpness was returning. "I got it from my mother. Now shut up, there will be plenty of talking this afternoon."

"What was your father like?"

"You never know when to shut up, do you?"

We rode on in silence. Such a long ride for a picnic. I thought of reminding Florence that she hated the outdoors. But I might start her being nervous again. Also, the set of her lips, the three bars she hummed, the tightness of her curls—made me reflective. I tried to think of three old men—Edgar, Hamish, and

Simon. I made them old. Bertha was the young sister—in a sheer cream-colored blouse.

The train stopped. "Quick!" Florence ordered, never a good traveler. "Look around—don't forget anything."

Strangers left the train, paused on the platform, and scurried off. You can't imagine what I thought. I thought someone would meet us—someone like Mr. Luzinzki, who lived in our building in 15C. I considered a black Ford, one door battered by indiscretion—inside on a dusty seat sat a plump, bald man waving. That would be a cousin.

No one was at the station. No one knew we were coming. We stood there, city refugees. I thought Florence would be upset. Let's get the hell out of here, she would say. But no, the scene was expected, anticipated. She marched us to the curb, waved into the air, and suddenly we had settled into the back seat of a local taxi.

You have to understand—I hadn't asked Florence for any more information, and she hadn't volunteered. So I thought a cousin or two. The taxi took us to a house where two huge chimneys loomed like overseers. Winter abominations in the August heat. I would have stood in the driveway, stood there forever. I never challenged crowds.

But Florence had a firm hold on my elbow. We didn't ring a doorbell, we walked around the side of the house in the direction of the noise that blew and billowed toward us. Sound that sprang past the leaves, the bushes, the bricks. The lawn swept us on. The picnic was everywhere. People shifted, passed, spoke.

Women bent over tables, their bottoms firm in their slacks; they dashed freely in their slacks, and they grabbed children who also wore slacks.

Half the women fluttered mothlike back and forth between long tables festooned with paper cloths, and placed bowls, trays, baskets. The air was peppered with barbecued meat, cucumbers glistened with oil, the lettuce grew in colors carried forward from antiquity, tomatoes trembled and blazed in their bowls. Triumphs of the bakery built loaf-shaped cities. The men ate. Men ate everywhere on that lawn, dipping their heads over mounded paper plates, their lips flipping droplets of strange juices.

No one spoke to us. We were invisible. I thought that fine. Florence would have none of that.

The heels of Florence's freshly polished white pumps sank into the manure-richened soil as she moved forward into the crowd. All the women were thin, belted, pinched, sucked inward. I looked at Florence. She fit. It was a swarm of forty, fifty people—more children.

Florence stopped, took her bearings, her eyes narrowed to periscopic focus. She sighted her prey.

"Linney," she called. It was one of her special voices—the one saved for demonstrating silver polish.

Someone named Linney turned around. She had gray eyes— later, I learned those were the family eyes, borne also by Florence. Linney's forehead was dotted with a melancholy sweat. She did not look pleased.

"Florence?"

"Yes, indeed. Decided to rejoin the clan." Florence laughed— that, too, was special—the demo laugh, an upper-register tinkle.

So these were cousins. I wandered undisturbed past people. Everyone wanted to be near a large jovial man called Dr. Bob. Hi, Doc, they called. They reached out as if touching his back were a cure. Someone called Tante was upstairs resting. Dr. Bob's Tante, I thought. There were several stout men with fringes of hair who seemed uneasy. Perhaps they were new to the cousins.

"How did she get here?" someone said. In the crowd, voices blended. Sound met no resistance.

"That has to be Barbie's fault."

"Well, she hasn't changed. What is it—a family curse?"

The laughter rose like a plume of glee.

The food was too much. I could make scrambled eggs when I got home. I decided to go into the house. If anyone asked, I'd say I needed a toilet. But no one stopped me. I took the back door, which led into the largest kitchen in the world. More cousins, smiling indulgently at each other. Fay and Anne and Toni and Grace and Libbie. Here, too, salads waited their turn for slaughter. The women, who were shifting and mixing and reprocessing, all wore brilliantly colored slacks and white cotton tops; their wrists clanked with golden armor. One woman, wearing a genuine maid's outfit with a cap such as I had seen only in Joan Crawford's movies, peeled vegetables at the sink. I realized after a moment that the women in slacks were only rearranging, adding a spray of parsley, a sliver of chives, there an olive. Who was I to them? Some child's friend? A neighbor trespassing?

"She brought potato salad all the way from the city unrefrigerated," said blazing-red slacks.

"You're kidding?" said yellow slacks.

"No—look. I swear the stuff is already tinged with green."

"For God's sakes, don't let anyone eat it. We'll die of botulism," said powder-blue slacks.

"No," I said. "Ptomaine. You'll die of ptomaine."

They stopped, looked at me.

"Ask Dr. Bob, if you don't believe me," I said.

"Who are you?" said yellow slacks.

"Melvina Winthrop," I said, and skipped outside.

As I left, powder-blue slacks was scraping two quarts of deli potato salad into the garbage.

*   *   *

"Bernadette!" Florence called in a powerful voice. "I've been looking for you."

I walked toward her, a phantom cousin, I thought. Florence's gray eyes glowed. She balanced a paper plate with food in one hand and a tall glass of tomato juice in the other. I was proud of her. Lots of women were already drizzled and grimed. Florence didn't have a spot on her.

"These are *our* cousins, Bernadette. This is Olga and Henry, and this is their daughter, Helene."

I stared at restive people, squinting in the sun glare. The woman in true-salmon-pink slacks twisted a string of pearls that hung beneath the collar of her white cotton shirt.

"Be careful," I said.

"Bernadette," Florence said.

"Well, if you twist pearls—the string snaps. I've seen it happen."

The man nodded. "She's got something there, Olg. Be a tragedy."

His wife took her hand away from her necklace. She must be the blood relative, I decided. She looked displeased. I thought that in a moment they were going to excuse themselves, say how they must go and speak to so-and-so. I guessed that Florence thought that too.

"Bernadette," she said, "why don't you and Helene go off and have a talk or something."

That was the first time I looked at the kid. I figured she was about eight years old. I wasn't planning to baby-sit through the afternoon. On the other hand, that would get me away from Florence.

"Sure, come on, Helene."

She followed me without objection. We made it to the trees, fifty yards from cakes galore—little tents of bug-proof netting protected sugar from itself.

"How old are you?"

"I'm twelve," Helene said.

"You're never," I said.

"Yes, I am. The doctor says that I will grow—he measured my bones. At my own rate of growth, he said."

"I'm twelve," I said. But she was more than small, I realized, she was basically not pretty. Not little-girl pretty. Her head was large, the shoulders narrow. The nose a questing bone. Was it possible to grow up and into your face? Size meeting its match.

"I've never been here before," I said. "To a Cousins—picnic."

"It's a club," she said, her voice gaining in authority. "A Cousins Club. Are you really a cousin?"

"Beats me. If Florence says so—I guess so."

"My father says the cousins are Long Island jewels."

"Yeah—well, they all look rich."

She giggled.

"Well, cousins or clubs don't exactly interest me. Just the stage. I'm going to be an actress," I said. "I had really good roles in three school plays this year. I played in *Inherit the Wind* and *Bus Stop* and something stupid called *Rinses*. It's my calling. A true actress—*n'est-ce pas?*"

"We study French in my school—you have a lousy accent," Helene said. "Anyway, my mother doesn't approve of the theater as a career—to act is a waste, she says. But we go to plays. I've seen plenty—real plays. Still, I wouldn't want to be an actress. I wouldn't mind reading plays—we have plays in our library at home. Plenty of plays. I don't know what I'm going to be. They give aptitude tests in my school."

I looked at her. "I bet you didn't make it into the Drama Club. Come back when you grow, I bet they said."

"Are you related to that woman who was talking to my parents—or did she just bring you here?"

"What woman?"

"The funny one with the weird voice."

I pushed Helene down. Her forehead only hit the side of the tree—no damage. Just a little blood.

"The bully!" I heard.

One of the women spoke—maybe Linney. "She has to apologize," the voice said. "No one behaves that way here."

There wasn't anybody to listen or I would have explained. It wasn't what they thought. After all, we were both age twelve, so I wasn't hitting a younger kid. By then Florence had grabbed my arm without watching where her nails went. Clearly, we were leaving.

"Why did you do that?" she shouted at me. We stood in the driveway in full sight of the chimneys.

"Because she was a prick," I said.

Florence sputtered. But she never hit you in public. That saved me. She had those moments to reflect, the thinking pause. Possibly I was right, she might think—that other kid was a prick.

After a while, Florence realized that she would have to go back through the cousins and into the house and use the telephone. Taxis didn't cruise these streets.

"Don't you move," she ordered.

If Florence hadn't been angry, I would have told her how I saw several boxes ripped up and carefully crushed—from Foods Tooo Goood, from Bakes, and Belly Up. So much for the homemade theory.

I waited, some people might say I waited a long time. It was after Labor Day. You can snoop and see something and not know what it is. I knew where Florence kept her address and telephone book—small black book. It was in the third drawer of the dresser, left side near the five embroidered handkerchiefs that were being saved. I never knew one single name in that book, so it hadn't mattered. But now I reexamined it. Yes, there was a name—that was probably the Dr. Bob. I didn't have a last name for Helene, and the book had three Henry something or others. First Henry didn't know who I was talking about. Not a relative, I decided. The second said I had the wrong number and that I wanted the other—the last Henry. That may be average in any determination of three sets of numbers. It will always be the last one.

They put her on the telephone. Must have been the maid—my name drew no reaction.

"Listen," I said quickly, "I'm the one who threw you down at the Cousins picnic. I shouldn't have. I planned to practice pacifism and so I shouldn't have thrown you down. I should have kept it verbal."

Now, I hadn't expected anything from her.

"Look," she said. "I shouldn't have said that. The woman wasn't weird—she was perfectly nice. Who was she anyway?"

"My grandmother."

"Are you in any play right now?"

"No. But in November they are going to put on *Joan of Lorraine*."

"No kidding?"

"Did you take the aptitude test?"

"Yes."

"Well?"

"Literature—or something like that."

I hesitated. Nothing had been cleared with Florence—this was dangerous.

"Next week—no school on Monday."

"Me too."

"How would you like to come over—spend the weekend."

"I have the dentist on Saturday. But you could come over

here for the weekend. I'm positive. I'd just be at the dentist for a half hour."

"Sure—I'll come."

This I suspected would be all right—getting in thick with the cousins.

Florence was surprised and suspicious. "Her? I never expected you to speak to that one—Little Miss Perfect, she was."

"Well, she called me with the invitation. Said she was sorry too. Can I go?"

"Listen, Bernadette, they're relatives, but I tell you honestly they can be snotty."

"That's all right—I can manage."

"They going to pick you up at the station?"

I hadn't asked. "Definitely."

Even at age twelve I understood what bound us. It wasn't blood. Just read "The Early Outcast." We were isolates. If it weren't for that, if it weren't that Helene needed someone, certainly Olga and her Henry would not have let me near their little girl.

But we were alone and scrawny and unchosen creatures at that—there was no option. Each other or no one. So Olga called Florence. Florence was fit to be tied. The bitch, she said, after getting off the telephone. That woman actually offered to pay for your train ticket.

I left the train at the Port Washington station. Florence had written all the directions down on a piece of paper that I didn't have the courage to refuse. For Sands Point, get off at Port Washington.

Henry and Olga met me. Helene, they said, had a piano lesson. I sat in the back seat of their green Buick. They pointed out the sights. Here was Helene's elementary school. And there was the school where she went now.

Helene was waiting for me. It turned out that she had rooms
all to herself on the third floor. A bedroom, a playroom, and a
room with couches. She had a bathroom, too.

"It's like your own apartment," I said. "You could do anything
up here and they wouldn't know."

Helene nodded. "Like what?"

"We'll see."

I toured the rooms. Helene's books filled four bookcases.
Florence was never big on actually purchasing books. That's
what God made libraries for, she said.

I took a book from a shelf.

"I don't know if you'll like that," Helene said.

"Yeah, why?"

"It's poetry," Helene said. "My school has a special class for
that. Anyway, let's go downstairs and eat. One of my favorites
tonight—little hens stuffed with wild rice and lingonberries."

What I learned that weekend: how to inhale smoke, what
masked the smell of vodka, and what to do with the vibrator
that Olga had brought back from Vienna. I already knew how
to dodge the patting hand of Henry.

It was time that improved my cooking skills. In truth, I could
have survived on tuna fish salad, but Martin couldn't.
He bought me three cookbooks. Later, I bought more.
Martin wasn't a picky eater. He liked a lot of onions and
garlic.

When we had our apartment in Washington Heights, Paulette and Gene lived downstairs. Paulette was a trained nutri-
tionist, and she was always on the propaganda trail. Make it at
home, she insisted, then you know what's in it. She was persuasive. I started my baking then—pies, cakes, breads. I pureed all
the baby food fresh. Then one evening at a party I went into

Paulette's kitchen, I opened the cupboards. Paulette ate food that came in cellophane packages. Two to a package.

A romantic interlude

Ellen Kealer was going to Miami with her parents for winter break. She said that she didn't want to go. An endless drag, she said. Louanne was working for her aunt. Myra's boyfriend was coming home from Potsdam. That left me alone with a fanful of twofer coupons. Even Jack, the doctor's son, was going with his grandparents to Fort Lauderdale.

That settled it. I would do my senior year papers. Florence snorted. Winter breaks, summer breaks. She, she insisted, got no breaks. So I took my notebook and went to the Forty-second Street library. The reference rooms were filled with high school students. Any book I had in mind was unavailable. I knew the rules. High school students weren't supposed to use a college library. Someone was always being humiliatingly removed from the libraries at Columbia or NYU during winter break.

That was because they didn't know how to do it. First of all, they either dressed up or down, so they weren't at ease in the library. Then too, like fools, they carried too much—high school texts or the wrong notebooks. Also, it paid in winter to look a little cold, as if you hadn't come a great distance.

I settled on one subject, one effort. I knew which paper I was going to work on. On adoption practices in city orphanages. My personal topic. When I was eight I had this fantasy in which I was Paulette Goddard's daughter or Merle Oberon's. Just an illusion. I mean I wasn't nuts—I didn't believe that.

Another fantasy was a game called Meeting a Man. This was a game played with your friends. I usually did my Doris-Day-on-a-cruise routine. Everyone laughed. I did a good Doris Day imitation. But when I played the game alone—internally—I thought differently. Then I imagined I slipped on an icy sidewalk on Fifth Avenue. He would catch me, his hand supporting my arm, his odor of tweed and fires and some rich cologne.

There was never a cruise. Instead, it was ten o'clock in the morning when I crossed Washington Square and headed for NYU's Bobst Library. My accoutrements were carefully chosen, the effect examined in a mirror. I practiced my walk—independent, jaunty. My manner pointedly brittle. I carried one notebook, a purse that hung from my shoulder by a wide strap, no bookbag or briefcase. Beneath a short plaid skirt my legs chapped in the wind. A gray wool jacket, a flapping scarf, and no lipstick. I looked like anybody. I was at home in the neighborhood. I could be sixteen or eighteen or twenty.

He picked me up. The young man suddenly trotting at my side. His stride soundless in thick, rubber-soled boots. He pretended for a moment that our pace was the same. Chance, coincidence. I gave him a quick glance. He had a thick brown mustache trimmed by someone partial to barbershop quartets. He carried a knapsack from which protruded a notebook that advertised *New York University*. Mine said *Readease*.

"Cold, isn't it," he said.

"Yes." I computed the odds—broad daylight. And with him I could get into the library.

"I guess we're both heading for the library," he said.

"Yes."

"Really cold out. Would you like to go for a hamburger?"

"It's ten o'clock in the morning."

"At noon?"

"All right."

Together, we entered the library, and no one paid us any attention.

At noon we went to Chock Full O'Nuts for hamburgers and coffee. I had no special sensation, no glimpse into future possibilities. I had been picked up before. The choice of a place to eat was mine. With experience you knew that not much could happen sitting on stools at a counter, even elbow to elbow.

I thought the man's face looked right, square and firm, with a short nose, an eastern European face that I understood. I toyed with the idea that like me he might be an ersatz student, then abandoned it. He was too old, and it had been a really cold morning for a walk to the library unless you had a purpose.

We ordered hamburgers and coffee. He talked. As he spoke he made wide sweeps with his hand, assaulting the salt and pepper shakers, rattling the catsup. His name was Martin Marr-key. He was twenty-three years old.

Now, some men were into young girls. I suspected that if this one knew I was sixteen, he would be out of here like the lark at dawn. So I kept my mouth shut.

He said that he lived with his mother and two sisters in Brooklyn. A third sister was married. Then he put down his hamburger and wiped the grease from his mustache.

"What I want you to know," he said, "is that I am a veteran."

"Yes."

"The army—I served. You understand? Got discharged just before the start of the semester. Back injury—but it does not interfere with life. I wanted you to know—I'm up front about things like that. About the army."

"The world," I said, "is one place—I'm another."

He stared at me.

"How did you hurt your back?" I asked.

His cheeks reddened. "I slipped," he said. "I wore a brace for a while—not anymore. Look, would you like to go to a movie tonight?"

"Or maybe we could use one of my twofer coupons."

"Yes," he said. "Anything."

It was only sensible to meet at NYU—after all, he lived in Brooklyn and I lived in the Bronx. I considered this as the affair of a winter break. That I liked him surprised me. I usually liked only my art. But there it was.

During the remaining eight days of winter break, we met every day. He didn't have a room or an apartment. It was always cold. We went to movies and kissed passionately. His hand beneath the sweater troubled the straps of my bra. I wondered if I could keep him from knowing much about me until I graduated from high school in June. I wouldn't be able to enroll in NYU, though. It was free schooling or no schooling.

Martin told me all about his life. He told me that he used to be fat. Fat kids carried that weight forever—even though he wasn't fat anymore. When his mother became pregnant with him, she was almost fifty. You can imagine, his mother told him, what everyone said. They gave me everything—castor oil, Epsom salts, everything. He was the last child. He was close to one of his sisters, the others always seemed like aunts to him. He wanted an ordinary life, he didn't mind saying that. A good life—but an ordinary one.

I told him the cunning lie that I was going to be an actress. I wrote poetry also, I said. I had to be careful, because the more I liked him, the greater the deterioration of my guile.

Martin's friend who sat next to him in Management Theory

lent him a room. But he could only have it between four and six
P.M. That seemed odd, it wasn't quite twilight. But we took the
room anyway. We had coffee, and then walked until it was time
to make love. A pause between lunch and dinner. Martin kept
asking me if I wanted anything, and I kept saying no.

His friend's name was Fred. A great guy, Martin said. The
borrowed room was in a standard rooming house. But no one was
in charge, Fred had said, no one cared. Nevertheless, we were
uneasy. On the other hand, we didn't see anyone. So Martin took
my hand and we marched up the stairs. He had a key.

Fred's room looked fine. Neat. There were posters taped to
the walls. One from a production of *Aida* at the Met. A photograph of a mother and a father in a generic family pose.

I wanted to ask if the sheets on the bed had been changed,
but I decided not to. We noticed right away that the room was
cold. Martin tried to turn the valve on the radiator.

"It's open as far as it goes," he said.

"That's all right," I said. Anticipation made you shiver too.

Martin unbuttoned my blouse. I wore a white cotton blouse,
my plaid skirt, and navy-blue knee socks. I told him to lift up his
arms, and I pulled off his sweater.

We were naked together. Goose bumps rose on my arms and
my shoulders and my back.

"Bernie," Martin said tenderly. "I think I love you."

I didn't know what he expected. Was it a confession of true
emotion? But boys said that. A lot of people thought that boys
didn't say that. They were wrong. Boys said, I love you, Bernadette. I love you, Bernie. I love you, sugar. I love you, honey. It
came as easily to boys—those words—as any other ones.

If a man said, I love you, was that stronger? Or was it still
what they thought was expected? How did I know?

"I love you too," I said.

"You do?"

"Yes."

"I'm serious about you, Bernie. Like I have never been before, Bernie."

"Look," I said, distracted. "A cloud."

It was true, his breath was a pearl-gray cloud in that room. It was tangible, it even floated—his words.

That did it. We lost our sense of formality. We began to giggle, we fell together on the bed, and made love quite simply and easily, but even the pressure of our united bodies couldn't trap any heat. I wondered then if that was an omen, a warning from the city.

We had kissed that afternoon—and somehow it was a parting. I thought I would die if I never saw him again. Florence was suspicious. Who studied all the time? She smelled something. She spoke about a thousand girls whom she knew who had thrown away their lives. Try living on nothing, she said. Nothing is good for nothing. There are a lot of things you could be, she said to me. Actress or teacher, for instance, or nurse.

I thought that Martin Marrkey was a calling. If ever I had a calling, he was it. I put my emotions—those of that period—into a series of poems. I called them "Calduran: An Unknown City." In these poems the lover is visualized as a well-endowed naked man who speeds through Calduran in a sleek car and is glimpsed through a veil of water. Sometimes he is shadowed by scarlet neon and appears captious and grieved and in stocking feet. I created Calduran as a city behind an ancient, ruined wall.

I thought that with the coming of love I would need truth. I read *The Tragic Muse* where James said "*that oddest of animals the artist who happens to be born a woman.*" I planned to use that in a conversation with Martin. One in which I explained myself. But the right moment didn't occur. I wanted him to know that essentially I was a poet—that was what I was.

I would have tried anything. For instance—that book. I almost forgot that. The book hadn't been lost—*Thoughts of Ancient Women*. I found that book in a bin of thirdhand books put outside the Strand Book Store because they weren't worth stealing. On page 37 of *Thoughts*, the editor had transcribed the notes of eleventh-century Sister Veronica. An unknown woman except for her writings.

Sister Veronica's advice was that to find yourself you had to learn how to leave your body. I thought that her advice reflected her times. She suggested mortifications—oozing, breaking, humiliation. Directions on how to position yourself, how to swing the chain for a blow right in the middle of the back. Also, she offered plans for the creation of wounds and open sores, all to be picked at until they festered. The ingestion of spiders. The tongue to the icy path. This, she swore, ultimately led to clarity of vision beyond the body.

The simpler—albeit longer—path to such vision was by walking around on your knees until the pain brought purity. I considered that. In my visions Veronica was a blonde. One of those skinny, Waspy, naturally neurasthenic blondes. Anyway, it was probably too late for me to try even the crawling when you considered that Veronica had performed her feats from age eleven onward. How bad could you have been at age eleven?

Before he went into the army, he had studied physics, Martin said. One semester and then he enlisted. Now that he was back in school, he had different ideas. He had taken some advice from an uncle.

His uncle owned his own business—the richest man in the family. That uncle was helping Martin to break the family mold, to escape, to grow. Take my advice, his uncle had said, and study accounting. His uncle offered him a position when he was finished. He paused to see how I reacted to this. I didn't. Not a two-bit accountant, he continued, but someone worthwhile. I have ambitions and desires, he said.

Suddenly, winter break was over. I would no longer appear in the NYU library. Ellen Kealer was back, her face softly tanned. Louanne returned too, with a new red coat. School started— my school. My life was no longer my own. Florence had to know where I was now. Day in and day out. I was less available, my time no longer my own. I thought that I would die if I didn't see Martin. I called him on the telephone. He called me too. Getting telephone calls didn't bother Florence. I can't see you, I kept saying to Martin. Maybe on Saturday.

One Sunday, uninvited and unexpected, Martin showed up at Florence's door. I could hardly estimate the length of his journey. He, too, suspected something.

It was Florence he spoke to. But from the other end of the room, I heard.

"What have I done?" he whispered. "What have I done?"

He was guilty of molesting a child.

Reflections on being zonked

God, I was tired. I had no idea that recalling life was so exhausting. If only I had been one of those children who kept a diary— but no, I wasn't. Therefore this. Actually, I was amazed that I never had kept a diary. You could buy diaries everywhere when

I was growing up. Their puffy covers came in many colors—leatherette with gilt edges. My friends kept diaries. Not me. I suppose at that time the poems were enough. And if my life had been long—why then, a line of thought, a progression of images would have emerged. But now, it won't. I must force it. Be young—think young for the sake of the journal.

I packed all day. I staggered around—but I had none of the symptoms of the last stages. Alois' last stages. At the end of each day I wanted wine, soft music and dancing. Wasn't that definitely a thirties movie? Not possible for me—except for the wine. I loathed the soft music syndrome—and I never danced much. Now, of course, I would slide away from my partner as I descended downward, knees at the bent, until I puddled on the floor.

I've taped boxes, numbered boxes, provided appropriate journal entries—I was up to schedule. To want more was greedy. What more can I want? A completeness. I feared that I was not showing myself as I wished. Where was total openness? Was an internal censor ever at work—cutting, pruning, changing? But I was fighting back. Damn the censor. Why not? My executors can tone down whatever they wish. I won't be here to complain.

I rolled my childhood back and forth. Snake eyes, I shouted. That child was me. But I found the backward glance not easy. I yearned to approach adulthood. How many more boxes until then? Who can tell?

I've ordered lots 27 and 28 from storage. Found receipts for R. & L. in Queens. Not certain what's stored.

I always thought that childhood wasn't a beginning but rather a separate entity. You know—you were a child, then you weren't. And the *weren't* truly was a different person. Separated from.

Now logically I understood that wasn't so. I could easily draw my own psychological lines and knots backward. But nevertheless, the journal convinced me to see that what I was, I am no longer. I am watching over myself.

My illness today stumbled forward. No child in me leapt out. My body churned beneath the skin. I held a magnifying glass up to my image in the mirror. I thought I was less recognizable. I was soft-pedaling the truth with illusion, artifice, costumes. I had found a bottle of makeup melting in the back of a closet. An all-day foundation in "Bright Light Pink." If I stood in the bathroom, at a certain angle I saw the stunning translucence of my skin. How thin, how traditionally ghostly. Eventually they'd notice, so I covered the face carefully. A layer of makeup, a puff of talcum—white was fashionable. I saw that in a magazine.

Ages nine to eleven, Boxes 7 to 16, have burned me up, but I cannot afford a day's rest. I glued a calendar to the back of my closet door, and with a secret code of dots created a time line. So much to do each day. I could tell that a pause now was unthinkable.

Chronological order—that was the key. I must move on to ages twelve to sixteen. Life had been more complex during those years. The number of boxes needed to cover that span was staggering. But I must not consider that. Not my chore to determine whether the number of boxes was either wrong or right. A megaskyscraper of boxes should be used if needed.

JOURNAL

Entries to cover Boxes 17 to 43. I
see in front of me a substantial
effort. I feel like a rousing shout—
Pack onward! This beats trying to
be jolly. So—Pack onward!

"I heard that Fred Allen died," Florence said. "That show will never be the same again." She stared at me. I grew nervous. Should I have changed my shirt? Florence hated dirt. That's why she was so good at demonstrating cleaning supplies. She believed. But if it had been that, she would have started right in on me. Comb your hair—I don't need another rat's nest. Or, Who needs to look at yesterday's tomatoes on your shirt? So that wasn't it.

"Money," Florence said clearly, "never grows on anything—forget moss. Some of the girls at the Kregers'—that's where I'm showing Crystal Klear Glassware Shine this week—tell me that you should be old enough. How old is she? they asked. Nine, I said. And a big nine. Well, she should be old enough."

I was never one to miss my cues. "Old enough for what?"

Florence cleared her throat, a phlegmy cougher's throat. "To have your own house key—and let yourself in after school."

My blood rushed, the dam of joy cracked. It was power that I was being offered. "Sure," I said calmly, suddenly a student of benign tranquillity. "I could."

No more dumb neighborhood women, no more no you can't, no more could you help me peel the potatoes since you're doing nothing. Nothing! Was that nothing when I was thinking? Let them call it what they wanted. Daydreams! Dawdling for what! I was thinking. Yes, I could stay by myself. You bet I could.

Florence twirled one of her short, tight curls. That implied a difficult decision—she tried to preserve curls. "Listen," she said, "there will be rules. My rules. And Miss Smarty, the first time you step out of line—I take back the key."

I nodded. I knew when to argue. Sometimes you kept your mouth shut.

"Well, if you could be trusted—and that's a big if. Still"—Florence calculated quickly—"that would save me twenty-four dollars a month." We both stood in silence. That seemed like a lot of money to recover just by the exchange of a key. What would we do with the money? Save for what, was Florence's motto. Death comes soon enough—and *he* can spend his own money.

It was agreed. We went to Santino's on the Concourse and had a duplicate key to the apartment made. A shining gold-colored key with the sharp edges of the newly created. A chain was purchased—sturdy. Florence gave it several experimental yanks. It could have been used to walk a bull terrier. The chain bearing the key was to hang around my neck beneath the dress, beneath the undershirt. The metallic chill faded. It was freedom.

Unfortunately, the timing was bad. The very day I showed it off to friends who were unlucky enough to have mothers at home was the day Lea Berg got blood between her legs at age ten. None of us had that, all of us wanted to see it. Everyone knew what a key looked like.

At age five, I started school. But before that, what a burden I was. What could Florence do with me? She had to work. That's how I met my first mentor—Mrs. Talmadge.

I had made the rounds of several neighbors. No one minded earning a little extra cash—but occasionally their own lives interfered. Once, Florence actually had to miss an assignment—a day of wiping on and off dabs of Mazic Jewelry Sparkle for Your Rings at Macy's. Why? Because Mrs. Hueblimintz's brother died in Queens. My day at her house was canceled.

So Florence searched for someone without a life. It was luck that such a person lived in the building.

Mrs. Talmadge claimed to be seventy. But her memories made her at least ten years older. An androgynous old woman with rusty-colored hairs sprouting from her moles. Her body was permanently fixed in a black dress with a shiny and sagging seat, wrinkled lisle stockings, and shoes that laced around surprisingly trim ankles. She was powerfully built, one of those old women whom children were afraid to bother. There was a rumor that with one blow she had broken the jawbone of Luzinzki's terrible nephew.

The truth of the matter was that Florence had never spoken to the woman—even when they passed on the stairs. Mrs. Talmadge was also not apt to be found in the local Laundromat. Perhaps she was one of those who washed their clothes in the bathtub. Who knew? But what Florence did know—Mrs. Talmadge was always home. No children with demands on her, no relatives to die unexpectedly. Alone, the neighbors swore. Not crazy—just alone.

We went to her apartment. It was almost an interview. Florence made the arrangements. I was told to behave while we sat side by side on chairs in Mrs. Talmadge's apartment. With her professional cleaner's eyes, Florence made a merciless tour of the living room. What was there and what wasn't. Five dollars a week and Florence would provide my food.

Mrs. Talmadge said, *"Liebchen."*

I gave her my razzle-dazzle smile.

Florence and Mrs. Talmadge shook hands. I would spend the next day with Mrs. Talmadge. But once outside in the hall, Florence started in. "Listen, Bernadette," she said, "you keep an eye out for dirty dishes in the sink, and for cats. You let me know if that old woman has got any cats. More than one cat, anyway. And any cup that shows signs of green mold—I showed you what that looks like. Also, check around for newspapers. You ever see more than say two, three days lying around—you tell me."

"Why?"

Florence snorted. "Craziness—the sure signs of a loony." Then her voice became sterner. "Meanwhile, you behave."

What lasting damage could be done to such a little kid? Florence supplied my lunch each day in a brown paper bag—the bag was to be folded and returned for reuse. The old woman could not take her eyes off that bag. She watched that bag with witchlike vigilance.

"What you got?" she asked regularly.

"An egg, apple—one slice bread."

"Trade?"

I hesitated. "For what?"

"I can tell you beautiful things and secrets—also, I got books."

I always gave her the egg, the apple. She said I could keep the bread.

"First secret," Mrs. Talmadge said, "my real name is Gerta Wein. Never tell a soul—I'll know if you do. But worse—they will get me. The Nazis will chew me up. But not if they think I'm Bertha Talmadge. Get it?"

I nodded.

"My husband was—why not admit it—was a gangster, a hoodlum, a regular Edward G. Robinson. In Chicago. But to me—never a syllable that wasn't honey. We had a house. You should see such a house. Red carpets darker than blood, silk wallpaper like baby's skin, mahogany tables with lion's claws for legs. And my life—never lifted a hand—why should I? I had maids to fetch, cooks to prepare. Food—fried eggs, boiled eggs, egg noodles, whole eggs buried in chopped meat, kugel with eggs."

I listened and nibbled the slice of bread.

But even with stories it was hard to keep me quiet. I wanted to dance, I wanted to sing, I wanted to go outside. Mrs. Talmadge would have done anything to avoid going outside.

"You know how to write your name?" she asked.

I shook my head.

"Four years old and already a dummkopf. Go to the table— over there—in the drawer, a pad of paper and a pencil."

She held my fingers. Hers were thick and red. We worked for a long time on the letter *B*. It took me two days to do the entire name. She said I was slow.

"America," she said. "A good country but so little learning. Not like Munich—such a city, Bernadette. Grow up and go there and see for yourself—then you'll say that Mrs. Talmadge never lied.

"In Munich I had everything. Gowns, balls, even a private tutor from the *Universität*. Then at sixteen, I was sent to New York. My mama said it was for the best. I was like a country girl in New York—no, more like one of those sleeping princesses. But a peach—yes, a fair and ripe peach when I married my *Bürgermeister*—a big *macher* named Lattimore. Get that?"

I nodded.

After lunch, we listened to the radio. When the radio played the slowest music, the old woman would fall sleep. Then I would

walk around the apartment, open drawers, peer into cabinets.
Not much to find, not much to see in Mrs. Talmadge's
apartment—two cold-smelling rooms. She had a kitchen table,
and on the top someone had scratched a heart and the initials
J.R. beneath it. I did that, Mrs. Talmadge said to me one day, my
very self. Maybe you'll learn why and maybe you won't.

The three unmatched chairs that surrounded the table
swayed if you fidgeted while seated. It was basically a room that
heaved. The bookcase was the best—tall and narrow and six
shelves high—thick with books. With permission I could take a
book and sit on the curved couch, which had softened from the
weight of many bodies. That couch was no identifiable color
but the outlines of distant dark roses could still be seen.

In the beginning I was frightened by the woman. But later I
realized how easy it was to get what I wanted. I needed only to
whine, "I want to go outside!" That always worked. Outdoors, it
was cold or raining or too hot for Mrs. Talmadge. She complained about her ankles—they resisted.

What I craved was entertainment—more stories, more attention, something new. So she taught me to read. "Forget everything you have learned about reading," she commanded. That
was easy, I knew nothing.

"The alphabet," she said, "we learn like this—B, R, T, M, Z, Y.
No order. Then you really know the letters. Listen, did I tell you
about the time my Mr. Lattimore took me back to Munich? No?
Well, he did.

"Was a mistake—but he didn't know. We went to dinner with
Göring—imagine that. I wore black lace—what a picture I was.
A heart-shaped neckline—pearls. Göring kissed my hand. I was
something—I had blond hair from my father's side of the
family. I was courted. Lattimore was happy. Lattimore, you see,
suddenly saw big money.

"Then my sister came to me one morning, pushed past the

maid. I was in bed being served coffee and sweet apple dump-
lings. Get the hell out of here, my sister said. Are you mad? Go
back to New York.

"I told my husband. Lattimore said never—I stay! You stay!
Let your family leave if they want to—don't see them going!
You stay! Pooh—that was all I had to hear. I booked passage to
New York—then he did. Lose me? Not him. Afterward was
when he said it was a blessing. Your doing, he said to me. And
it was.

"This book, Bernadette, is called the *Thousand and One Nights.* I
am going to read to you. If I think you should know the word—
I'll stop, and you'll tell me what it is. *Verstanden?*"

When I was five, I started school, and stayed with Mrs. Talmadge in the afternoon only until Florence arrived home.
"Don't tell anyone that you can read," Mrs. Talmadge counseled
before my first day. "They'll make your life hell. A little dumb
goes a long way."

When Florence gave me my own door key, it was an initiation
into freedom. There were rules, but basically I was my own
person. The apartment—our apartment—was mine. I spent
one entire afternoon trying Florence's makeup—red lips, eyes
stabbed with mascara, rouge. I spent one afternoon sipping cold
coffee. Then I lost interest; after all, I could do anything I
wanted whenever I wanted.

I have no idea why I began the routine of the eggs. Perhaps
because I could. Three times a week, I boiled two eggs and
brought them to Mrs. Talmadge. I knocked on her door like a
real person. "Oh ho," she said, "Miss Smarty Pants." She repeated that each time I came, and her eyes mocked me. Run, I
told myself—smash the eggs on the landing. But I never did.

"Here," I said.

She took them.

I kept up that practice for almost a whole year. Then I stopped seeing Mrs. Talmadge regularly—she never went outside unless absolutely necessary, so our paths widened.

"Look," I said. "Suppose I wanted to borrow your apartment—you know, like for an hour. Could you take a walk?" I spoke quickly, I was nervous. I knew I hadn't really thought this through.

Mrs. Talmadge stared at me, her eyes seemed to have faded into the palest blue—hardly a color at all. I thought for a moment she didn't know who I was. "Who you going to bring here—my Lattimore?"

"What?" I said. Was she crazy already?

Then she laughed. "Sure—take the apartment."

"Tuesday—the day after tomorrow—at four?"

"Why not—I'll maybe have an appointment."

"Thanks," I said.

That had been easy. The boy's name was Jack. He was the doctor's son. The doctor was nothing special—he was a garden-variety doctor. The family couldn't move away from the neighborhood—the doctor's practice was in the neighborhood. Also, he lacked get-up-and-go—that was what Florence said. Go to him, if you're not sick.

Jack was a feeler and a looker. We were in ninth grade together. He liked to go down to the storage room and unhook my bra and then stare—sometimes he made little moans. He kept suggesting the possibility of more. I told him about this apartment—how maybe I could get it. I didn't dare use Florence's—what if something got broken? Anyway, she had this nose. This professional cleaner's nose—she could sniff out any aberrant scent. She'd know.

On Tuesday, Mrs. Talmadge opened her door, she winked, she left. I just stood near the door waiting. Well, I was nervous. Jack came late—then he stayed about ten minutes. He didn't lay a hand on me. Maybe he was scared. Afterward, I heard what he said to others. Bernadette is off the wall, but she puts out.

I stayed in Mrs. Talmadge's apartment for one hour—I stood at the window, didn't leave until I saw her walking down the street coming back from—where? I had enough time to look around, though—dirty dishes piled in smelly chaos in the sink, jungles of newspapers and magazines in the corners of the room threatening to grow toward the couch, three cats acting as onlookers as they dried their fur to the sizzle of the radiator.

For my junior high school graduation, Mrs. Talmadge gave me a single strand of pearls in a blue velvet case. Florence examined those pearls under the light in the bathroom. She often demon-strated jewelry cleaners. She scratched at the clasp, sucked on a bead. "I tell you, that's pure costume at perhaps a dollar fifty."

"They are not," I shouted, and snatched back my gift.

"Knowing and yelling are two different things!" Florence said.

I wore those pearls every day for a week. But then I was absently twirling them, when the string broke, and the beads, the color of fog, skittered across the classroom floor. I stepped on a single pearl, and it crushed to powder beneath the weight of my foot. I certainly never told Florence.

I forgot—the Halloween poem. I brought Mrs. Talmadge a copy of the school newspaper. She read it. "Don't do that again," she said. "Have some respect. Pumpkins and nonsense! Nothing to do with the ripeness of life. Save yourself for importance.

"Listen to this—listen to what happened. My Lattimore died

in a room while making love to a young girl. She opened her legs to him as I had done. Sex is always going to be a woman's fate. Write poems about that."

When I asked to borrow her apartment may be the very last conversation I had with Mrs. Talmadge. Yes, it must be. I hardly ever saw her afterward. But then she had never walked much. Perhaps she was afraid. An old woman on the streets. Once though, I thought I saw Mrs. Talmadge leaving the grocer. Sarrano's Quik Stop. Yes, Sarrano's. It didn't have to be her. An old woman wearing a coat with a torn hem that dipped to the curb. Could have been any old woman.

Florence told me that Mrs. Talmadge had died. She heard it in the hallway from the new woman in 16B. Someone in the building had called the police about a smell. They broke in and found her. Florence went downstairs hunting for details. It turned out that Mrs. Talmadge had belonged to a burial society and there was an already paid-up funeral. Good thing, everyone said. I was at school the day of the funeral. Florence had to work. "Anyway," Florence said, "it's not like we were family."

"She must have had two husbands," I said. "A Lattimore and a Talmadge."

Florence shrugged. "Maybe. Anyway, I never saw anyone come around."

We thought that was the end of Mrs. Talmadge, but we were wrong. I got home before Florence, so I opened the letter. Addressed to me. I was exploding by the time she came home. "Guess?" I shouted.

"What?" she yelled.

"I'm an heiress!"

Florence paled, clutched her neck. "Who died?"

"It was *her,*" I said. "Mrs. Talmadge." I waved the lawyer's letter.

It was true—technically I was an heiress. The letter from a lawyer said that Mrs. Talmadge had left an estate of one thousand dollars and the contents of her apartment to Bernadette Amy Berne.

"I never would have believed it," Florence said, rereading the letter for the third time. "Let's find the super. He has got to unlock her apartment and let us in—we have rights, we have the letter."

"You bet," I said.

I was surprised. The super unlocked the door, grumbling at being called from his table. The rooms had lost their flavor. It must have been her. What had I expected to find? I knew what was in the apartment. No hidden treasures. Still, we looked.

Since I had last been in these rooms the bookcase was gone. Sold perhaps. Too bad. I coveted that bookcase. There were no cats. The ancient couch remained.

Florence was disappointed and sniffed with disapproval. "Stinks in here," she said.

I opened the cabinet doors in the kitchen—chipped dishes, cups, dime store silverware, pots.

"Someone got here before us," Florence said, "and swiped everything."

In the back of the bedroom closet I found three books—the English version of the *Thousand and One Nights,* a novel called *Passion,* inscribed to "my loving wife, Bertha," and a book in German that I could not read.

"I'm going to take these," I said.

"Some inheritance! Anyway, they got to be sprayed with Raid before they're coming into my apartment."

Inside the front cover of the book written in German, I found a sepia-toned picture of a baby. On the back someone had written "Gerta, age eight months." But it could have been a photograph of anyone—that didn't necessarily mean that it was a picture of Mrs. Talmadge.

The super cleaned out the apartment. "She left a mess," he said. "Mouse droppings from the year one. Worth your life to go in the closets. Dried cat shit. And newspapers—a regular Collier brothers. Look at these boxes—piles of nothing."

I sat on a chair and went through the boxes. Old bills from Con Edison, rent receipts, shopping lists, notes. One said, "Midnight blue was my heart." No real personal mail.

I told my friend Louanne that I felt like a snooper—but on the other hand, I was the legal heir.

Florence encouraged me. "Look," she said. "Who knows. Maybe stuffed in an envelope, maybe wrapped in news-paper."

But there was nothing to find. I was certain that personal papers had once existed—papers in drawers, letters, even photographs. Florence had tons of stuff. So I thought that Mrs. Talmadge must have dropped these leavings from her life down the incinerator. Here a picture, there a letter. My friend Myra thought that was sad. I didn't know. Maybe Mrs. Talmadge was just careful.

When the check for one thousand dollars arrived, Florence made me put it in a bank. Open an account. It was clear to her, she said, that I was not the most reliable person, and eventually I was going to need money. Never mind what I wanted. I thought you hated banks, I said. I don't need to hear anything from you, Miss Know-It-All, Florence said. The money went into the bank.

Myra asked to borrow *Passion*. "I love old books," she said. She returned the novel within a week. "Crap," she said to Louanne and me. "Listen to this." She opened the book. " *'Oh my beloved, my own Elsa. If I could touch your handkerchief—that would be life enough for me.'* "

We giggled.

"That's high excitement," Myra said. "In this book, the exchange of glances gets you pregnant."

When I was a senior in high school I took that novel and dropped it into a Salvation Army collection box. I didn't want anyone to see it, and think it was mine. The other two books I kept. I thought that one day they might be left to my children, if I had children.

In my 1977 notebooks were the poems "Germany, 1937" and "Trying to Love Göring." Martin's mother said that was what she would have expected. Martin asked me if I was out of my mind telling his mother about those poems. But she asked me what I was writing—it was October of that year. I looked up from the pink chicken awash on the plate—it was at her dinner table that I told her. If I lied, the poems might have died. You can risk just so much.

Göring wore a uniform fashioned from his dreams, and the woman had a vigorous manner and blond hair that lashed across her face.

*   *   *

I've read about the lives of poets. Lives that I can't hope to match—who they studied with, what they learned—even the extent of their experiences in the world. And love for some of them was fantastic, occurring as it did with an air of exotic truth.

It's not that I didn't love or wasn't loved. All right, not always loved in turn. If I were to start—why, it must be with Eugene. He rises up before me, pouting mouth of discontent. Plump-necked Eugene. A reclusive rider, stolidly hard core. Love? Was it the short curls of his pale brown hair? The arrogance of early good looks? I fell in love with Eugene in fifth grade. He was the boy the girls loved that year. We loved him, we treasured him, we hoped for a sign. But I was the one who loved him the most, and in return, he offered me only a spiteful hate. But still, my love lasted through that entire year. I wrote a poem for Eugene—not delivered—no anonymous caress—just a whisper aimed in his direction. I had read William Vaughn Moody, and snippet that I was, I thought my verse as good.

> To Eugene, a beloved.
> What is that on my sleeve?
> Is that a cat's print of good-bye?
> Is that all she will leave?

Two years later, Eugene became a constant shredder of food, a lumpen, the groans of middle age alive in his mouth. Soon he had rolls of itching flesh. A paunching, stained body. His hair darkened. The girls said it was a shame. I, on the other hand, thought it justice.

This, of course, is merely the lead-in to the next mentor who waited for me. I might add that mentors were to be found in unlikely corners.

Our building had a new super. Florence said it was about time. The heat being an occasional thing. Some said old Nun-illo had gone mad and had walked off with the secrets to the pipes, the faucets, the entrailing ducts.

We waited—the children of the building. The style and disposition of a super were important. The new one looked all right—less frowning than Nunillo.

The man and his family would live in the apartment next to the boiler room. That always sounded bad, but in truth, that apartment was large and sunny and painted each year in "Winter White."

The new super was a small, tightly built man whose broad-hipped wife looked stronger. He turned out to be more like the old super than different. He angered easily, language and hearing were subject to the weather. He had a war injury that sent torrents of impurities snaking through his body. His wife was proclaimed to be moderately tolerable.

They had a son—seen briefly on the first day when they wheeled him into the building, his nose running, his hands jerking. His name was Bertram. Light of their eyes. God's gift to encourage humility. He lived at age thirty in a wicker wheel-chair, its high back an expression of the builder's art.

There was a physical reaction on seeing him. His body an armature, his hands stiffened hooks, his face a torturous ride. People crossed themselves when they saw him. And he noticed. You could tell that he noticed. His eyes mocked and watched.

He took the air in the courtyard during school hours only. The mothers objected otherwise. Not for themselves, they swore. But children—what did children know? They were frightened.

The super's mother accepted that. God's gift. God's pain. She spoke freely about Bertram's birth, happening in her forty-fourth year. Her splitting body that didn't open until the tenth day. The women of the building listened and murmured. Still, the mother was surely to blame. Look at her. A woman so fat must have crushed him in her womb.

"He's smart as a whip," the super's wife said, and patted Bertram's head, the brown hair that she combed each day. "He talks."

Of course he did. With care, you could hear every word. I brought Florence's canvas-covered folding chair to the court-yard and sat beside him. It was a school day, but I was home, having developed a passion for monthly cramps.

He was almost a prisoner. He couldn't escape me. Go where? I, on the other hand, breathed freedom. He was somebody and he wasn't. I could talk to him. Maybe tell him anything.

"I'm a poet," I said by way of introduction. "Bernadette Amy Berne."

If you didn't listen carefully, all you could hear were gurgles. The words were drawn out—each syllable stretched as far as it could go. But I didn't embarrass myself. I didn't say anything like, What? What? No, I extended myself. I tried.

This was what I heard.

"Ambition? Or fact?"

"Fact," I said. "I am a poet. What do you do?"

"I read," he said.

"Did you ever go to school?"

"The city paid for a tutor—a long time ago. Who is your favorite poet?"

I snorted. "I have a hundred, a hundred fifty."

"You can't answer the question?"

"Louise Bogan."

"Not bad. Can I see your poems?"

Now, considering my youth—I was into the age of secretiveness—I could say that most of my poems were private, and whether meant for the world I was uncertain—but the poems were never hidden. I always wrote in front of Florence and suspected that once in a while she looked in my notebooks. But their very openness gave them freedom.

"They are about my life."

"I should like to read them. A poet writes to be read—isn't that so?"

I hesitated. "I'll show you two—all right, three."

I ran into the building and up the stairs. Which three? I wasn't going to give him an entire notebook—I didn't trust him that much. So I recopied "Reading Profumo," "Jack, A Doctor's Son," and "Pictures from the Movies."

He was still in the courtyard when I returned. I knew how he read. He had a tray with a clip and a stick to hold in his mouth—the stick raised the clip and turned the pages. His father had made it, he told me.

"Three poems," I said. I was flushed. After all, what did he know? What could he know?

That was Wednesday. Thursday, I went back to school. I had to go—Drama Club had a rehearsal for *You Can't Take It with You.* I was fidgety on Friday—especially after school. I went over to Louanne's to help her give herself a perm. I thought about going to see Bertram. Should I? Louanne yelled, I was pulling her hair. But I didn't want to rush him. A careful reader needed time.

On Saturday, I waited until Florence left for work. I didn't do anything strange, I stayed in my pajamas, I yawned, I spoke about hanging around. I had to do the shopping. It was one of the rules.

"Here's the list," Florence said, and plopped a sheet ripped from my pad in front of me. She sprayed her hair with extra-hold and her dress with the scent of lilacs.

"I left twenty in the ashtray. And pay attention to what the hamburger looks like. You hear?"

"Hear," I said. My soul whispered, Go! Go, Florence!

The door closed. I counseled patience. Sometimes, something was forgotten, and the door could suddenly swing open. I checked the clock. Five minutes, ten. Safe to shower. I would dress and maybe wait just a bit. Until nine o'clock. Didn't the super rise early? He'd have to. Bang at the pipes, bang at the boiler, swear incantations at the furnace. Nine o'clock was plenty long enough to wait.

I went downstairs, took the basement corridor that was a dead end to the super's apartment. As I said, that apartment was light and airy. Five good rooms, including the kitchen. Bertram's mother opened the door. She was already dressed, a slipshod arrangement of safety-pinned skirt and blouse from another time. Her rooms, though, were clean. Cleaner than most they serviced.

"Could I see Bertram?"

She smiled. "Sure."

"Bertram," she called out, as if he might be God knows where. He was in the dining room, his chair pushed up against the wall that had a window, the sunlight from the floor of the courtyard surely as bright as that found one flight up.

"You," he said. "I read the poems. You have an intimate tone. You are also salacious."

"What?"

"Salacious means—"

"I know what salacious means." I was wounded. "That was what I saw, what I knew—those poems were the truth."

"The truth of your poetry—you immediately assumed that by salacious I meant bad. I was only surprised."

"By the poems?"

"By their source. Their source surprises me. How old are you?"

I considered lying—but the women in the building talked. "I'm fourteen," I said.

"That's close to what I would have guessed. So I was surprised. I would like to read the poetry that you like—as well as more of yours—if you'll let me."

A man wanted to read my poetry.

"Listen," I said. "If you want me to get you anything from the library—I know your mother goes—but I can travel elsewhere for more stuff. Forty-second Street library. Just give me a list."

He did. He dictated, I wrote. Some of the books on the list were for me. No one except a school reading list ever had suggested any books for me. So I read Gertrude Stein, Jean Cocteau, Balzac, Lovelace, Moliere, Leopardi.

Oh those Saturdays—long winter Saturdays when I sat in the super's kitchen and spoke to Bertram. We went over my poems, line by line. Once, standing near him, my hand touched his arm. It was a warm arm—it bespoke humanness. I was ashamed that I would have thought otherwise. It was an arm—as white and skinny as mine. Yet different. I rocked back and forth on the balls of my feet.

"The world," Bertram said to me one day. "Why don't you explore the world?"

"What?"

"What happens in the outside world—don't you care?"

"No," I said. But then suppose he was right. I started buying the *New York Times*. Florence said *that* better come out of my allowance.

I gave Bertram my first poem from that period—"General MacArthur Falls in Love."

*   *   *

Florence asked me how I could understand what that poor unfortunate soul said. I told her I could. She said maybe. She was suspicious. I heard her question the super's wife. How much could Bertram move? she asked.

Twice a day, Bertram used two aluminum canes and stood up. He was supposed to balance himself for five minutes, but two was his limit. I was standing beside him the day he crumpled. I caught his folding body and shoved him back into the chair, which bounced from the impact. His legs had been close to mine.

I knew I was in love with Bertram. It was real love—I wanted him physically. I wanted him. But I didn't know what to do. I didn't think his mother monitored our conversations. Anyway, half the time we were alone in the apartment. So I did what I could. I wrote a love poem. A disguised love poem called "To Mysterious B."

It was stupid of me. I offered it, trying to be casual, in the company of two other poems—all for him to critique. I waited the usual number of days. Still, it was stupid of me.

He guessed.

It was Saturday. His mother let me into the apartment. I knew something was wrong—I saw that in Bertram's eyes. In his silence. Long minutes before he spoke.

"You think," Bertram said, "I love children? Did you think that I was a man who could only love children? Go away, Bernadette Amy Berne. Get the hell away."

I thought he would come around. His mother said he got moody from time to time. But he didn't come around. I was *persona non grata* in the super's apartment.

Still, I am not apologizing. Bertram was an influence. Afterward, I could never look at a hand or an arm or a leg without understanding the power within them, the erotic possibilities, the black dreams. I have an entire series of poems—although disguised—that are the result of having known Bertram. I believe that the images in the poems "To Mysterious B" may be an important focus for future studies of my work.

To Mysterious B

Is virginity mandatory? If so
I am terribly sorry Should I
open a vein and let that stand for
virgin's blood. Listen B, cease
your lunatic silence Are you not
the fox in hiding? Surely you dreamt
of what I could do even as I lie
in my bed coolly reciting footnotes
from books of advice Offering
intimate details of one-night stands
minus benedictions So, B, let us
make love Forget the pleasures of wet
dreams No matter how treasured
Come feel where my thighs enter the body
As I play the role of your trembling girl.

Make your way down the hall I can
whisper for you sixty words you have
never heard Oh, how honey soft are
your hands Come B, rattle the bones
and drum away B, understand, for you
I would do anything B, you recognized
me when others pulled away You gave me
room and place B, suppose no one else does?

—BERNADETTE, AGE 14

(This is an early draft of part 1, found in Box 23, section 14. Note how this draft differs from later versions—see Box 29, section 8.)

I thought that one day I would need true criticism, a definition of what I had done—a mingling of our tongues, deep plumbing of syllables, avid mauling of meaning. The problem was that this analysis usually came after you were dead.

But the first time I thought about criticism, I wasn't considering death. I sat in the very dell of my kitchen in a trance of solitariness. Thoughts awakening. I was already into the period of having time for my work. How hard for a woman poet. How old were my children? Paul was ten and in school all day. Ruth was six, she napped in the afternoon.

Yes, I was in my kitchen. The passion of the day still mine. I had a pad of paper. My teeth circled the eraser on the pencil. Criticism, I thought. I wrote the word—a newly born shaman.

It was then that Toby called.

"Bernadette," she said, "I am reborn."

"What?" I hadn't yet left my reveries. "What?"

"Politics. Returned, Bernadette—you wouldn't understand—to the true inamorato of my youth—politics. A first love."

Her voice jangled past me, through me.

"And sweets, I am giving a party. It's going to require donations. The party is to help with Koch's campaign expenses. So come with an open purse."

"I thought you were a Republican."

Toby sighed. "Not for ages, Bernadette. That was just an unfortunate period of my life—I'm surprised you would bring it up. I blame all that on Raymond."

"I'll send a donation," I said. "But I don't think we'll be able to come—Martin doesn't like politicians."

"Pooh on Martin—you come. It's more than the money, Bernadette. I will need warm bodies. Couldn't you? You owe it to friendship."

*   *   *

Martin said he'd stay with the children.

"You'll hate it," he said. "A bunch of handshaking strangers."

"I know," I said, and wearily buttoned my best cloth coat, lime green.

It was a February night, the light moon-pale and the chill fierce. I took a bus downtown, walked two blocks east. Toby lived on Seventeenth. As soon as I saw the elevator crowded with strangers, heading for the fourteenth floor—I knew that I could have stayed home. I would not be missed. The body count guaranteed a success. But there I was in the elevator going up.

But you couldn't enter the apartment. Two women whom I didn't know sat at a card table and guarded the entrance. It cost one hundred dollars to get into Toby's black and white living room. The women took credit cards or checks with identification and shrieked with pleasure when change was required.

Right from the elevator you went to the line. Five steps in and a sign announced *Cash Bar*. The man in front of me turned around when he spotted that.

He grinned at me. "No way," he said.

"No way," I repeated.

We pushed past everyone, traffic in the wrong direction, to the elevator. We were the only riders down.

"C. S. Wellington," he said and offered a leather hand.

I presented my woolen one. "Bernadette Amy Marrkey."

You think I would have known who he was? He was C.S. He was a critic, he was a man of known qualities. I even owned his last book—*Sounds of Poetry*. But I never guessed—C.S. was such a common combination of initials.

"Can I buy you a cup of coffee? A place right across the street. Damn cold out."

"Sure," I said.

C.S. looked old in the light from a sodium arc lamp. His skin had the silky glow of someone who had given up efforts, and his voice had already grown shivery. Yes, he was a man valleyed and creased and crevassed. I was amazed to note that he wore a skullcap; he didn't explain. Of course, later I looked him up. He was only sixty-eight—but at the time I was thirty.

We sat in a red leatherette booth. I believe that all the booths I have sat in in my life were red. I sincerely believe that.

We ordered coffee. He added a piece of blueberry pie.

"I don't feel bad about skedaddling," he said. "Foolish efforts anyway—political things. But then I shouldn't have gone—I'm moving out next month—before the election."

"Where are you going?"

"Going to California." He winked at me. "My twilight years will be spent elsewhere. Received a lifetime pass to a good library—and I am getting married. Misogynist takes the leap."

"Congratulations."

He examined my face. "Well," he said, "and who are you?"

I repeated my name.

"What use is your name to me? Offer a better definition."

"I am a poet."

He flinched as if struck. "You *followed* me?"

"What?"

"Don't pretend—I know the sort you are."

I pulled on my gloves. At least there were other people around. On the other hand, he was possibly crazy. I dug a dollar from my coat pocket and dropped it on the table. "For the coffee," I said.

"Where are you going?"

"Away."

"You didn't follow me?"

I stood up.

He frowned, leaned forward, looked up.

"You don't know who I am?"

I shook my head.

"Sit down. I apologize then—I think I do. I'm C.S. Mean anything to you?"

I sat down. "You are *that* C.S.?"

"Yes. People follow me. But you didn't look the type—you looked like a simple married woman—children, husband. They always looked different—the scribblers who pursued, harassed, demanded. A bloody lot of maudlin versifiers."

"Nevertheless," I said. "I am a poet—even if I didn't follow you. I would have thought you would be the last person to say or imply that someone didn't look like a poet. There is no such thing as the look of a poet. That is romantic rubbish."

"I like you," he said. He reached over and patted my hand.

I felt his touch through the wool, cranberry-colored wool.

"Too bad I'm going to California. L.A. Yes, I'll be there. Marrkey? Well, I never read your work, did I?"

"No."

"All right—you may send me two poems. No more—or I'll flip them all into the garbage pail."

"Two."

He handed me a card. "This isn't my California address. I don't give that out. But you can send them here—they'll send envelopes on."

April 14, 1978

Dear C.S.,

I am taking you up on your offer. Remember me? I am the woman who did not follow you. We had coffee together after that political party that we did not go to. Anyway, C.S., you said that I could send you two poems. Here they are—"Night Out" and "The Chalk Boundary." I await your comments.

Sincerely,

Bernadette Amy Marrkey

7/10/78

Dear B.A.M.,

Enclosed please find your two poems. What do I think? I consider "Night Out" to be a five-dollar-an-hour hotel room and "The Chalk Boundary" is pure hopscotch. Housewives!

Yours in poetic pain,
C.S.

September 2, 1978

Dear C.S.,

You arrogant scumbag! You dirty dishrag! Poetry does not belong to you. Enclosed please find "The Victim's Cry" and "garden of hope."

Yours in critical pain,
Bernadette

12/12/78

Dear Bern,

"The Victim's Cry" requires that you listen to Ernest Chausson: 2nd Movement—Piano Quartet in A. It will give you the needed sense of da-da-da in ³/₄ time. Re "garden of hope"—read (or dare I hope, reread) Sidney's "Defence of Poesy."

Yours,
C.S.

March 8, 1979

Dear C.S.,

I am glad that you liked "Vinegar's Appeal" and I truly appreciated the way you annotated it. But in the margin at the twelfth line—the line that began, "A joy drawn from dark wormwood"—I cannot read what you have written.

Best,
Bernadette

Dear dette,
I wrote "too long."

Y.t.,
C.S.

These are all of C.S.'s letters re poetry that I could locate (my replies are carbons). Perhaps other letters exist in his estate.

C.S.'s wife left him that spring. I saw her picture in the *National Enquirer* at the supermarket. She was very thin. *The Candy Queen Tries Again,* said the newspaper. *Done with rowdy so-called intellectuals, she said.* C.S. appeared in a sliver of a picture—looking like an out-of-focus archaeological find.
This was his last letter to me.

7/1/80

Dear Bernadette,
Ding dong—the witch is gone. I now invite you to come to L.A. We can cohabit or marry—although I advise the former. Don't be in a hurry to decline—as you already know, my advice can change your life. I can give you a visible life as a poet. Who else can do that? Me. And age as a factor in life decisions should be ignored—our life together can be a priapic dream—bumps of sweat and mesmerizing chill arise at that thought. . . . What I know, my dear, you cannot even guess. I would only confess to you in the intimate circumstances of erotica. Then you would know.

Yours,
C. S. Wellington

This was my reply.

August 12, 1980

Dear C.S.,

My life as a poet belongs to me. I cannot imagine living with a critic.

As ever,
Bernadette

I was certain that he would understand. But C.S. didn't. I sent two more letters, tried for a chatty tone, accompanied my notes with six poems—I believed in the magic of that number. He did not respond. Still, he had offered much useful information. During the two years of our correspondence, we exchanged sixty-three letters. I have these letters from C.S. plus the carbons of mine and, of course, the annotated poems that he read and commented upon. I predict that they will be useful for future scholars. Once, C.S. sent me a package containing translations of rare Arabian texts. Thus, my knowledge and vocabulary increased.

I have always regretted that our correspondence ended before I wrote my "Nights in Berrasban" cycle. C.S. could have set me straight on the sexual practices of the six-armed god.

Illusions in a teacup

I made myself a cup of tea. Black tea, richly dark, and with a fragrance of mystery. Martin and I bought that tea in Chinatown on a Sunday after we had dim sum. It was called Invigorating Tea, and the label said that the leaves were commingled with herbs. Martin said I should never use any product with an amorphous designation of ingredients. Herbs? he said. Which herbs?

I didn't know.

I sipped the tea. No real chance that it contained anything potent—anything magical. Time to read the journal. I didn't intend to have the journal recount illusions—so one of my favorite reveries was deliberately absent. A typical child's delusion. Not the adopted-child or the mixed-up-babies one. Mine was the bastard one. I used to wonder if Ursula had actually been married to my father. Was Ursula ever really married to anyone? I was curious.

A mistake. In a fit of lack of caution I had asked Florence whether her daughter had ever been married. Florence flung wide her arm with maniacal fury and slapped me, not across the face, although it had looked as if that was where the blow was intended to land, but the smack ended up inappropriately on my forearm. Who do you think you are! she yelled.

Now it wasn't that I was unduly cynical. Not at all. But tell me—where was the father? He wasn't found. My exact feelings during these illusions were difficult to repossess. Different times, different people. But I knew that when I had asked Florence that question—in my heart, I had long ago accepted the fact that there was no father—except as the sperm-dropper.

When she was in a good mood, Florence implied that someday I would know. But I thought that suggestion was a leftover from some movie. You'll know, the old woman told the girl up there on the screen—both of them bigger than life.

Prier that I was, I went looking. In a shoe box, the family pictures were kept. A tumble of pictures, piles of the unknown. Three were once singled out. My daughter, Florence said, pointing at tiny heads, and that was your dad.

I stared at Dad. The photographs were box-camera-type photographs. You had to look closely to see the faces. These weren't pictures in good condition. The corners were broken off. Snatched perhaps from some album—the fact that they were gone perhaps a secret. And thus mutilated, the pictures looked old.

When Florence was at work, I studied these pictures. I took the magnifying glass that Florence used to help her thread needles. In one, Dad kissed Ursula's cheek. What was I looking for? I was uncertain. Maybe some familiarity of gesture. Anyway, I never wondered what happened to either of the people in the photographs. I hoped they were dead. But, of course, I was only eleven.

It's very hard to trace people. And a disappointment. I have no idea what happened to Ellen Kealer. Lea became a teacher and, as far as I knew, never married. One day when I was out walking with Ruth—who rode in her stroller—I suddenly realized that I had completely lost touch with Lea. Myra Davies became a social worker with a master's degree from Columbia. She married another social worker. Someone named Joel. The marriage took place in an afternoon ceremony in an apartment on Riverside Drive. I was there, pregnant with Paul. A woman whose head was wrapped in a strawberry-colored veil poked my belly and whispered, The punch—don't. I remember looking into that bowl—something at the bottom hadn't dissolved. I was afraid to drink any. Afterward, I forgot to send a wedding present, and by the time I remembered, it was too late, so I never called Myra again.

Until Paul was two years old, I faithfully glued little black corners in an album to hold our pictures—the pictures, though, were still removable. That first album had a navy-blue leatherette cover, and *Our Family* was printed in gold letters. Orderly, I was orderly. I wrote on the back of each picture where it was taken and Paul's age at the time. I even kept a running list of all the places written on the backs of the pictures. They had a rhythm. I recopied them in lines without commas. *Macy's Christmas Parade Central Park Zoo In Front of Sam's Golden Gate Bridge Old West Park Near Florence's By the Library Tucson The Nite Motel Next to the New Dodge In the Hospital Close to Enid's The Grocery Hartford.* Eventually the list filled two hundred and seventy-three lines.

One day I stopped putting pictures into the album. When Ruth was born, her pictures were everywhere. You could open any drawer and Ruth would be there.

What was that noise?

He stood in the doorway, tousled hair, blue cotton pajamas. The effect was boyish and the appeal immediate to a primitive maternal instinct.

"You," he said. "You!"

My emotional reaction (which I had before) was originally recorded in 1971, and again in 1980, in the two poems "More Winter Weather" and "Tie Hard the Mother Strings," respectively.

"Martin," I said. "I'm sorry, did I wake you?"

"No," he said bitterly. "You didn't wake me. Why should you wake me?"

"Sorry," I said.

"You know where I was today?"

I shook my head. I suspected. Oh, I did suspect.

"You pushed me to a scene of embarrassment, Bernie. I went to see Clive—that Waspy caricature. I hate that effete creep—your doctor."

"You looked him up in directories."

"Personality—I'm talking about his personality. Acts like I'm somewhere north wind of him on the evolutionary scale. Makes me feel like a goddamn peasant—as if I ate meat before it was cooked. But I went there, Bernie. Do you *know* why?"

I nodded.

"Well, I didn't beat around the bush. He expected animal. He got animal. My wife refuses to fuck me, I said. I swear, Bernie. I looked right down into his eyes and said that. She says never again, I told him.

"Clive stared up at me and said, She's into relapse. She took a turn, he said. What the hell does that mean? I said. I tell him how last week—it was last week—you climbed on a ladder and put up heavy drapes. And two weeks ago on a Saturday—when I didn't want to—we walked home from the movies. Cold and windy. I was tired—you weren't. Explain this turn, Clive, I said. Does it mean that we can't have sex? No, he said. But I don't make Bernadette's personal life decisions, he added. Who asked him to? I never.

"That's how it was left. That's it. God, Bernie, you have been in and out of remissions and relapses for years—this will be another one. I want you, Bernie."

It was a hard moment in my life. I saw Martin. It was man looking lovable and vulnerable. I considered the possibility of leaving him a note suggesting which of my poems he ought to read after my death. The strings and knots of this ancient and primitive whirlwind pulled tight. To go in the other direction required great strength.

"No," I said.

"Whatever happens now—be it on your head!" he replied.

Martin once told me that when he was a small boy, his mother woke him up one night. She actually pinched him awake so that he awoke startled and crying. She looked wild, he said, like a madwoman in her torn nightgown. Get up, she commanded.

Up, up, up! He was afraid that he would wet his pajamas as she dragged him down the hall to his sisters' room. She woke them up, too. And then she made them all kneel. The girls whimpered. Promise me, their mother said. Promise me all of you—that if I die you'll get the silverware from the drawer and my diamond ring from the box and Aunt Hystil's brooch from under the lamp base. And pull out all the money from inside the covers of the *Reader's Digest* condensed books. You'll grab all that and run. Or you'll be left high and dry—I know *him*. You won't let him have any of that. Promise me! They promised.

JOURNAL

———◻——

I find that I have many papers in Boxes 44 to 67 that will illuminate my life. The rest can be found in these pages. Future biographers will have to trust my perceptions—and my memory.

"I didn't see your la-di-da Helene," Florence said.

"No," I said. We were back from a Cousins Club dinner in Great Neck. It had been a buffet supper with card table seating and place cards. My chair? I landed out on the back porch. "Helene is away. They sent her away to school. Boarding."

"Couldn't stand her, eh?"

"Probably."

Helene. Florence never forgot anything. Anyway, Helene and I didn't see much of each other anymore. Not for years—except at Cousins, there we talked sometimes. They sent Helene to school in Vermont. For winter break she met her parents in Miami.. For spring break she went with them to Puerto Vallarta.

We almost met at the Cousins summer picnic, but I had a better date. Then the next year I went to City College, and Helene took a year off for language study. She went to France for French and Germany for German.

Helene—just another cousin.

I learned a lot after I got a key to the front door. I found Gertrude Stein in the library. I memorized "Tender Buttons." I wondered whether by reciting a poem often enough it somehow grew inside you. To write poetry you had to be disciplined—plenty of other things to do.

What was great about being alone was that I could recite out loud. No one to yell that was a waste of time. Forgotten women poets were the best to read out loud. The card catalog in the library had lists of forgotten poets. That designation was funny. Surely someone remembered—otherwise those poets couldn't be gathered together in anthologies and labeled as forgotten. Think of Lizette Woodworth Reese, Esa May Carteret, Isabelle Parker. Poets like them.

You have to understand that I wasn't thinking Helene. I never thought Helene. Out of sight.

"You'll never guess who called," Florence said.

I hadn't even taken off my coat. Although you didn't have to do that too quickly—the steam heat wasn't great. Florence had a special look. You could tell that she was waiting.

I had come from the library. This was the schedule. I went to classes in the morning, sold shoes in the afternoon, and studied in the evening. It wasn't actually bad. The store gave thirty percent discount on shoes to employees. That's because the shoes were so expensive. Even with thirty percent I never bought one single pair.

"Who?" I said.

"The Princess of Oyster Bay—Helene."

"Yeah," I said. "Do we have any tuna left? What did she want?"

"In the square plastic container—the one from lasagna. Sounded in an uproar—imagine that—a Great Neck uproar! She said please have Bernadette call. Puh-lease, she said."

I looked at my watch. "Too late. It's eleven-thirty already."

"It didn't bother her to call during *my* supper. Who calls at the dot of six? I ask you—who!"

"All right." I made a tuna sandwich and carried the plate to the couch. The telephone was on the end table. A sheet of paper half stuck under the telephone. Call *H.*, it said, and gave the number.

I bet it was a number for that telephone on the third floor. I dialed. It only rang once. "Hello," I said.

"Bernadette? Is that you?"

"Yes. Long time no see. How are you?"

"Fine, yes fine. Bernadette, I have to see you—tomorrow. I have to see you then."

Florence was listening.

"Yeah, well I'm tight for time tomorrow, Helene."

"Please—it's important. It's truly important."

I thought I knew what that must be. I thought it could be only one thing—listen to the tension in her voice. Yes, she must be pregnant. She figured that if anyone knew what to do, I would.

"Look," I said. "The only time I could see you is at lunch."

"Fine—swell. I'll buy you lunch."

"Okay. There's a Chock Full O'Nuts—"

"No—we need a booth."

"I won't have much time—all right, got a pencil? A place called Del Roy. Look up the address—no, there's only one Del Roy near City. I walk there by instinct. Noon."

I hung up. Bit down on the luxuriant mayonnaise that glazed my tongue.

"She's in trouble," Florence said in satisfaction.

"I didn't say that."

Florence snorted. "Some people were born yesterday. I wasn't."

So Helene was in trouble. So what. Happened to a lot of people. I sat down to study. Nineteenth-century Russia. The Duchy of Posen. I liked the sound of those words.

Now I never expected *not* to recognize Helene. But I almost missed her. I guess I did what everyone does under the circumstances—I took my last image of her and elongated it—but I was wrong. She had grown together—proportions altered. The head, the neck, the body, all met. She was unified. She hadn't turned pretty. Maybe it was the clothes. She was smart-looking, though.

Helene wore a beige pleated skirt. My eyes went to her belly, but you can't always tell with pleats. Especially those skinny pleats that whirled at you.

I was seated in a booth already. They didn't want to seat one—but I swore someone else was coming. Need two glasses of water, I said. I had the menus.

I stood up and waved. Maybe she didn't recognize me, either. There she was—trotting over. We leaned forward, we kissed cheeks.

"Honest to God," I said, "you look great."

Helene smiled. "Thanks. Your aunt said you were in college now."

"Aunt? Florence is my grandmother."

"Grandmother—said that you were in college."

"Yes, I'm at City. And you?"

"I'm transferring to Columbia in spring—I've been studying in Paris."

"Great—wonderful. Waitress!"

"Could we talk first?"

"No—we can talk while we eat. I have to be out of here in forty-five minutes, Helene. I have a job—time is money. Medium hamburger, french fries, coffee—bring me two coffees."

"The same," Helene said.

I bet with myself that she would leave all her food.

"So," I said, "you might as well tell me."

"Tell you?"

"Come on—you had to see me rush-rush. We haven't been

together for a month of Sundays. When did I last see you? So—
I guess pregnant."

She shook her head.

I was surprised. "You're not?"

"I was."

I thought right away of complications. I was not equipped to
know about medical complications—I had no experience in
that. "You better see a doctor, Helene."

"Be quiet," she said abruptly. "Oh hell, what's the use? We
have—what?—thirty minutes left."

"Then tell me fast."

"I was pregnant—I met this person. I was pregnant last
year."

"Last year?"

"Yes, last year."

I looked at my watch.

"Couldn't you call in sick or something?"

"No," I said. "I get paid by the day. I get five-fifty an hour." It
was an exaggeration.

She didn't hesitate. "I'll pay you then—right now. The day's
pay."

Florence would have had a fit. Never take anything from
them. But Florence wasn't here. I hadn't any intention of re-
fusing.

"All right, I'll call in sick," I said. It wasn't a question of
pride. I considered the money. She could afford it. Why not? I
got up. There was a telephone by the door. I was too sick to
work.

"All right then—you were pregnant last year," I said when I got
back to the booth. "Who? Who was it?"

"It was terrible," Helene said, and sucked in her lower lip. "I was home for the summer—I met this person. Christ, I got pregnant right away. Then I told him—and he said he'd marry me. So we did."

"You're married? You're kidding! Not an abortion?" I was incredulous. Not a word had leaked at Cousins.

She shook her head. Her skin was deeply white, her neck long, she looked high-strung, well bred. I thought that only through optical magic could we be related.

"No one knew, Bernadette," she said. "I thought I loved him. I married him—my fear was like a fever. Then afterward—like a couple of days—I wasn't pregnant anymore. You understand—we were married and I wasn't pregnant. And suddenly I couldn't stand him—I didn't want him at all. I didn't know what to do—I just packed up and went back to Paris."

I whistled softly. "What about him—the person? What did he do? Disappear?"

"Sort of. Then I came back home. Well, I always planned to get a divorce—I thought maybe later. I'd manage. But two days ago he called me—at home. I don't know how he knew I was back. He wants to be married, Bernadette. He says he'll tell my father—he says he'll get me pregnant again. I hate him."

"Listen, Helene, tell your father yourself. He'll arrange a quickie divorce—one, two, three."

"Bernadette, he has never been too fond of me."

"Who?"

"My father."

"You're kidding!" I thought of her father. Jovial Henry. Henry of the stroking hands and greedy eyes.

"He thinks disgrace—publicity—is the worse thing in the world. He never gives interviews. He's got a lot of money, Bernadette. And his ideas—he's nineteenth century. Didn't you always find him nineteenth century?"

"Definitely. Want do you want from me, Helene?"

"I'm going to see this person—this evening. I tried to put it off. But he wouldn't."

"Is this like extortion?"

"Yes."

"You have money for him?"

"What I could manage—five thousand."

I whistled again. "You think that's enough?"

"I don't know. Will you come with me? He said alone—but another woman shouldn't bother him."

I hesitated.

"I'll pay you five-fifty an hour right through the evening. And I'll drive you home," she said.

"Sold."

I couldn't believe it when Helene told me. We were going to a park. Suppose I wasn't going along—she would have been crazy to go somewhere so isolated by herself. That showed the difference between city bred and raised in the sticks.

A small park, Helene said. Like a square of green in the suburbs with a cut-out pond and a pair of rented geese. I thought it a mistake, two shiny cars parked together in a deserted park on a November evening. But I hadn't done that. This wasn't a tryst that I had set up. I was an observer—a neutral Switzerland.

Helene picked me up at the library. I used that time between lunch and assignation to study, since I considered the evening a sacrifice, although a paid-up one.

I tossed my knapsack in the back seat. It was the kind of car I thought Helene would have—gray, new, and essentially boring.

Maybe it was nerves, maybe it was the way she always

drove. Her nose an inch from the wheel, hands welded to the leatherette. I thought at once about the disinherited heroine, I thought about movies in which the daughter lost every thing.

"What are you studying?" Helene said, her voice stiff and cracking.

"Drama major. And you?"

"Nineteenth-century British literature."

"Very interesting. Who is he?"

"Who?"

"The person you married."

"I met him at the pool."

"A swimming pool?"

"Yes."

"He worked there?"

She gave me a quick glance and then turned back to the road. We had reached the Whitestone Bridge.

"No, he was a guest. It's the club pool. He was a guest. Someone's guest."

"What does he do?"

"I don't know?"

"You don't know?"

She shook her head; her voice became thin and piped, like the intercom voice at a door.

"He was on vacation—he was looking around. Planning to settle down, he said."

What an idiot! I couldn't have imagined before that she was such an idiot! This was her affair. This wasn't mine. I promised myself that I would be an observer to whatever happened and not a bona fide participant.

"We're here," Helene said, her voice suddenly stronger.

*   *   *

The park had lights—but the atmosphere was dark. The other car was already parked, pulled off the road onto frozen ground. It was a better car than I had anticipated.

I looked at Helene. Was she scared? Hard to tell. I felt imprisoned in a spy story, my arms pressed against my chest, bound there despite an atavistic desire to flee. I shivered, concentrated on the scene before me.

"I'm going to crouch down," I said. "I think we should let him think that only you are here."

Either she agreed or didn't hear me.

She parked the car, got out, left her door ajar—but that was not on the side where he was. So I stayed concealed.

"Helene," the man said in a stranger's voice. "All right, what's this about?" The man made a sound like a belch, but perhaps I was wrong.

Now they were walking away. What was the matter with Helene anyway? She should have stayed near the car. Speak louder, Helene!

Her voice was lower than expected. His too. All I heard were murmurs. I presumed this was the point when cash would be offered.

I tried so hard to make out words that I jumped when Helene suddenly gasped, followed by a gulp, then an unrehearsed squeal.

"I won't," she said.

He spoke or mumbled.

For the first time I was aware that struggles made a noise—not voices. The impact of bodies, the slide of feet. Someone was hit. Now in all honesty, I didn't know whether she hit him or he her. They were by the car—no, behind the car. The car gave a wild bounce. I danced upward in time to see them clutching at each other. He was pulling her coat. He was shorter than she—but he carried more bulk.

"Hey!" I shouted in a voice as eerily clear as the winter air.

He turned toward my protest, and taking advantage of that, Helene's fist shot out, connecting with his evening-shadowed jaw. The man fell forward—it was as if Jack had dropped from his beanstalk. Bang!

In my momentary bewildered vision, bolstered only by lamplight, I saw that his eyes were unprepared for the occurrence, they meditated on other matters and, in collapse, had frozen with that stare. He was not young—perhaps forty. A thick man who had fallen as if in a trance. His arms hung straight down, lines of scalp shone in the moonlight, his scarf tangled with his legs. His hands in pugilistic knots.

"My God," I said, and then caught a fender to keep myself from slipping. The winter grass had a sleety coating. The concrete path glowed, a shimmering furrow.

We stared down.

"I hit him," Helene said, puzzled, dismayed. She clutched her coat closer.

"Maybe he slipped."

"What?"

"Well, you hit him, and then perhaps he slipped—he fell forward. I think otherwise he should have fallen backward."

"Is he moving?"

I bent over, but touched nothing. I had never felt for a pulse—not even mine. He wasn't moving, but then the black overcoat was thick. Would it have sighed above the beat of a heart? He lay belly down.

"What?" Helene said. "What?"

"We should leave," I said, although thinking out loud. "What was he doing—before he slipped?"

"He said he would make love to me—make me do it."

"Here—in the park?"

"Yes—he said I was his wife and he had the right."

"I say we leave."

"They'll find me," Helene said, her voice curiously unin-
flected.

"I don't know," I said. "Maybe they won't make a connection.
Look, he wasn't robbed. He fell facedown—maybe hit his
chin."

"But what was he doing here in the park? They'll wonder."

I squatted. I was frightened. Suppose he moved? Those
clenched hands raised, and it was me they clutched, grabbed.
You, you, he screamed—as in a horror film. But he was still. I
wiggled my fingers under his body, met no brutish resistance,
reached the zipper on his pants and pulled it down. He was
warm—did that mean alive? When did you turn cold under the
circumstances—if you were dead?

"He stopped to relieve himself in this deserted park," I said,
and as I said it, it acquired a late night logic. Yes, it could have
been that way. "He stopped to pee. Why not? Let's go."

"He's alive, isn't he?"

"Can't be sure."

I bought the Long Island newspapers for three days. I read
Newsday thoroughly. He wasn't actually news.

He was dead, though. Body found in park. He fell. No hints,
no scent of the killing. He had been found intact—wallet, keys,
watch. His sister in New Jersey told the newspapers that her
brother was a solitary person given to long rides.

"I ask only one thing from you," Helene said. Her voice was
muffled. She must have held the telephone receiver too close.

"What?"

"Promise that this will remain a secret—you still write those
poems, don't you?"

"Yes."

"Promise me—not a word about this. Nothing—ever, ever."

"Oh for God's sake, Helene—I'm not going to send us to jail!"

"Promise! You have to promise—I'm terrified, Bernadette. My life is changed forever and forever. I can't bear the thought of it being in writing."

What could I do? She was a new widow. The man's eyes—oh, how I longed to write about them. About what he saw. A man given to solitary rides.

"I promise."

I'll mention something really strange. A trip to Chicago—the Windy City. A business trip. Martin said come on. You'll have fun. So I went. He was in the city on business. I wanted to go to the art museum, I wanted to buy something at Marshall Field's, I wanted to walk along the shore of Lake Michigan.

It was about two o'clock in the afternoon on the second day of the trip. I was by myself, growing tired, walking more slowly, when I actually remembered the building where I once lived—a part of my life I referred to as the haze. And I swear that in front of me suddenly—the building where I had lived with Ursula Marilyn Berne, and perhaps Dad. Up to that moment I had never known that I had lived in Chicago. But now I knew. There had been rooms in that building where Ursula danced—ah one, two, three, bump kind of dance. And the man had said, Let it rip, baby. Ursula gave me a Coke and a cheese sandwich. A rich golden mustard spread on the bread.

I stood in the middle of the room holding the sandwich. That room—the walls pale green like grass faded in the sun but not actually burned. Must have had a bed somewhere—but no bed in the sight of the vision. A table with legs that folded—of course, a card table. A card table with a hot plate on it. A curtain on a string. A curtain printed with orchids. And me behind the curtain. I was certain that this was the building—gentrified now—but basically the same.

Remember the promise of a sheetless Stearns & Foster mattress and someone named Shifton laughing at me, taunting me, Come on, baby, oh baby. Did you think I had forgotten? Right away it would seem that the mattress and the laughter occurred simultaneously. Well, they didn't.

It all happened the year a wild restlessness came over me. The year I turned twenty. I was pretty then—twenty is pretty. Good chin, aided the profile. Smooth black hair.

Maybe I didn't dress right. Yes, my clothing was a problem. I had found this place—up above a fish store on Mott Street. They made strange-looking tights. I bought five, six pairs— different colors. I wore a pair of tights all the time. Lime green with black stripes, orchid and white, chain gang tights. What kind of job can you get if you dress like that? So I did back room work at an insurance agency.

All I needed was a high school diploma, and to show up. My fingers touched tissue copies—tender pink, summer yellow, desperate blue. Separated and collated. The forms stacked in piles, making small villages, actuarial mountains. Sometimes I read the forms. An accounting of troubled times, black days, bafflement, windfalls. My hands were carbon-grained, finger-prints in color; any place I pressed, my hand left my permanent mark. She was there—see the whorls. I could be caught imme-diately. It was a job that made you think of death.

I had left college—time off I called it. Florence tried to persuade me to try demonstrating, she would teach me every-thing she knew. With my dramatic training, she swore, I could rise to the top.

I moved out—too far to travel, I said. Where did I go? I read advertisements in the newspaper, looking for what I could afford.

The advertisement required no specifications—no cheerfulness in the morning, no nonsmoker, no caffeine-free beverages.

Roommate, 1½ rooms. The girl's name was Sammy, the place was a Fourth Avenue dump, the dresser was cardboard, the double mattress was on the floor. I got the cot. We paid our rent jointly as C. Claudine. Maybe a sublease's sublease. Two weeks into our mutual home, Sammy got picked up by the police. I didn't know what happened. I found a fresh cardboard box and carefully packed her possessions and stacked them in the corner of the closet. There was no door on the closet, it separated from the rest of the room by a curtain on a string. The curtain was dirty, but the pattern was all right—blue dots on a purple background. I was now the sole owner of C. Claudine.

Louanne called me up. I couldn't believe it was her—I hadn't seen her for years. She got my telephone number from Florence. We met and had coffee together. Louanne kept up, she said. So she knew what had happened to a lot of people—many of whom I could have sworn I never knew.

A month later, Louanne offered me a gift. She was marrying and moving to Cleveland. I could have her role, she said—she would tell them. Off-off-Broadway.

I wasn't lonely. My evenings were my own. But I went to the audition. The part was small, a handful of lines. The alienation theme was popular that season. A play gritty with city pain.

Shifton wasn't in the play. Shifton was a designer. That was his set—mouse-gray backdrop with three red stripes.

After I took the role of the girl named Flower, I tried to go backward, tried to remember whether Louanne had actually disliked me. Nevertheless, I left work at five and went to rehearsals.

Shifton hung around evenings—maybe he had nothing else to do. Nothing better. No, the woman playing the lead said, he is working his way through the cast. Twelve women and one man. I wondered if my turn would come up before the play opened and closed.

I never had luck with real good-looking men, drop-dead men. So Shifton seemed a good bet—my kind of man. Adolescence had left him pitted, life experience as if patted on by a makeup man. But I should have been cautious. His type of looks was just beginning to be popular.

This was what happened when we went out to a coffee bar on Sixth Avenue.

"Sweetheart," Shifton said, "I divide the check—every time."

I smiled. "Why not." I ordered a double cappuccino and rum baba with whipped cream. He had an espresso.

Shifton worked as a waiter in a sporadic fashion. He lost jobs for picking fights with the customers. Pricks, he said. I hate waiting on pricks.

I characterize our affair as experience. I think I make him seem coarse and hard. Yet he once brought me two clear goblets for our wine—wrapped in tissue and red ribbon. He even sang to me in a voice keen and sweet. He didn't have a place. He slept in the rooms of friends. We went to C. Claudine to make love. Shifton was a fine lover, may have been my best—perhaps the artistic temperament. He was skilled, he created designs, his technique changed a little every time.

"Move in," I suggested.

He kissed my nose. "Tomorrow."

Shifton didn't need a car or anything. All he had to do was make two trips from the apartment of someone named Cliff who lived three blocks from C. Claudine—because everything

Shifton had came in two liquor store boxes. We folded up the
cot. It was Shifton who took off the sheets, baring the mattress.
That mattress was old—a nesting spa. It smelled like the third
day of everything. The stains were ancient bruises that had
melted into the stripes.

"I can't sleep on that," I said—descendant of Florence, professional cleaner.

"Yes, you can," Shifton said. His ankle came behind my knee
and I flipped down. He came right after me. We tumbled on
those tufted hills, studded with prongs and buttons. I grew to
like it, a new dimension to love.

The play opened and closed on a Tuesday. An audience of
friends and derelicts. Nobody even wanted my Flower costume.
They tore apart Shifton's set. Our evenings were suddenly free.
I had expected nothing, but Shifton was incensed. He stormed
the rooms. "I am going to make it," he declared, and pounded
the kitchen table. "I will!"

I nodded. I wanted him to succeed. But I thought he didn't
know how. Anyway, I guessed that he thought the same about
me. Only I was silent.

"Don't you want to be something?" he accused. "God, you are
so bloody content, Bernadette. As long as you can scribble—
you want nothing."

I was upset—how to tell him the strength of my position
when his direction had not yet come? I was something—I was a
poet.

I don't know what I expected. Love wasn't a set piece in a
museum. We weren't joined. He loved me or I loved him—
neither seemed to apply all the time. He slept away the mornings on the premises of C. Claudine. I got up and pulled on the
striped tights, over which I wore a black tunic. I took an uptown

subway and then walked three blocks. Did it sound arduous? It was nothing. All day I heard about life. My co-workers. Their loves, their abortions, the state of their bodies. Nothing can compare with the intimacy and confessional of the working environment.

"He lives with me," I said.

"Lives off you," LindaLee said.

"Well, I sympathize," Meta said. "Once, my best boyfriend— best I ever had—had a hard time. What could I do? Let him starve? So what can Bernie do?"

"Let him starve," LindaLee said. "Sorrow starts with an s— don't forget that."

No one told me what Shifton did during the day. He never did. I thought I would come back and find him fucking on the Stearns & Foster mattress. Without a sheet. Once, I called up and said I had to work late, until eight. I sat for one hour in a luncheonette at Columbus Circle, until the waiter told me to go and peddle else- where. Then I took the subway downtown. At six-thirty I crept up the wooden stairs and silently entered the room. Shifton was in bed, propped up on cushions watching the news. Even with his elbow was a paper plate, the red sauce of the spaghetti soaked through. He turned to wave, shifted the plate. Lava entered the mattress. A stranger, I thought, would take that for blood.

I never caught him. I suspected, I sniffed his body. Love left a trail. Three times, I came home late. I never caught him. So that's not what happened.

They made me work until eight. I was so surprised I forgot to call. A tragedy in California the previous week, thirty-four cars rear end to front end in the mountains. The paperwork had reached us—an avalanche to be collated pink with pink, blue with blue, yellow with yellow. It used to be harder, I was told, before colors. Someone received fourteen hundred dollars for that suggestion.

I got home close to nine-thirty. Shifton wasn't at C. Claudine. I knew where he was. The bar we liked, where we went, an out-of-work theater bar. I didn't waste time cleaning up—washing my hands was pointless. Who would see me in the bar? A room always dark and smoky and crowded. It looked like a standard pickup bar but it wasn't. Nothing gained here.

The room was filled, as a bar should be, with a collection of half-known people bouncing between booths, tables, stools. I blended. I was in black, my face another white face. You maybe had to see the tights to be certain who I was in that room. I exchanged smiles with some of the half-known people.

I heard Shifton laugh—his laugh was uncontrolled. He had once been someone's darling and that gave the laugh confidence. I headed for the sound, my path constantly impeded.

I believed that hearing in a crowd was a trick, requiring super concentration on a certain set of decibels. I followed that laughter. It was, of course, the moment when I acknowledged love. I loved him. He was witty, he was funny, I could talk to him. I loved him as he laughed—uncontrollably. So I stood in the bar shivering. I must have suspected. Did I? Else why had I stood there, my teeth pounding, my fingers holding tight to my arms, keeping them from flying away.

What was I to hear? Unprotected—no premonitions, no augury. I was being given up, served up, carved up. I would have shouted quite without dignity. Love me!

I tried to move quickly, my path barred by the weight of strangers. It was a good night. It was a Friday night. I had to reach the table.

Too late.

SHIFTON: It's a scene like you wouldn't believe. Look, I know she's almost a basket case. But you got to get the whole fuckin' picture. We have finished our two laps, see, and she sits up and switches on this shit lamp with a one-watt glare. She's got this notebook—a fuckin' child's spiral notebook. What was it like for you? I swear—the bitch is taking notes for a poem. A screwing poem. When I wiggled my cock, how much of her can I touch? Did it have colors?

MALE VOICE: Dirty red.

(Laughter)

WOMAN: Every time?

SHIFTON: Every fuckin' time—pardon the pun. It's the craziest thing. When you vibrated my flaps, did you see my reactions? It's a sex quiz. She sits bareass, knees up— nothing to imagine there—and asks these questions.

WOMAN: Honestly she writes poems? Dirty poems? I wouldn't think Bernie had the vocabulary.

SHIFTON: Who says they're poems? The late night muse.

(Laughter)

MALE VOICE (new one): How is she—by the way?

SHIFTON: It's a living.

(Laughter)

I left the bar. Felt in the bottom of my purse for change, a folded bill. I needed darkness. The theater around the corner. The marquee promised that back by popular demand was the latest rerelease of Barbara Stanwyck in *Double Indemnity.* I saw it twice. Do nothing in haste—Florence said that she had tried to teach that to her own daughter.

So I waited two weeks. I did it on a Saturday. I made a good breakfast. Bacon drained on a brown paper bag, scrambled eggs with tiny bits of sweet red pepper. Bagels purchased and carried all the way from Broadway and Eighty-second. Shifton ate well.

He finished, and slowly with the corner of his thumbnail picked the sharp edges of bacon from his teeth.

"Sweetheart," I said evenly, "I think you have to pack up this morning and leave."

He stared at me. "What?"

"Normally," I said, "I would give more notice—but you have plenty of friends, so you can be put up somewhere without too much trouble."

"What the hell is going on?"

"I can't get any more information from you," I said. "You're used up."

I waited around the halls of C. Claudine even though I had laundry to do. I didn't trust Shifton. I watched him fill two cardboard boxes—he had to get fresh ones from the all-night liquor store across the street. He called someone. Yeah, he said. Yeah. A man I recognized came upstairs and carried down one box.

"Hi, Bernie," he said nervously.

"Fuck her," Shifton said.

That evening I rode the IND to see Florence. When she opened the door, I started crying.

"What happened?" she said.

"My hands," I wailed. I held them out.

She pulled me into the bathroom where the light was better. "Christ," she said. "Look at those stains. You got to find a different job." She bent over and rummaged on the wooden shelves beneath the sink, behind the curtain that hid their existence. She pulled out bottles—The Industrial Man, NO Stain, and a powerfully green liquid soap.

Within two hours my hands were burning and raw—and pink.

*   *   *

I reenrolled in City College. Night classes were hard on me—
the concentration seemed to require a yellow dawn. Even the
young looked old—perhaps it was the cast of the light, a blue
tinge that created veins where shadows would have been
enough. People had responsibilities that they spoke about—the
intimacies of the evening student. Husbands abandoned, the
boss that hated you, money problems.

I got a job waiting tables at the Oh You Deli, and I also had a
new roommate. Her name was Patricia. She wanted to be a
dancer, but meanwhile she worked in a cafeteria on Seventh
Avenue. We both carried big purses lined with plastic bags. We
never bought groceries.

It was Patricia who took me to a party one evening. I was
depressing, she said. Her men came and went, she didn't care.
Come on, she persuaded this one. Let her come along—it's a
party. She can get lost there.

I could tell right away that it was a middle-class party and I
should have really known someone to be there. But there I was.
The host brought me a drink. The party wasn't that large, only
twenty, twenty-five people. The house was in Queens. I couldn't
get lost. I wasn't planning to eat—I ate all the time. I would do a
bottoms-up with the glass and find out how far to the subway.

The man walked over to me. He wore a plaid jacket and
necktie and pressed pants. He was a stocky man with a long
torso. What Florence called hunky.

"Hello—I'm surprised!"

Surprised at what? I had a go-away stare—I had perfected it
by practicing in a mirror.

"Yes?" The voice, too, was a studied chill.

"I do know you," he said.

"Pardon?"

"Bernadette—Bernie?"

God, he did *know* me.

"I'm sorry," I said. "Must be the lighting in here."

"Well, I guess I've changed. But you—let me see, it must be five, six years."

"Yeah—maybe."

He kept staring at me. He was wounded, anyone could tell. He hadn't been remembered. I had no idea who he was.

"It's me," he said. "Martin—Martin Marrkey."

A lover of my youth—he had done a bye-bye act.

"Oh yes," I said coolly. "And how are you?"

"Fine—I'm an accountant now. You?"

"Still a poet." I looked at my watch. I'd find the damn subway myself. "Listen, excuse me—but this was just a stop. I have to go."

He reached into his pocket, pulled out a golden pen, a rectangle of pasteboard. He held them out. "Write your number, please. Maybe we could go out for coffee sometime."

I imagined a small collection of pasteboard rectangles shuffled periodically in search of a winning hand.

I smiled—this was the smile I had used in two different plays. It was the dismissal smile.

"Telephone number in the book," I said. I didn't even offer my last name in case he had forgotten it.

The naming

Two things have happened. First, I realized that I shouldn't delay in the naming of a literary executor. I needed someone to be in charge of the future. My future. The future after I died. Of course, I meant reputation and works. The future of a poet. I was occasionally astonished by the scope of what I had collected— the artifacts, the footprints of my life. Abundance. And still the material grew. Material that explained, showed, added. Notebooks, pads of paper, scraps of paper written border to border. I packed the poems as they appeared. My tally was rough—to date, approximately one thousand six hundred and seventy-three poems. Give or take.

I achieved contentment by my actions—the tying up of the ends of my life. I procrastinated then and buried the thought of executor. To let someone in—now. Wouldn't that mean relinquishing my power over what was here? Probably. This was the second thing.

A will? It could be done in a will—the naming. Why not? Wait a bit and let the final details be presented in the will and read after I was dead. On the other hand, didn't that defeat everything that I intended? No, the naming must take place now. I required the assurance that what I have left behind will be set free in the right direction.

Who should it be? I knew who not to select. I thought about everyone I knew. First I considered the possibility of two, then three caretakers. Then I decided that would not do—three constitutes a division of authority. It must be one person who would have the unsquabbling right to keep or discard.

One person. I felt better having made that decision. Anyway, it would have been hard to find three people. It wasn't a case of any three. It had to be the right three. But one—I could find one. Although the selection would be tricky. I'd think it through—maybe just a trifle hurried. I'd find the right person.

Right in the middle of this problem, Martin started speaking to me again—directly, that is. He always spoke to me in front of Ruth—why should she suffer?—but those words had the effect of an overheard conversation.

He spoke to me—freely. This was like saying, Up yours! What started this? A return to small civilities, accounts of his

day, advice requested, minor anecdotes. For instance. I ran into
Brodlan today, Martin said. On the street. They're moving to
Florida. Really? I said. What about his business? Martin smiled.
That's it—the bastard sold out his partner. Just like that—and
he and Joel were friends—tight friends. It's up yours—that's
what it is.

I thought affair. I thought affair at once. Martin must be
having an affair. He was talking—but not looking directly at
me. Definitely an affair. Well, I ought to understand. And it was
on my head, wasn't it?

Clive missed a call. I almost telephoned him of my free will. It
was yesterday, when I swear that my soul for a moment circled
the room. What a horrendous feeling—not elation, or exhilaration. But awful. I wasn't into Tarot cards or revelations, nor did I
believe that this was only one of my many lives. What happened was that I went liquid, hot metal to be poured, my body
squeezing itself together.

When the soul had found its portal and reentered, I high-
tailed it for my copy of Älois. It wasn't enchantment or an early
intimation of existence on another plane. It was definitely and
simply the turn. That settled it.

I had planned to call Ruth's teacher and protest her edict that
my daughter comb her hair—but now, forgive me, Ruth, I had
another, more important call to make first.

I suppose I had needed a precipitating event—such as the
soul hallucination—an occurrence before the occurrence to act
as prod. I needed a) a will and b) literary executor(s).

Martin had a will. I had seen it. He left everything to me and
upon my death to Paul and Ruth. His was not a complicated
will. But he ought to change that will, too. I was definitely not
going to be his beneficiary.

I had to have my own will now.

I wasn't going to write my own will—no sick-lady attempt. I wanted something *official*. So I required a lawyer. Who did I know? The real estate lawyer who handled the buying-selling of our apartments. All I recalled of him were his eyeglasses. Huge lenses with coppery battlements, sitting triumphantly and claiming his plainsman face. I abandoned that thought. Then there was Don who came twice a year to dinner. But Don belonged to Martin. That left me with the telephone book.

What about family? What about the cousins? Yes, among the cousins were lawyers. Kay's husband, Hiram, was a lawyer. Kay had become the matriarch of all cousins, picking up her mother's guardianship of the Club after Linney died. Yes, Kay's husband was a lawyer. What kind of lawyer—I had no idea. But all I wanted was a simple will—a family matter. Hiram was worth a try.

I had the fall Cousins Newsletter—names, addresses, telephone numbers, were printed each fall. That's how you knew who got divorced. *True* blood cousins were printed in capital letters—spouses in small type.

I was uncertain whether the journal should have covered more of Florence's life. Not, of course, that I knew that much. Consider the year that she became evasive. I was fifteen. Could I take care of myself for, say, a Saturday and Sunday? She would be back by Monday. It sounded pretty good to me. And that first Saturday alone, I got up late and ate a slice of American cheese. I took a leaf of lettuce and was about to chew it, when I turned on the faucet and coated it with water—Florence said that no one knew what could be caught from the unwashed. Anything was possible.

I thought those days alone could be spent in writing—poems

about shadows and heavy boots and trespassing. But those hours passed instead in a daze of television.

Summers were tricky. Maybe it was the time it took twilight to fade. Florence sat at the table drinking her coffee. Do you know what my life has been? she said. Have you any idea? I looked up. Heat had misted the room, but Florence looked parched. What? I said. Florence sloshed coffee into her saucer as she reached up for a circling bug and swatted it into a feathery pattern on the table. She blinked then. My life has been all right, she said. Then she stood up and got the sponge from the sink and wiped the table.

I thought about whether I should call Hiram in the morning. No, Martin said that mornings were hell. That was probably true for Hiram as well. After lunch—I would call after lunch. How did I know his office telephone number? From the Cousins Newsletter squibs column. Hiram had joined the firm of Johnson, North and Ravich.

"Who?" the secretary said in a trained voice.

"I'm a cousin—a relative. Tell him a cousin—Bernadette Amy Marrkey."

"Hold please."

The question was—was Hiram available? Would he know who I was? Cousins were everywhere.

Then he was on the line, his voice vigorously friendly.

"Bernie," he said. "How are you?"

"Fine," I said. That still didn't mean that he had differentiated me. I did the requisite family line. "How's Kay and the kids?"

"Good—very good. Everyone growing up."

"Hiram," I said. "I need a will for myself—I need it now."

"Now?"

"I have been sick. I am sick. So—yes, now."

"All right, Bernie," he said. "You want to make an appointment? I'll transfer you to my secretary—have her fit you in."

My soul took that very moment to bang against my rib cage.

"No," I said. "Could you come here? Could you possibly?"

He didn't hesitate. "Well, I could stop by, Bernie."

"In the afternoon?"

Now he hesitated.

It wasn't a secret, I would have said. The will. But no need to worry anyone—yet.

"All right, let me see—Friday. Yes, Friday at two."

"I'll be here," I said. "You know where?"

"You in the Cousins address list?"

"Yes."

I knew full well you couldn't just name someone as literary executor—that someone had to agree. On the other hand, I could name the person for the will and lie to Hiram about prior agreement. Get agreement later. I had to consider this decision—it was truly important.

To whom does the artist bequeath his life?

Always forgetting

I can't open up the right box again. That box was already in the cave of Aladdin & Sons. But here was a poem—carelessly misplaced, ignored, abandoned. It belonged in Box 22. The high school contest poem. Try remembering everything!

The bulletin board on the third floor had contests posted. The citywide poetry competition didn't exactly offer prizes—all you received was publication in a Multilithed spiral-bound booklet. I had submitted two poems. They accepted one. It wasn't even the poem I liked best—"Deceiver" was that one. Haiku.

Deceiver

Wise death. . . .
To seek its victims
By subtly wooing them
Until they drop Life's hand—
Blind fools!

The poem they took was "Precious Moment," a tale of the loss of youth. The English teacher said wasn't that wonderful. She regularly wore purple lipstick applied with no regard for the natural lines of the lips. Louanne said that the woman was either a lesbo or a nympho.

We had to read the prize-winning poems in class. Three other students had poems printed in that booklet. Marilyn Rose had two poems accepted—one was about spring and the other about seeing the pyramids for the first time. The class liked the poem about the pyramids best. Marilyn Rose smiled, neither a shy nor an affected smile. Egypt, she said, was great.

All those people are elsewhere. The English teacher married a man who worked in construction or maybe owned the company. The day before graduation Louanne was found by her brother in the back of a closet and acting as if she were out of her mind. She yelled, Assholes! Assholes! She was sent to live in Chicago with an aunt who was a bitch. The iron maiden, Louanne's brother said. If Marilyn Rose became an actress, they probably changed her name. I imagined hearing one day that

our high school had honored its distinguished alumna—
Marilyn Rose née her acting name.

I knew Arthur in college. We used to talk. He wore strange
clothes for the times—capes, a hat with a brim, huge sweaters.
He believed in destiny. He believed that he was a writer—that
no other fate for him was possible.

We drank our coffee together at the Student Union. "I will
write and write one day," he told me. "The time will come. That's
why I plan no family—I plan to create a world in which poetry
is all—in which my poetry is read."

I sipped my coffee. "Yeah. But how can you know for certain
that you will succeed?"

He smiled. "The sense I have of being willing to dedicate
myself. I'll go to Italy, Bernadette. That's what I'll do. The fresh
air of another language. And you," he said kindly, "why, you
have the theater."

"I have my poems, too," I said.

"But it is different for you," he said.

I looked at him. "You don't really think I'm a poet, do you?"

"You might be," he said, "but you lack ambition—and Bernadette, I don't know if anyone has ever told you this, but you
are not driven. The drive to succeed is necessary in life. I have
that drive, and I know that I will be famous, Bernadette. That's
not conceit, I swear."

Later we went up to his room and went to bed. He made love
at a mighty pace.

His was not an uncommon wish. Even in high school I knew a
girl named Louise who was going to be a famous writer—more
specifically a novelist, although she left herself open to other

forms of writing. She had a reclusive manner and hairless arms. We took the same IND subway line—the D train. Whenever we were in the same car, we spoke. You have to be open to life, Louise said. I know exactly where I'm going—the college, the graduate school, the postgraduate training.

Once, Louise put her hand on my thigh, a blunt-fingered hand. After a moment, I reached over and lifted the hand from my leg. She brought to mind the girl who had grabbed me in the girls' room in seventh grade and kissed with premoistened lips. I explored this in three poems called "The Non-Ur."

I might add at this point that a man named Shifton once said that I was essentially a middle-level clerical person. Accept that, Bernadette, he said. Your temperament is not artistic. I'm afraid you lack those special sensibilities. On the other hand, he concluded, there is plenty of room for the ordinary in life. That's what makes a world.

The Will

Hiram was once sicced on Martin. It was at a Cousins Club party. Was Martin supposed to take Hiram to the john? No, to the woods behind a house. Clean him up after he puked. Were they crazy? He wasn't even Hiram's relative. He didn't even like him. But there he was by his side. His hand perched on Hiram's elbow, guiding the man's elbow.

This girl, Hiram was saying. She keeps my marriage alive. Yes, definitely. She is a doll. Before her—Marion was fuck of the year—a definite title. Who you got, Martin—Marty?

Hiram leaned forward, swayed toward a tree, cautiously rested his forehead against the rough bark. God, he said, oh

God. Then he let loose. Martin turned away. The man was a pig. Indescribable bits flew. Something imprisoned on the tassel of one loafer. That's it. Martin backed off and vigorously rubbed his shoe against a tree. He walked toward the house. He left Hiram, moaning alone in the orange-gray twilight.

I didn't blame him a bit.

Some families were big on birthdays, some weren't. I always had birthday parties for Paul and Ruth. Paul had one every year until he was twelve, then he didn't want any more. Ruth stopped earlier. After her tenth birthday, she said—I call it off.

Hiram's fiftieth birthday had been last August. Normally, I wouldn't have remembered that—basically, I knew zero about Hiram. But I heard talk about the party. A surprise party that Kay held for Hiram in Garden City to celebrate the event.

This was a *special* party—not to be considered a function of the Cousins Club. The party was discussed at the Cousins Fall Festival dinner in Huntington. This, of course, was after the fact. Would I have gone? I wasn't asked.

A cake decorated with silver dragées for that birthday. Seashells filled with beluga caviar. A string quartet followed by the Chas Rockers. Sixty-five people.

Some cousins weren't invited to everything.

Hiram rang the doorbell at ten to two, he was more than prompt. The peephole in the door exaggerated his lack of height and made his stocky frame rotund. I saw him adjust his tie, assume a solemn expression, check his watch. Thick gold. He looked fifty—maybe fifty-five. His hair held a crimping wave despite the lacquered finish. His sleeves bore trenches of wrinkles.

This was what I wore: First I thought which bathrobe. I rejected the usual one. I selected my lemon-green robe and new black slippers. I coated my face with suntan. Cherry-red lipstick. No one could tell, I thought.

I opened the door.

"Bernadette," Hiram said enthusiastically. "Good to see you."

I leaned forward and his lips provided a sucking smack against my cheek, followed by a sharp withdrawal that released a puff of talcum from his collar.

I led the way to the living room.

"Nice place," he said, and really looked around. "Do you miss the city? Yes, you have a nice place. We haven't been here. I don't think I have ever been here."

"New. We moved last year," I said. "Not quite a year. You want a drink? Coffee?"

"Well," Hiram said, "I've packed it in for the day, Bernadette. Yeah, a Scotch, if you please. With just a tender splash of water."

"Coming up," I said. From the kitchen I heard the click and then a flap of papers. He had opened his briefcase. Business. I made a careful but generous drink. This trip to my apartment was a special favor. I understood that.

Hiram sank down on the couch, the cushions parted. I sat next to him.

"Good drink," he said. "Good stuff."

I waited until he had taken several swallows. "What I want, Hiram," I said, "is a will—nothing elaborate."

He smiled. "I figured that, Bernadette. What are we talking about here?"

I wasn't unprepared. I had a list. I pulled a piece of paper from my pocket and unfolded it. "This is what I want," I said, and handed him my list. "I leave Ruth the brooch known as Aunt Hystil's. I leave Paul my collection of books. My other jewelry and all personal effects I leave to Martin."

I paused.

"Except for my personal papers and poems—those I put in the custody of a literary executor. All that material—those papers and everything—will be in storage in Brooklyn—Aladdin and Sons. I want the literary executor, Hiram, to have the sole right to determine the future of my personal papers and poems."

"A literary executor, Bernadette?" Hiram smiled. "Well, I'm glad to see that your career took off. You'll have to forgive my ignorance—I don't keep up with that kind of thing. Anyway, we'll put that in the will—the literary executor. Fix it up just right. Who do we name? Who is it?"

"Helene."

"Cousin Helene?"

"Yes, *her.*" I hesitated—then the lie. "She has agreed."

"She agreed? *Our* Helene? Then no problem. I'll have this whipped up for you. Maybe you could stop by the office to sign it?"

"Yes," I said. Favors were over. Anyway, that meant that my disguise of health had worked. I'd pick a day when I felt intact and take a taxi. "Just one more thing, Hiram. I would rather Martin didn't know—he hates wills."

Hiram nodded. "Sure thing, Bernadette. And I might add that you are looking fine right now. I mean really great."

"I'm into a good period, Hiram."

"I always liked you, Bernadette," he said. "I guess you knew that. Will Bernie be there? I always asked Kay before we left for a Cousins Club."

His hand played a recitative across my shoulder. I detected the scent of caraway seeds not overtaken by the artificial fragrance splashed across his cheeks.

"Yes, I admired you, Bernadette," he said. "You among all the cousins have style—you have a beautiful complexion. Your spirit—your spirit is free."

He shoved his sleeve up. The watch showed two-fifteen. He probably understood school schedules. For instance, when my Ruth was likely to arrive.

One of Hiram's hands now carelessly lay in my lap, the fingers trying to pinch open the zipper of my robe.

"There hasn't been a single time that I've seen you—that I haven't wondered what it would be like," he said. "You understand?"

I had kept my mute vigil long enough.

"I'm celibate, Hiram," I said.

"What?"

"Doctor's orders."

JOURNAL

---□---

*Settling the matter of the literary
executor has been a great relief.
And my choice was splendid—
even inspired. I am ready for Boxes
68 to 79.*

"Listen," Florence said. "If you decided that you wanted to give this Martin the heave-ho, you can."

I shook my head.

"My sister, may she rest in peace, might have had a much better life if she had given her husband, Ernie, the heave-ho before she married him," Florence said. "But she was kind of a wimp. A damp dishrag. Lacked courage. You—you have courage."

"Sister?"

"Half sister."

"How come I never heard of her? You're making this up."

"That's what you think—Miss Sure of Herself." Florence got up and took the photograph shoe box from the closet shelf. She dug past people. "Here," she said. "This is her and me. Hardly more than kids."

It was a photograph of two young women standing arm in arm and smiling. It was true that they did resemble each other.

"My half sister from my father's second marriage," Florence said. "Christine. Dead now."

"Died from marriage?"

"Don't be a smart-ass, Bernadette."

I examined the picture closely. All young women looked alike at one point in their lives, I thought. I knew that right now I looked like my friends Lea, Marsha, Bonita, Amy, and

Charlotte. We could have fooled people. We could have claimed kinship.

"I suppose he must come to dinner," Florence said.

"Yes," I said. "When? Friday?"

"Saturday."

"I'll help."

"Some help."

Florence made baked chicken, mashed potatoes, and peas. I didn't expect any trouble. Martin was a talker. That was not unusual in a household with a silent father and a ranting mother. Perhaps not so common for the sons. Sons were supposed to take after the father. But Martin swore that his father had been conditioned not to talk. His sisters spoke, but mainly to each other. Martin kept right on talking, though, even in a household without listeners. It was his theory that ectomorphs liked to talk. And that was his shape.

Martin didn't bring candy or flowers or wine. He brought a miniature pine tree in a tiny blue ceramic pot speckled with yellow. "This," he said, and handed it to Florence, "will live forever."

She eyed it. "Thanks."

"Want a drink?" I said.

"Sure," Martin said.

We sat side by side on the couch. Florence sat across from us.

"I guess you want to know about my family?" Martin said. "Poland. Where's yours from?"

Florence got her queer look on. "From here," she said.

"My grandfather worked for a cousin in St. Paul," Martin said. "If you're not careful, that's what happens to strong-looking people. Ox jokes. They have to survive that. My father ended up hauling furniture for a brother-in-law. They were strong Poles, not city boys. Came from a family that thought Prudnik was big-time and Cracow beyond possibility.

"My father's name was Milo. In America, he lived his life in Polish—family talk, books, *The Polish Hour* on radio. No one would have believed he was born on this side. My mother, though, she didn't speak a word of Polish. Kids pick up from the mother. I can't put together two Polish words."

"Let's eat," Florence said.

"I have nearly three thousand dollars," Florence said. She had a copy of one of last summer's bride magazines, borrowed from an employees' lounge.

"Keep it," I said. "We'll do a justice of the peace, and then we'll all go out to dinner."

"Well, if that's what you want. What about the cousins?"

"Have we ever been to a wedding of a cousin—ever?"

"Probably not—anyway, I'll spring for the dinner."

This was what I heard. I heard that Martin Marrkey's mother had to be bodily lifted to her feet and carried to the ceremony, all the time sobbing, "I'll kill myself, I'll kill myself. My son—my own son condemning his sisters to unmarriedness—cursing them. Wait! I begged him! Wait!"

Her tears flooded the taxi, frothed waves in the Rumanian restaurant, drizzled a shower on the tablecloth. "I can't eat!" she swore. She was able to swallow only a little brandy.

One day I sat at the kitchen table yielding to my terrible passion for chewing on pencils, chipping away at toxic yellow. Have you noticed, I said to Martin, how the fashion now is for women to die? What? he said. Really, I replied. Women are dying everywhere. On television everyone is a widower. Stories about how a widower bravely raises his three kids. And look at Paul's friend what's his name—yeah, Dale. His mother died two years ago. And Breyer's mother is dead. Simon's wife too. Women are dropping like flies.

Martin's sisters Ida and Ada visited our new apartment. Their mother, they said, had a slight case of a virus. Something was running around. The sisters brought towels and a set of salad plates in clear green-tinged glass. They pronounced our apartment darling. I have always remembered that apartment, although in memory I made it bigger and I added a window. Also, I did away with the neon sign one floor below that cast an unhealthy sunburst glow upward.

Martin worked for his uncle. He gives you peanuts, I said. The man exploits youth. I wrote a poem "In Family Debt." Martin said that he owed his uncle a lot. Advice, I said, was free. Anyway, just compare our wedding with that of your uncle's son Artie—a full-blown triumphal procession that culminated at a catering hall in Queens. And a five-piece band. In November, Martin quit. He was scared. I wasn't. I knew they would love him in the city. And they did.

Florence came to dinner at that apartment. "Very nice," she said. She brought a box of chocolate-covered cherries. She wore one of her department store navy crepes with a starched white collar. In the kitchen, she whispered to me. "Be careful—his mother will make your life hell." I nodded.

You think I didn't know what happened? When I was pregnant—they all counted backward. After the tenth month, they lost interest. Then they wondered what had been the rush. Things were difficult, though. So many changes. I wrote "Unscheduled Happenings" and "To Hospital." Florence had a stroke one night. She was alone in the apartment. Mrs. Luzinzki from downstairs 15C called me. I rode alone in a taxi and clutched my purse, my raincoat. Martin was in Cincinnati.

In the hospital, Florence recognized no one. I stayed in the waiting room for hours, nibbling the edges of paper cups, scrawling words on a napkin—I sat there for eighteen hours. And before she died Florence cried out, "Herbert! Herbert!" I didn't know who that was. The doctor told me not worry. Her mind, he said, had wandered. Herbert could be anyone.

I named my son after his great-grandmother. I named him Paul and that was because Florence always wanted to be named Pauline.

Christ, this man was breathing down the collar of my dress. "Bernie," he shuddered. "I want you. I'll get a room, an apartment. I have sweated dreams of you, Bernie."

"You're drunk, Randolph."

"No, I'm not. Here—smell my breath."

We were in the hallway of a house in Roslyn. Alicia was listed as a full member of the Cousins Club, Randolph was the spouse.

Look at this man—trying to hump right here in the hall through clothes, fully upright, and in full view of children chasing each other in some horrible game. My turn, one of the boys yelled. I choose Taff! I choose Taff!

I inserted my elbow between Randolph and my waist and jabbed. "I," I said, "do not choose you. And I always do the choosing."

"You came on to me—" he complained.

"Not to you—you're a relative."

*   *   *

Martin's sister Ada went into management training at Macy's and then moved to Dallas and transferred to Neiman Marcus. It was apparent that she was the happiest of the sisters. The oldest girl, Mirla, lived in San Diego and couldn't afford the trip back for our wedding.

Ida hated her name. Said it typed her. I told her to change it. Change your name, I said, either legally or not. She and I were uneasy with each other. I couldn't believe that Martin had actually damaged her by marrying first. Anyway, Ida married the very next year. So how bad could it have been? She took an old boyfriend. He had inherited a house in Ronkonkoma from an aunt whose only son had died in a skiing accident.

I wrote a poem for Ida about her new house. "Optimum Room" it was called. I realize that it should be here, or at least a copy of it. But that poem cannot be re-created. Ida put it on a closet shelf, and one day her son took it and drew with crayons across the words. By the time I saw it, Ida said, the poem was lost in a wash of blue wax.

The newspaper had a picture of him. *Tennis player scores*, it says. That was Joel. I met him in a line—not a restaurant line—a movie line. We started talking about how stupid we were to stand in the line. Then they said seating in the first two rows only. Joel said, Want dinner? All right, I said. We left the line.

He took me to a place in the Village. He ordered figs to start. I had never begun a meal with fruit except breakfast. Then we ate fillets of sole princesse and asparagus tips that stuck out of little pastries and, finally, thick coffee in tiny cups. The meal cost Joel sixty-five dollars. I wondered what he wanted for that. But all he wanted to do was talk. He said that you could make a fermented drink from figs and one day he was going to do that. He said that the sole was coated with a sauce made from concentrated cooking liquor and someday when he had time he was going to make fillets of sole with oysters. He was the first person I had ever known who could talk about food. He wasn't curious about me, though.

Life always improved. I believed that, and often, this was true. Martin did a favor for a client and in return he was rewarded with five and a half rent-controlled rooms in Washington Heights. Rooms so big. Space, space, I sang and whirled around. Martin sang back and twirled me. We had a picnic on the dining room floor. That client later made the newspapers with a terrible scandal, but by that time Martin was employed elsewhere.

Losers, Weepers

I have been working steadily, stopping only when necessary, and even then I was always trying to recall everything that I should enter in the journal. For instance, my desire to be alone. It was amazing that, by nature a solitary person, I had actually spent my life surrounded by people. When Paul was seven and Ruth four, I hired a cleaning woman who came Mondays, Wednesdays, and Fridays. I never knew what to tell Tilla to do, so she made her own way. But one Friday she didn't appear.

I had depended on her. You grow to depend on someone. I was abandoned, the house smothered in chaos. Here it was two o'clock in the afternoon—the beds huddled loosely in their sheets, the dishes adrift on the table, the floors attacked by toys.

Tilla was lost. I tried to call her but her telephone was disconnected. I called Martin at the office. Lie, he said. We must.

We were expecting four for dinner. We said the stove

collapsed and took everyone out to a restaurant. Five or six similar experiences are in "Strangers, People, Others."

Then we hired Dela, who was not as good a worker. She banged the vacuum into the soft wooden legs of chairs. She broke a bottle of perfume that I had been saving. It wasn't particularly expensive perfume; as a matter of fact, its label had fallen off. But the scent was special.

Martin said do what you want. I decided to do without household help. That way I could recite my poems out loud. I kept pads of paper lying about—I could write in every room. Anyway, it was good for children to have duties.

Paul was given three tasks and Ruth, two. Paul complained that no one he knew had to do anything. I began to serve steak and french fries on Monday; franks and beans, Tuesday; take-out Chinese, Wednesday; pizza, Thursday; chicken, Friday. Saturday and Sunday—it all depended.

Toby telephoned and said she was getting a divorce.

"Listen," she explained. "We were standing in a line on Second Avenue. Waiting for a table at that new seafood restaurant that Claiborne said was the best. Do you know what? That bastard husband started to yell at me. There on a Friday. You are a spendthrift, you are a shrew, you never cook. I died, Bernadette. I died. You know what was funny? I'll tell you. It was my money that was taking us out to dinner. Miss Spendthrift's money. Then—oh, life is like this, Bernadette. You are indoors so much—you just don't know. Al Knotts and his wife were across the street—moved closer to the curb to hear and see. It must be all over. Everyone must know."

"You're the first to tell me," I said.

*　　*　　*

Then the question always arose—did dreams belong in the journal? Forget Freud. Ignore the followers—puss breaths! But still—all right—I was in this desolate forest, not completely desolate—somewhere near Petrograd. I was being chased by peasants, by noblemen, by men on horseback. Yelling, they were all yelling. Drop the book! *Intelligentsia!* It sounded like a curse. Then—for shifts follow the pattern of dreams—I was in a café or at the very least in a large cafélike room. I was neither greeted nor ignored. As a matter of fact, the ease of my acceptance by the group assembled in that room was calming. They were speaking, sometimes one at a time and sometimes a cacophony of sound. Writers, they declared, they were writers of the common people. Who? I asked. A tall man spoke. He's Herzen. I'm Dobroliubov. And that one over there, he's Uspensky. Here—and he handed me a pile of sheets—Read this, woman. The papers were headed: "Is it not the beginning of a change?" I was impressed. I'm a poet, I said. Show credentials, one of the men said—I think that was Uspensky. I searched my pockets—but I was wearing only a bathrobe. Wait, I said. I'll go back, I'll bring proof. They shook their heads.

Then I woke up. I was in a sweat. Martin wasn't home. Could I blame him? I couldn't be still. I started cleaning, dusting, straightening. I started on the closet.

Another journal. I wasn't snooping. I swear. But suddenly I found a journal in the apartment—and it was not mine. It was Martin's. Martin was keeping a journal. I was startled. I nearly fell from the shock. I thought about the length of time left to me—then I read his journal. The contents could go with me to the grave.

Only a few entries in his journal so far. But it was essentially about me. I felt that. I sat down that very night and recopied what he had written into a notebook—so that it could be part of my life. How many ethics violations in this? That's for the literary executor to decide.

Martin wrote his journal in a bound book meant for figures. The word *Expenses* printed in gold letters on the cover. If he had asked me, I would have told him that those tactics did not work. Be open, I would have said. And no one will notice.

JOURNAL

———■□■———

This is neither a play within a play nor a poem within a poem. It is, however, a journal within a journal.

EXPENSES [Martin's Journal (recopied)]

I have begun this journal at the suggestion of Hiram. I'll recount the circumstances. Perhaps it will help me to get into this.

I am a talker. That was the difficulty. Ectomorphs were talkers. And I had this problem. What could it lead to? Impotence? Pain? God, how I needed someone to talk to.

I made a mental list of confidants—each name yielded a problem. And I hadn't time for psychoanalysis. Hiram? Yes, Hiram. It was amazing—the name came to me that way. Why not Hiram? I could see myself confiding in Hiram.

Where did Hiram live? I had to locate him. I didn't exactly know him very well—we weren't friends. He was essentially Bernadette's cousin. Yet somehow I was going to have to find an excuse to see him, or maybe I could run into him by accident. Nothing professional—not I need a lawyer, Hiram, old boy. Why would I use him?

Actually, it turned out to be easy. I remembered the Cousins Newsletter. They list everybody—spouses, business addresses. As soon as I saw his address, I realized I knew that office building. All right, I knew where he could be found. What to do? I decided to plan an accidental meeting at midday.

The weather had turned crisp, the leaves turned brittle. There was wind in the city. You could get something in your eye just walking down the street. I understood that I was playing against the odds. No reason why Hiram wouldn't eat lunch in his building, even at his desk. Who knew anything about him anyway? Only that he was married to Kay. That he was unfaithful. It was desperation or madness that had led me to hope to meet him this way.

What I knew for certain—Hiram was in town. His secretary said so. Who's calling? she asked. I hung up at once.

I wasn't even embarrassed—me, a busy man, a man with an active daily life—sitting in a restaurant on Lexington Avenue, drinking coffee, twisting around on my stool like some crazy to watch the door of the office building across the street where a conveyor belt crowd exited for lunch. Maybe Hiram never ate. Maybe at three P.M.

It was him. My God, it was him. In a navy-blue suit. Squinting into the sun. And alone. I dropped a dollar next to my saucer. I sprinted across the street pursued by a squall of car horns. It was the noise that made Hiram look up.

"Martin?" Hiram said. "Were you the idiot running that way?"

"Yes," I said. "I'm surprised to see you. Work around here?"

"Here," Hiram said.

"Lunch?"

We ate corned beef sandwiches, soda, french fries. I felt an intestinal burning, but that didn't stop me. I was determined to speak, to cleanse my mind. I told my tale, my fear. I told him everything.

"It's when I'm making love—I think that my wife is going to die," I said. "She is going to die at the exact moment—that's killing me."

"Listen," Hiram said. "You've got a natural libido. What were you supposed to do? Wait forever?"

"Perhaps I should have."

"Crap," Hiram said. "I understand how you feel. Your wife is sick. Bernadette is a wonderful person—fact. But life, Martin, is life."

"True."

"Look, I've got clients. Divorce is a traumatic thing— sometimes they eat themselves up with guilt."

"I'm not getting a divorce."

"I know that—but the analogy fits. So these men—I'm speaking here just about men—they are torn up. Unrealistic, Martin. Suddenly the inaccessible wife becomes some idol, some marvel they can't possess. So I tell them to rethink their marriage in realistic terms. The pros and the cons. See her as she is. Write it down."

EXPENSES—Journal

February fourteenth, I thought about committing adultery. No one will ever persuade me that this was a dormant desire. Yet even as I admitted to the thought on that date—to be followed by the commission of the act—I suspected that this will be used against me. How? I don't know.

Why did I say that? Because it was a secret. I know about secrets and their short lives. As an accountant, I have had secrets given to me—no, not those that are obviously told to you but rather those still believed to be secret. Numbers reveal much. For instance, my father told my mother that he had only ten dollars on him. We had returned from a store not five minutes before that conversation, and I had seen his wallet. Only age five, but I could count, and I counted the bills in the wallet when my father paid the grocer for a loaf of bread. One of those long crisp breads sold by this grocer but baked elsewhere. My father had broken off the end and given it to me. I sucked the bread until it softened. That's an ugly way to eat, my father said. I was embarrassed. Still, a front tooth was loose and wiggled dangerously against the bread, so I let the saliva moisten the crust, but I did not explain this to my father. Dumb kid, my father said. But I knew that more than ten dollars was in his wallet. Already at age five, I understood the unraveling of a secret.

On February fourteenth, Bernadette wore black stretch pants, worn thin at the knees to a milky gray color, and a bulky white sweater. She moved around the kitchen, noisily, maybe clumsily. "Hell," she said, "I think I burned the potatoes."

It was a family evening. Later, we watched television. Bernadette sat scribbling on one of her yellow legal-size pads. Paul walked over to a window. The snow is really coming down, he said. Stay the night, Bernadette said. Paul nodded. It was already after eleven and still snowing.

I didn't think of my home as a cave. All right, once in a while. Then the world seemed to be outside—like in a snowstorm, yes, it seemed like a cave. The effect was pleasant, warm, reassuring. I even enjoyed the way it felt. Snug as a bug in a rug. What did I do? I turned on the electric blanket a half hour early. That way the sheets would have time to grow warm and inviting. Bernadette didn't like the cold, and sometimes by the time the bed was warm enough, I would be asleep.

So there I was on the night of February the fourteenth. My hand moved down her thigh with a slightly circular massaging motion, I kissed her neck, my other hand slid up the hem of her gown.

Bernadette moved, and suddenly one hand was against my chest, a firm cool palm that pushed me back. It wasn't coy resistance. Her eyes were open. Moonlight in the room, enough to see by. No more ever, she said.

Bernadette turned away from me after the pronouncement. I was stunned, stared at her back, searched for clues. The gowns, for instance. She knew I disliked those three long-sleeve gowns sent to her by a lunatic cousin. Made of a cheap satin material that rasped across my fingers. When had she started wearing them? I sat up in bed. Bernadette was motionless, her hair swept across her forehead, her shoulder buried in the pillow. I looked at her and had one of those prescient moments—that this was the future.

Had she meant it? Of course she meant it. This wasn't the result of an argument. I hate you, she might have yelled. Or, Marriage stinks! And I would have screamed back the same words and then left the apartment and slammed the door. Ultimately finding myself outside. But not knowing exactly where to go.

Those times had occurred mostly when we lived in Washington Heights. I would stand outside the apartment building, angry, and with my breath coming in esophageal gulps. Well, you couldn't just stand there like an idiot. Usually, I went to wherever I had parked the car and sat inside and listened to the radio. Once, I thought the cops in a circling patrol car wondered about me. But they must have seen plenty of men who sat like that—behind the wheels of parked cars. I used to smoke in the car. Half a pack and then I went home. After I gave up smoking, my timing was off. How long was half a pack of cigarettes?

February fourteenth was the date on which I thought about committing adultery. By February fifteenth I had already committed the act with a woman whom I met in a snowstorm. This woman wore a full-length silk slip—no bra underneath. I never saw one like that except in the movies. First off, I insist that this woman looked nothing like Bernadette. The woman had short black curly hair. And an amazing fine down, also black, grew between her breasts. The woman said her name was Elaine— maybe she didn't tell the truth but it certainly began with that letter. Erin or Ellen or Edith. She wore a gold chain with a gold filigree letter *E* dangling from it.

How experienced was I? I met the woman in *my* own neighborhood. Trudging toward the subway. It was a tryst—we were both heading into the city, snow or no snow, and we agreed to meet that evening. Who will know how my hands trembled? I called home. My daughter, Ruth, answered. Everything all right? I asked. Sure, she said. I don't know if I'll be home for dinner, I said. Count me out.

Calling in old debts

I finished recopying Martin's journal entries to date. The copy I will pack in the appropriate box—not up to that box yet. Then I almost delayed important matters, for I started at once to write the poem "The Hirsute Woman." I saw the black down, petals of hair, and a voice husky. Too husky.

I stopped everything. I was in the midst of a kind of denial. Else why hadn't I called Helene? I had to face the fact—I had to call Helene. She, too, was in the latest Cousins Newsletter. They had welcomed Helene back to their midst in the last issue. Welcome Helene, they said.

Our Helene back from L.A. is now teaching at Balmont College on the Island, the newsletter informed. The actual address/telephone listing told the real story. She had returned to her maiden name. That meant a husband I had never met— her second—was gone. Once widowed, once divorced.

It was two o'clock in the afternoon. I traced her to the college. A secretary took down the message. Please call Bernadette, I said. Urgent.

She called back at two-fifteen.

"Bernadette?"

"Yes," I said. "Me." Actually, I didn't recognize the voice, it had deepened, sharpened—grown, I thought, rather querulous.

"It's Helene."

"How are you? Long time."

"I meant to call," Helene said, with cordial insincerity. "I was just getting settled. I reopened mother's house—you know what that's like. Anyway, I was planning to call you. I have this enormous list of calls."

"Doesn't matter," I said. "But I need to see you. Tomorrow."

"I can't make it into the city tomorrow, Bernadette. Can't you tell me over the telephone?"

"No—this is for me of great importance. Life or death."

"What?"

"Come, Helene."

There was a pause. I thought her breath was exhaled.

"All right—I'll try to manage. It will have to be morning—I teach in the afternoon. At ten."

"Fine," I said. "The address is in the Cousins Newsletter."

I had never—not even before I told Hiram—doubted my choice. Helene was to be my literary executor. Helene was neat, orderly—and once into a cause, relentless. She will know what to do with the papers. Some people had an internal coding. They knew how to manage—plan a wedding or what to do when the baby came too early. Or a funeral. Yes, even if they had never been involved before—all of a sudden they put together a list of whom to call, in which order, what must be done first. I believe that Helene can do that. Oddly, I can trust her in these matters.

Everything that will happen will do so after my death. It's not ego. Not totally. I have written my poems—I want them to have an existence. And after I'm dead—well, I suspect I have been a hindrance to my art. Possibly they were right—possibly I didn't look the part.

The next morning I dressed in slacks and a blue and yellow diamond-patterned sweater. The robe I usually wore was certainly the most comfortable garment to wear and it was clean—I tried not to be slovenly—but I thought that the robe signaled depression to Ruth and Martin. She never dresses, they would say. Clive would call that a signal. No one ever thought comfort.

I combed my hair, put on lipstick. Added a coating of makeup. Six months, I thought. Approximately six months left.

I prepared a fresh pot of coffee. I bet with myself that Helene would refuse a cup.

I was about to start the compilation for the years seventeen to twenty-four. I decided reluctantly not to begin until after Helene left. The sorting was a mess. Papers and their dust. Then too, the billowing plastic bags for what was discarded. Old newspapers. I had discarded many newspapers.

Helene didn't arrive until ten-thirty. She was annoyed, flustered. Her earrings shot daggers of glitter.

"Traffic," she said. "It was hell."

I nodded as I examined her. She was now in a state of completion, I could tell that. Her face settled into firmness, her chin pulled in, her thinness treasured. She wore a startling yellow sweater and a gray skirt.

"You look fine," I said.

"You too," she said in counterfeit of truth. Then she frowned. I thought perhaps I had underplayed the makeup.

"So you're back," I said.

"Yes."

"Coffee?"

"No thank you. Listen—Bernadette. Considering the traffic—my time is short. I have a class. What is it?"

I decided not to put the request into the form of a repayment of favors—not unless I had to.

"I want to name you my literary executor."

"What?"

"Literary executor—I'm making out my will."

"And we couldn't discuss this on the telephone?" She was annoyed. "That would have saved both of us time—I'm the wrong choice. You probably didn't know—but I changed my major years ago. My degree is in history. My doctorate dealt with the suffragettes in Liverpool, 1870 to 1900. Not literature—certainly never poetry."

"That doesn't matter," I said. "You can bring in someone to advise you."

"Advise me? Bernadette, I am sorry—but I really can't do this. It's impossible. I didn't know your poetry required a literary executor."

"It does—it will," I said. Sometimes you have to be direct. "You heard I was sick?"

"Yes, I am sorry. Kay said something. Is it a return of what you used to have?"

"Kay doesn't know from shit. It's death, Helene. I am dying."

Depending on the circumstances, that can be a very melodramatic line—and so I intended it. I was certain that sentimentality lurked in Helene. It was a cousin trait. They cried during television shows.

"What?"

"And soon. I never asked a favor, Helene. Did I ever ask a favor? This is important to me."

"Dying—really dying? I don't know, Bernadette. What would I do as literary executor?"

"Take charge of my papers and poems—make decisions about them. Nothing else."

"You are making this very difficult for me, Bernadette. I truly am busy."

I gave her my Bette Davis stare. I was annoyed that it worked. Helene should have seen through it. For a moment I doubted the soundness of my choice.

"All right—yes, I'll do it," she said. "But you understand, I am truly not knowledgeable about poetry."

"Don't worry. It's agreed then. Just one other matter—don't mention this to anyone except maybe Hiram, who is writing the will. It will get back to Martin—he hates wills."

"All right—I promise." She hesitated. "Bernadette, you really don't look bad."

"I know."

JOURNAL

———■□■———

More of the journal within the journal.

I began to recognize that certain look. The writer's eyes. Martin must have been working in his journal. I waited patiently for the opportunity to check. We spoke now, we were civil. There was Ruth to consider. But Ruth was always in her room, the level of her music a classical pestilence. Still, we spoke. Evenings, he went out. I waited.

Yes, he had been in the journal.

Martin took the journal away with him every morning. Clearly, he didn't trust me. It was in his briefcase beneath the newspaper; the briefcase itself was in the closet concealed behind his raincoat.

While waiting for my opportunity at the journal I wrote "Confessions, True and Necessary," "No Orphan to the Heart," "Promises Unpromised." These, my most recent poems, I have laid aside for the last box. I put this note here in the journal in case the poems got mixed up—they belonged in the last box. These three.

211

EXPENSES—Journal

I can end the evening of the fourteenth of February and go right ahead to the fifteenth because on Hiram's advice I have begun to write this down in search of truth and everything has already occurred. But if I did that then I have made myself into some kind of cunning devil. Everyone free to say well he was just waiting for a chance to take another woman. Or worse yet, they think backward and misconstrue. Alicia, for instance: Well, he kissed me once. Sure, it was a party and all that—but he kissed me for a very long time and I am certain that he felt my breasts—I admit I was a little tipsy—but yes, now I am certain. He felt my breasts, through the cloth—my blue velvet dress— and I had to push him away.

I said nothing before, Alicia adds, out of consideration for Bernadette.

Yes, I can see this happening. And someone else saying that I looked up her dress—then everyone falling over each other to say what they had always suspected about me. That I was a lecher. That I could not be trusted. How could he have done that to Bernadette?

I faced celibacy as of Saturday, February fifteenth. Because on the preceding evening, Bernadette rolled over in bed and said, No more. The words came out of the blue. I knew that might happen eventually—but not yet. Bernie was sick, sick for years, getting sicker. On the other hand, she outlived the first doctor. Didn't she outlive Amberson? And she was still going strong. She was matron of honor at Toby's last wedding. Was that sickness or health? She had rumbaed—she was full of energy. She had looked terrific even in that ridiculous lavender matron of honor dress. She had danced and danced and then at home I undressed her. When was that? That was in October. October to February.

I indulged Bernadette—didn't I? For instance, that crazy day when she said that when she became sick enough to need chronic care she wanted Ruth and Paul to be able to visit her easily. By public transportation, she said. And so we would have to move.

Bernadette has many qualities that are difficult. She daydreams. She quotes poetry. Out loud. She didn't just remember what everyone learned in school when they were children. I remembered something that began "Samuel the Cam-uel." She knew entire poems. Quoted Byron, 1812. A distinctly irritating habit.

For some men—they meet a woman or pick up a girl or are smiled at during a dinner party. Their wife's dear friend or someone from the office. And they don't know how it happened—the affair, the liaison, the happening—dated in their mind only by credit card slips adroitly pocketed, hidden, flushed.

But I *knew* my date. I needed no credit card slip from a motel as a reminder. February fifteenth.

February fifteenth. I unlocked the door. This was a modern apartment, you opened the door, and there you were. The living room. Paul sat at one end of the couch reading the newspaper. Ruth was at the other end. The television was on. Bernadette sat in the wing chair. She wore a quilted bathrobe. She was writing. She paused, looked up and smiled. As if, I might add, last night had not happened.

I couldn't cross the room and kiss her. How could I kiss her?

She would smell someone. She would smell *E*. I couldn't just leap into the shower either. On the other hand, last night was my excuse. I nodded.

"How is it out?" Paul asked.

"Still rotten."

Paul had arrived for dinner on Friday. It was Saturday night. He had stayed over because of the snow. But I had managed to get into town the next day. It was Saturday night. That meant Paul didn't have a date. I felt terrible—considering that I had just crawled out of a woman's bed. And my own son didn't have a date. He was a good-looking kid too—he looked like Bernadette.

"I saved you a pastrami sandwich," Ruth said. "Paul went to the deli."

I wasn't hungry. I had eaten. I had taken Elaine to dinner.

"Thanks, honey," I said, and knew what I must do. I was going to sit down with the sandwich saved for me by my daughter and eat it—no matter what.

I was going to get away with this. I was going to get away with being unfaithful, because I was trusted. That was the key. No one in this room would suspect me of going off with another woman.

Hiram said to describe, to tell, to unburden. For instance, Bernadette wrote poems. Many were numbered in notebooks. On pieces of paper. Like number 113, 235, 671. I didn't know why. I could read them if I wanted to. Sometimes I read them. But so many. In truth, I was never much of a poetry fan. But they kept her busy. They kept her happy.

I don't know why this made me think of coffee. But Bernadette always made lousy coffee. She was in never-never land while counting. Sometimes five scoops, sometimes six. Also, she hard-boiled eggs until you could play stickball with them. And bacon, she burned. But give her something complicated—out came gourmet food, a feast, a celebration.

Amberson—before he died—said she might be sick for years. Ten years, fifteen years. Our lifetime—my lifetime. That, I could stand. But now Clive said there were atypical directions taken. She was following this particular atypical line. Illness went its own way. Bernadette's disease had taken a turn, Clive said. It was now in the realm of disorders called orphaned. What did that man know?

For the truth of it was, Clive, old man, that suddenly it was February fourteenth. Night, Clive. Get it? We're in bed—my bed. Am I embarrassing you, Clive, old man? Bernadette was beside me, I rubbed her shoulder, I kissed her neck. She turned her head and looked at me. No more ever, Martin, she said.

Did you hear that, Clive? We're not talking headache. I knew that if I touched her again, what I would feel would be stiff like leather. The expression on her face was determined.

Oh Bernadette, my Bernadette. Be all right. I swear I will never do anything again, I promise. Hope to die.

All the critics

Paradoxically, this is what my body did. The nerves buzzed and greedily danced to a heathen melody that I didn't control, a babel of tumult. Certain physiological events that were mine— not covered by Älois. Perhaps my disease had turned mutant.

Still, I was persuaded that I will complete my task. It was not false pride or a pastiche of hopes. If anything, it was a bet I made with myself.

I tried to be honest—turning the purse of my life upside down. Had it been what I expected so far? This American artist's life. Not what *I* expected? Where were the wonderful fireside chats? The gentle teas, the teasing conversations, the white linen? Nevertheless, this was where my poetry came from—this was the source.

I debated whether Aladdin should dig into its cave and expel one box to be sent to Helene. No, I decided against that. It was best for the boxes to stay together. Those men from Aladdin knew me, they have decided that it was a business. What business? A business. They hauled the boxes away with a cheerful contempt.

This is what I did. I had a copy of the set of poems "To Mysterious B"—part 2, third revision. I sent that to Helene by Express Mail. Here, I wrote, is a sample of my efforts.

Helene telephoned me the next morning.

"My God," she said, "when did you write this?"

"Age fourteen."

"This is what you write now? *This.*"

"Yes."

"I couldn't read the fifth line."

"*Catena Liborum Tacendorum.*"

"And who was that Sally?"

"She appeared on Dick Clark's *Bandstand* in 1960."

"Was this published?"

"Not this one."

"I'll be honest with you, Bernadette. I'm not certain whether you haven't stepped past the bounds here between erotica and pornography—the literary bounds, I mean. I'm not a prude. You know that I'm not a prude."

I wasn't surprised. "Helene," I suggested, "find someone to

read my poetry—maybe another faculty member where you teach."

"I have just arrived here, Bernadette. I don't know anyone at the college. They'll think I'm mad."

"Try."

"Maybe we should rethink this—maybe I'm not the appropriate person."

"You certainly are."

I hung up.

Blackmail. It was easy to believe the obvious. To recall that murder. To say that I was using that—that unmentioned but shared experience. But I swear I wasn't thinking of the man who was murdered that night or how Helene figured in that matter. I never alluded to it when speaking to her. Besides, the man was bones by now.

I admit one regret. Yes, a regret—I was never able to describe his eyes—crammed as they were with impressions. And those impressions preserved, embalmed, and saved. I thought of writing my poem—of trying to disguise the possessor of those eyes—but I decided that was too risky. And the poem itself could not be a secret.

Critics didn't frighten me. What could be worse than the lashing of C.S.? Nothing. From Helene—I wasn't interested in Helene's opinions—about poetry. What she needed was an assistant. Someone who would understand. Although the power—the final decisions—would belong to Helene. That would work.

Helene will find someone to assist her. Someone to read the poems. She was a true cousin, raised in the pattern of powerful women. They understood how to keep order. Her finger will point and single out. Someone will step forward. They have a way, those jewels of Long Island—bred as they were to rule.

Martin came home, he hummed, he did a strange series of dance steps. I visualized a lipstick stain on his collar, another streak running from breast pocket to tie tack. I saw this woman as a blonde, young enough to scandalize the sisters Marrkey. A chotchke. Did she offer to cook for him after they made love—slices of potatoes crackling on the burner, and fat, blood-red sausages dripping their juices into the pan after they had been suitably pricked? If I snapped my fingers, would he come back?

The assistant

His name was Nathaniel. Nat. He was uncertain, he told Helene, and she relayed that to me. He was astonished that this work, his sample, had been written at age fourteen. He doubted that strongly. At any rate, he admitted that the work in question was not running in the currents of established poetry.

I had no real basis for picking him, Helene said. I could tell she was anxious to be done with me. Bring him over, I said, come for cocktails on Friday. Ruth was going to Ronkonkoma to spend the weekend with her aunt Ida. Martin was never home on Friday evenings. Yes, bring him here.

"Sorry to be late. Traffic," Helene said.
"Bernadette," the man said. "May I call you Bernadette?"
"Sure."
I watched him, the shielded expression on his face. I thought

he was buried in his thoughts. I decided that he wanted a poet. Yes, he wanted a poet of his own. He was dressed for his part—the tweedy patches-at-the-elbows jacket with the sweater underneath that was lightly fraying at the neckline. He had a firm handshake.

There we were. The three of us. Bound by poetry.

Nat positioned himself near the treats I had prepared, and pawed relentlessly at spicy shrimp, crackers lathered with goat cheese, rolled anchovies. He had no obvious pretensions nor was he besotted with scholarship, although he bit off the ends of his words like a classroom lecturer.

All the time, I thought he evaluated my smallest movement. For this occasion I had forsworn my makeup mask. The effect, I knew, was appalling. Death's door, they must be thinking. He and her both. A prelude to stinking affliction.

But he—oh, I saw his eyes before he dropped the gates. A dead poet. He knew the value of a dead poet.

"Helene tells me that this is a sample—'To Mysterious B'—of many more. How many?" he asked.

"Lots."

"You publish?"

"In sixty-three small magazines—most don't exist any longer. Then there was a small collection—a booklet—put out by Oracle Press."

"Well, I was impressed—I want you to know that—yes, impressed by the raw talent in the poems I've seen." He reached for a shrimp, sipped his Scotch with its melting ice cubes. He tried joking. "I guess you can consider me the *first* Marrkey scholar, eh?"

Then I knew for certain. I was source material to him—he might have his hands on original source material. Was he holding it in then? A thirst for my crowd of poems. You could make a career with that. Who was he? I envisioned him as knowing people. Yes, he knew people—but no original material for him. After all, how much was there to go around? Doomed to a life of excavating secondary sources. Until now—until me. That wasn't so bad. I had been wanted for worse reasons.

We sat cross-legged on the floor, Helene, Nat, and I. I wore my robe for the occasion—comfort must triumph over convention, I had decided. The man—Nat—kept staring at me. I could tell that Helene found him an uneasy choice. And he had, of course, assumed that the poet would be like her cousin.

I offered manila envelopes. Twelve envelopes, clasps bent. In the envelopes were copies of a few poems—the originals were packed in their proper boxes. I wasn't about to give up everything. I had prepared for the evening a selection of the world poems created after I took Bertram's advice about seeking outward.

I had Helene and Nat read "Kennedys en masse," "Doxies of War," "Grocery Without Change," and the long "Leftists in Control." Papers spread around us as they were passed from hand to hand. Those papers appeared to spawn more. Soon we sat in a circle of arcane significance.

Nat rubbed his head. His hair was gray and thick and pulled itself into tight waves. "I've an idea," he said. "Now, I can't promise for sure. So don't hold me to this. But I am giving a talk next week at West Central. I might, just might be able to work this material in. Depending upon further close reading, of course."

Helene grew haughty. "How? Why? Is this a reputable meeting? How can this be done so quickly?" she said.

"The talk," Nat said, and tried to focus his attention on me, "is about forgotten women poets of this geographic area. Fortuitous. Yes, fortuitous. Maybe I could bury—forgive me—stick you somewhere in the middle. You did publish—I'll need bibliographic evidence—so theoretically you qualify. The talk is at West Central—a Currier and Ives kind of school. It's their annual conference sponsored by the Wickes Endowment. Of course, I would have to cut someone else out—but it could be worth it. Look, it would be an opportunity. Bernadette, what do you say?"

Helene intervened. "My cousin and I should discuss this."

I could see what she was thinking. He had been selected quickly. Had she made a mistake? I, on the other hand, thought he was perfect. I had no objection to an opportunist. After all, no matter what he did—ultimately, the bandwagon on which he climbed was mine.

"Helene," I said, "Nat's idea doesn't sound too bad."

She stared at me. Either the reins were in her hands or they were in mine. I dropped the reins.

The door to the apartment opened. Martin stood there and looked down at us. "What's this?" he said bitterly. "A séance?"

On a bus line

I knew that we had moved to this apartment against Martin's wishes. The truth was that I had never determined where we lived before. Martin liked to move. But this time—the selection was completely mine. Illness had its power, I knew that. I used that.

I picked the apartment because of its location, ideal location. Consider the bus connections. From here with two buses you could travel easily to Alcott's Chronic Care Facility. Alcott's, a business owned for ten years by the Oppenheim family, printed its enticements on glossy, heavy-weight paper—its brochure a sonnet to ill health. The building was at the end of a residential street, canopied by rows of military-straight but dying elms. Alcott's was built there because of an idle zoning board. Alcott's was on a bus line—bus stop right on the corner one block away.

This was what I planned. Ruth could visit on Wednesdays after school. Paul could come on Saturdays. And Martin was for Sundays. The idea of the entire family standing around my bed was depressing. Now everyone would be able to come alone and no one would have to wait for a ride.

Yesterday, I made a test run to Alcott's. I came by taxi—but they recognized me as a real potential customer—not a browser for the future. What a jovial and unctuous greeting I was given. What do I smell? I said. The day administrator sniffed. I don't smell anything, he said. A definite odor, I said. I decided that it was the scent of pine.

Clive said I was astonishing. I didn't pursue that. I believed that there was a survival psychology in having a purpose. I believed that with a goal you lived longer—lived to the completion of that goal. But, of course, the goal had to be real. That was what I believed.

Helene sat on the couch, her shoes off, her feet tucked under a cushion. "My life," she said, "my life sucks."

"Yes—how so?"

"Come on—look at the difference between us. You have a husband—the same husband—two children. Me—I marry badly. You didn't know him—the second one—but he was a bastard from the start. He used to yell at me—You're rigid, he'd say. Me? He couldn't do two things consecutively.

"Maybe I am blind—maybe I am judgment blind. But you—you succeeded. You won't mind—you know what Cousin Linney used to say about you. Well, she took me aside one day. You've been spending a lot of time with Bernie, she said. Don't, Helene. Don't do that. I see a long road of trouble for that young lady. She hasn't a chance, Helene. I wouldn't be at all surprised to hear—God forbid—that Bernie was in reform school one day. She actually said that."

I nodded. "Yes, that sounds like her."

"But look at the two of us now. Your Paul is quite the student, I hear. Columbia at sixteen. And your Ruth is an angel."

"Yes," I said. "Paul is a scholar and Ruth is wonderful."

"So here we are. The two of us. I would be different if I could, Bernie. I messed around, you know. Really, a lot. And I would certainly redo my life if I could—right from go—I would redo. And you?"

"My life," I said, "is what it is. Probably unchangeable."

"Nonsense, we could have been different."

"No."

O woman poet. Hidden like a bird in a room to whisper: *Who are you? / Are you nobody too.* Should she be like Amy Lowell and promote "Amyism"? Or minor like Sara Teasdale or Elinor Wylie? Or a lesser poet—coquettish and bookish with requisite nervous breakdown in preparation for the kamikaze attack. Be dead. That was an acceptable certainty—be a dead woman poet.

The story was out.

Paul called me. It wasn't the day of his usual telephone call—I was worried.

"What's wrong?" I said. Paul was consistent.

"I'm not certain," he said. "Listen, is this true—you named a literary executor?"

Secrets cannot be kept.

"Yes, Paul, I did."

"Mother, why? I couldn't believe it. Mother—with all respect—that's embarrassing. It's not that I'm putting your work down—but a handful of poems does not require a literary executor. I'm your son and you know that literature is my life. Contemporary American—so why didn't you ask my advice? I cannot understand this. I would have been pleased to receive your poems and I would have treasured them always. You could have counted on me."

"I'm sorry, Paul," I said. "I didn't mean to hurt your feelings."

"My feelings? My feelings aren't hurt. Unfortunately, it's almost a funny story, Mother. Unknown poet appoints literary executor—for what? Don't you see that?—a joke."

"In that case, Paul, the joke's on me."

"My God, Mother, aren't you listening?"

"I hear you," I said.

He paused. "Listen, how do you feel?"

"Fine. I feel fine. Mind intact, soul wandering."

"What? Look, I'll see you on Sunday. We'll talk further."

"Can't wait. Good-bye."

Who told? Could have been Hiram. Or Martin, guessing after viewing the literary séance. Could have been Helene. Helene drunk and soul-searching with a cousin. Could have been Nat. The world being circular, he would have known someone who knew someone. Ruth could have snooped. Had I ever told Toby? Not that I recalled.

*   *   *

"Listen," Toby said, "I'm hardly seeing anything of you these days."

"I've been busy."

"Bernadette, that's always been your problem—you stay indoors too much. Anyway, I joined a new therapy group—I'm sick of meditating. This group—I'll give you the address, if you're interested—is teaching me to face the truth. Face the truth, they say, and then tell it. They led me step by step back to my first marriage. Remember that one? Face the truth, they said. Why did you divorce him? Are you speaking the truth? So I realized I wasn't. I never even told you."

"No," I said.

"I was going to San Francisco. I was working for Plum's at the time. The trip was a perk. I bought my DelLiso suit—the red one—for this very trip. I was already at La Guardia when I realized that the papers that were the very reason for going were back in the apartment on the dining room table. Well, I couldn't tell anyone that I had been that careless. I changed my reservations. It meant losing an evening in San Francisco—but that was that. I took my car from long-term parking and drove back to the city.

"I unlocked the door. That soon I knew. I swear, Bernadette. As soon as I unlocked the door. The rooms were drenched, they stank. A scent like musk—like musk ox. You know what I found—no need to tell you what I found."

"Life is chance," Nat said. He wouldn't tell us any more over the telephone. He insisted that Helene come to the apartment all the way from the Island. He even offered her a ride. But she had her own car.

I was excited. I couldn't stand the wait. I went into the kitchen and prepared a small dish of mushrooms stuffed with seasoned breadcrumbs and parsley, prosciutto and slivers of melon.

Helene arrived first. "Is he here?"

"No."

"Then he didn't leave when he said he was." She stared at me. "You look flushed—Martin isn't home? I hate to see you here by yourself—anything could happen."

"Not that way—it won't," I said.

"God, can I make myself a drink?"

I nodded.

"Bernadette, don't be upset. I mean he—Nat might not have good news. We don't know that. We don't know him—hardly know him."

"I'm prepared."

Nat wore a dark gray suit. I scarcely recognized him. "Ladies," he said, and kissed our cheeks. "Please be seated."

"Crap," Helene whispered.

We sat on the couch. Nat stood in front of us. He didn't even ask for a drink.

"Chance," he said, "yes, chance. Months ago I read a call for papers in the *Chronicle of Higher Education*. The conference's theme was 'Forgotten Twentieth-Century Women Poets of the East Coast.' To tell the truth, I wasn't going to send in anything—but then there was a woman." He smiled at us. "And she was teaching at a girls' school right up the road from West Central. Bingo! I sent in an abstract of my proposed paper and, of course, it was accepted. Chance, you see, chance."

"God," Helene said, "what are you going to do now, give us a body-by-body description of your weekend?"

"I can't be annoyed tonight," Nat said. "Not tonight. So there I was, ladies. I had forty-five minutes to talk. Concurrent sessions—and I want you to know that I decided as a trial balloon to devote twenty minutes to Bernadette. If it flopped—well, it's not that big a conference.

"Let me tell you, I'm a pretty good speaker—not being vain. I play the crowd. Eye contact, pauses, the works. And my audience wasn't bad—no, it was respectable.

"Well, ladies, here's the kicker—let me read directly from my speech."

He pulled papers from his pocket, a bunched roll.

"Shit," Helene said.

Nat smiled at her.

"Now," he said softly to this attentive audience of two, "let us consider the work of Bernadette Amy Marrkey—poet born in the middle of this century. Marrkey is a difficult poet to classify—her work falls somewhere between confessional poets—those codifiers of mainstream American culture. Her ear is locked in the patterns of this culture as visualized in measured stanzas and cadences. Listen now to sections of 'To Mysterious B'— "

Nat paused and looked up. "The clincher was the question-and-answer period. Who they would focus on. A woman stood up first. She had a notebook. She had written down her question not to forget it. In the Marrkey poem 'The Maimed and Short-ened Lover,' she said, can you elucidate on the meaning of the words 'nocturnal pollution'?

"To that I replied, Saint Thomas Aquinas in—I believe—*Summa Theologica*. From that point on we were a hit."

"Fantastic," I said.

"We mustn't jump to conclusions," Helene said. "This all requires planning."

"Yes," I said. "And I have left it in your hands."

*   *   *

Maybe I should hurry with the filling of the boxes. No—I mustn't. Any faster, and errors will occur. The boxes must be packed at the proper pace and manner and, as always, accompanied by journal entries. I'll hold off outside influences as best I can.

For Box 76 or 77??—check

What goes around comes around—Florence said this
A pot   Like people when observed who act funny
Money   They say goes to the rich and absotuely never
Lands in the laps of those charming and clever
Death and taxes. Unpaid taxes were lost in the mail
Thus, extenuationg circumstances keep culprits from jail.

MAYBE

PICK UP
MARTIN'S
LAUNDRY

Sayings DRAFT—6

The camel's back. For which this was the last straw
The very last I put it there myself on skin rubbed raw
The rolling stone. I built a roadblock, stopped it cold
Ruined everything, they yelled   Now you won't grow old
The stitch. In time I snipped apart those threads
Causing wounds in four Jacks two Toms three Freds
A pot. I filled with water, stared full-face, proved the lie
Saw it roil and boil until that metal was totally burnt and dry
Death and taxes. I claimed unpaid taxes lost in the mail
Thus, these extenuating circumstances kept me from jail
Death. All sayings can be proven false as I can show
as for the certainty of this—I'll let you know.

Another Ocean

SEE IF
THIS
GOES

Once upon a time I was terribly good the
way girls are. I wore blue A good color
for me. I learned to dance to iron shirts
to darn pants

CALL
TOBY

the loved

Hands in his pocket, another cock-of-the-walk
Sir may I speak to you? Despite the fact you're uglky and blue
Blue's a good color for

JOURNAL

―――■□■―――

Here we go—Boxes 80 to 114.
Nevertheless, sometimes I tire.
What do I want? Sometimes, love.

I saw a woman crossing the upper level of Grand Central Station. I almost called out, Yoo-hoo. I was held back by the recognition of time. This large pink woman must be a stranger. My woman would be past ninety, an anachronism. Her talkativeness perhaps no more than an aching syllable. Her twitching smile and brilliantly red dyed hair no longer commanding respect. But in her time, in the tangle of my life, she taught, as such women often do, geometry. Such a fierce, hard woman must already be a part of folklore. It had been widely rumored that she was a communist and had been seen in the teachers' lounge reading the *Daily Worker*. One day the geometry teacher said, Attention everyone! Attention! There are only two ways out of poverty. There is crime and there is education. This is the lesson for today—for you in this room, there is nothing else. You think there is, but there isn't.

"When I was in the army years ago," Martin said, "I was seeing a married woman."

We were in the Village in the Cookery; we had come from a revival of *Leave Her to Heaven*.

"Her name was Clarisse," Martin said.

*   *   *

233

In my poem "Showing," Celia made the young man tremble. He never lost the vision of her when she knelt naked on the bed, hovering above him with the flat plane of her body—his fingers crushed to her breasts. The room where they made love—a chilly, exulting place, its only color found in a blue-red chenille bedspread. The whistling shabby parakeet. Touches of feathers and tassels of paper were found even on the pillows.

"What do you know?" Martin said.

My God! "You mean am I a virgin?"

"Don't be a smart aleck. I mean sex beyond the quick moments of college bedding or even after. A sensual life, I mean that. Yes, beyond fumbles and gropes."

We went to a bookstore and bought a collection of manuals and a copy of *Lady Chatterley's Lover.*

Florence paid for a set of dishes. Like a hope chest gift, she said. Also, she bought me a nightgown and peignoir of white satin trimmed with nylon lace in a pattern called point d'Angleterre. Florence wasn't on any department store payroll, she was paid directly by the companies whose products she demonstrated. But she had friends. One of them bought the nightgown set with his discount card.

Listen, when I first found out that I was truly sick, I was cheerful. "It's garden-variety illness," I said. "Many people get strange things. My cousin Reynold was sent to the jungle by the navy. He came back with a rare fungus on his hands—for fifteen years he suffered—but basically, he was all right. And as for me—this is the kind of disorder fraught with remissions. Lots of feeling-fine periods. Furthermore, I am only thirty-two."

Did I believe what I said? Hard to be certain. I thought I was fairly convincing. Still, Ruth locked herself in the bathroom. Paul sat on a hard chair in the living room and nodded at everything I said.

"Anyone can adjust," I insisted further. "See this." I held out my hand, my right hand, the hand I was self-conscious about, because the little finger was bowlegged. It curved outward.

"When I was twelve years old"—I spoke loud enough for Ruth to hear through the bathroom door—"I fell in the movies, tripped and caught my finger between the coils of the metal spring that attached the seat. Snap—like a trap. And when my finger was set—well, that doctor didn't know beans. It healed like this. Then that doctor told my grandmother that in time the finger would straighten itself. It didn't. It should have been reset. Now, for the longest time—are you listening, kids?—I was embarrassed and ashamed. I hid my hand, put it in my pocket. Wore skirts and dresses with pockets. But now I have adjusted."

Amberson told me to live my life as usual. So I went to the library. You can find out many things.

"You know," I said to Martin, "I have come down with this disorder at just the right age—and my symptoms are absolutely right on the button. I haven't got one tantalizingly different symptom."

"You're morbid," Martin said. "That can't be a good attitude. I read a lot of stuff about the effects of laughter—that's what you should try, Bernie. Groucho Marx movies—stuff like that. What the hell are you reading anyway?"

I held up my book. One illness had led to another. *The Case of*

Augustus d'Este. "In 1822," I said, "this man developed multiple sclerosis after a great shock."

"I'm up next for the Cousins Club," I said.

"You want to do that?" Martin said. "Didn't what's her name—didn't Kay say that you could skip your turn if you weren't feeling well?"

"Feel fine. I don't want to be a sponger—fair is fair."

I debated what to do. When it was your turn—you could make the choice. Several cousins called—Dottie and Lutie and Cush. Pass it up, they suggested.

I decided to do a luncheon. A Spring Luncheon. Martin said I was out of my mind considering the kids and everything. I thought this would be a good exercise.

The question of place. They couldn't come here to our apartment in the city. Cousins now numbered seventy-five with spouses and children. I bought a Long Island newspaper and read past the local events. You could rent halls, rooms, suites. I circled in red a variety of options. "Lovely garden-view room—for large parties." Or "See the Sound from our windows—a setting for Events of Distinction."

I found what I wanted. An American Legion hall located not quite midway between Quogue and Mattituck. What did it have? It lacked atmosphere—I ignored that and the smell of bleach-sweetened mops. The room for rent had walls of glossy white, paint heaped so thickly that tiny bubbles and pellets grew. I knew that I wanted that room. Yes, that was what I wanted. Think of the contrast—the repressed horror of the cousins on seeing that plain red brick building whose windows overlooked nothing—then walking into the room to be brilliantly decorated for the Cousins Spring Luncheon. Yes, I liked the effect.

"I'm doing a Spring Luncheon for my Cousins Club," I told Toby.

She sat restlessly in my kitchen.

"Don't talk to me about family," she said. "My mother—my own mother—told me on Saturday that I was a terrible mother. Her daughter, she declared, is a plague. Why? In these rotten days not one of my children has gone bad. Not one. Even those that don't live with me."

"Yes," I said. "That's true. Anyway, I'm doing a luncheon—for a lot of people."

Toby shrugged. "You're implying that I should forget what that woman said. You're right. A luncheon? God, what an effort. Do you want the name of the caterer who did my wedding? Except for that vulgar sweets table—I thought the food was pretty good. Duck is always a good choice. Although they stiffed us on the wine. Still, I was satisfied."

"I'm doing it myself."

"You're kidding! Hiring your own cooks and stuff? You really can't save that way, Bernadette. Anyway, I want to tell you something."

"Yes?"

"You went somewhere, didn't you? Last Thursday evening?"

I had to think. Not that I go out that often.

"Yes, to a poetry reading at the Y. Three young new poets were being introduced—"

She interrupted. "Stop. None of that shit sticks to me. But—you were seen. Bernadette, I keep telling you—the world is small. Yes, tiny."

"Seen?"

"Afterward—didn't you leave with someone?"

"The man who sat next to me. We both adored the second poet and couldn't bear the others. We went to have coffee and talk."

"That's it—sweetie. Adele and Peter saw you."

"Saw me?"

"Well, yes. They said that Bernadette and this strange man were sitting together—à la tête à tête in a very dark coffeehouse on First. I thought it wasn't you—but Adele swore."

"It was me. They followed me?"

"I don't think so. But Bernadette—discretion. I always say discretion is best behind closed doors."

The poem I wrote was "Helen and The Lover." In this poem (in four stanzas) Helen whipped off her dress. It was like giving birth—the way her body throbbed. Of course, Helen had never given birth—but it must be like this. Fame—she was giving him fame. She felt invincible with the power to impart immortality. He was the instrument—but she was the guiding force.

All through the years 1972 to 1984, I wrote poems. It was my hobby. I made jokes that I had to write poems because I was too clumsy to play tennis. I don't think that's funny, Paul said. People create literature out of creative need. I wanted to tell him that he was a jerk, a stiff-necked jerk. But I didn't want to hurt his feelings.

Look, it wasn't his fault. That was not yet a period of great confidence. I didn't truly understand, even though I was constant in my dedication.

I read the poetry printed in *Poetry, Nation, Partisan Review, Paris Review,* the *Christian Science Monitor.* I went so far as to address an envelope to the *Hudson Review,* but then the audacity of the gesture stopped me. It was not a right that I felt I had. So I discovered other magazines less fearful to me. Magazines that published three issues and then disappeared. These magazines published my poems. Then Oracle Press offered to print a small collection of my poems in a booklet. We have long been interested in your work, they said. Martin took me out to the Russian Tea Room to celebrate. I had shashlik.

My husband was always pleased when I had a poem printed. Ruth would nod. Paul always said great. But it was hard for them to sustain the interest. Once I had a very good year, and fourteen poems appeared in magazines called *Night, Slender, Capella, Seltzer, Sign, grief, Caporum, Arro, Treyf, FLICK, Slivers, Threads, smack,* and *vanish.*

That was the year I spent a lot of time sitting down. I developed a passion for candy and potato chips and soda. My clothes struggled with my body.

Martin brought home a pamphlet on exercise. I picked out an easy section. *Control Your Breathing.* I practiced inhaling, exhaling, holding my breath. This system taught you to think your breathing, see your breathing, feel your breathing. I kept at it. I practiced. Then one day it happened. I stopped breathing for a few seconds. It wasn't euphoria, but it was amazing. I told Martin. He stared at me. I can see it now, he said sarcastically, another back-from-the-dead report.

"I don't see," Toby said, "why I can't go. I am doing absolutely nothing that day."

"It's a Cousins Club, Toby. Cousins."

"Pooh—you're the hostess."

"The rule is no."

"With all those people—who would know?"

I hesitated. Whose wife could Toby be? Someone's new wife—not yet listed. "All right—but be prompt. Don't make an entrance."

"Lovely."

I was hot and sweating. It wasn't exactly a shower that was available; in fact, what it was—a pewter-colored, coiled hose in a mud room. Still, I planned to hose myself off after all the work was done.

I had hired two local people who were recommended by the janitor. Hard workers, he said. And they work cheap. I hadn't gone wrong with these kitchen-possessive women who pinched and poked and nibbled relentlessly.

They were the ones who set the bowls and platters with military precision. Mumbling in Polish about my extravagance. Look at the flowers. And it wasn't even a wedding. The flowers—the theme was daisies. They were a bargain from one of Martin's clients. He had a daisy overload. All I did was mention flowers to Martin and he had the man call me. Originally, I thought something blue. No problem, the man said. We'll dye the daisies blue.

The janitor moved the tables, three long tables in a U formation. He approved. "This feels good," he said. "We did this for the Legion Awards Ceremony. Best arrangement. Something friendly about it."

I wiped my hands on my apron. "Thanks—I think it will work. Enough room for seventy? Or seventy-five?"

"Sure, missus. Just watch out for the left-handers—they'll put your eye out with their elbows."

"Right."

"You the caterer?"

"Yes."

"Well, it smells good. Sometimes we get people who ask who's good. What's the name of your place?"

My place. I looked out at that U-shaped horizon with its fresh thick table linen, octagonal white plates, glistening rented silverware. The daisies bloomed immodestly with unnatural dyed-blue petals that tumbled forth a brazen bunch from clear glass mixing bowls. If I had a place—would this be my place?

"The Late Night Muse," I said.

The man was clearly disappointed. People wanted plain names, easily understood. Names with substance like Brown and Company or Good Food. The man didn't ask for the telephone number.

Neither Florence nor I had ever taken our turn before—always we had skipped our right to entertain the Cousins. Florence had always shrugged—she'd developed a finely honed shrug. Who needs it? she scoffed. I had agreed.

But now it was time. I admit to deception—but that of omission. I permitted Martin to believe that someone was doing the food. Martin would provide the liquor, and he had been told of a lame maintenance man who worked in his office building, who could be hired to tend bar.

I planned to cook. There was a kitchen. Why not? This was what I did, the two Polish women clumping after me. The menu. I made cold tomato consommé, coq au vin blanc, green beans, dandelion and bacon salad, and tart Tatin with apples. For the children there was also homemade praline ice cream.

The Polish women astonished me. With their thick and blunt fingers they delicately cut and peeled, they chopped and seeded, they coaxed and simmered. The menu seemed too light to them. For men, they said. For women alone, it was all right. Nevertheless, I said.

We worked side by side, thus camaraderie was built. Here, here, they insisted, and showed me how the platters should go.

They stood back, surveyed. Place a bit of parsley there, two ruby-red Tiny Tim tomatoes on the next.

The women had thought family style, but I yearned for presentation. They were agreeable. So the salads were mounded, molded, muzzled. Nothing peeked up. It was Versailles at the Legion hall. The breads pyramided, crumbless and butter-soaked.

A small blue van parked outside the kitchen door, the driver honked. Yes, it was the right place. He unloaded a monstrous weight of bottles—pink and yellow and white and amber. One of the Polish women herded the man. Put them so, she advised. The other counted the bottles. This much of this. Then they permitted me to sign the receipt.

Martin arrived soon after the van. His voice echoed through the hall as he searched for the right door. "Hullo, hullo."

Who could greet him? The women and I were at the tarts, glazing them with a spiritous syrup through touches from a feathery brush. We exchanged looks of triumph.

He made his way past the festive tables into the plain rectangular kitchen where real work was done. We all looked up.

"What are you doing?" he said,

"Cooking."

"Cooking?"

"Yes."

"Where are the caterers?" he cried.

"I am the caterer," I said.

"My God," he said, "Bernadette, are you mad, doing this by yourself? Are you crazy? Have you looked at yourself? Have you seen?"

There he stood, elegant in gray flannel trousers, navy jacket—to the party born.

"You're out of your mind—absolutely. People must be on their way."

The food he ignored.

"How can you see them like *this?*"

"I'm dressing—of course, I'm dressing."

The women shouldered me, they nudged, they whispered. Go, dress. This scene they understood. This was what they knew happened. They could finish, they understood what was yet to be done.

Martin turned and left our room, his hands shaking, his lips a stony silence of imprecations. He went to get a drink from the lame man.

It seemed incautious of me to reenter my dining arena. I pulled from my purse the last party touch. Place cards.

"Here," I said, and gave them to one of the women. She stared at me in despair.

"Don't worry," I said. "They are in order. Alphabetical order—start at the far end of the U and put a card at each place."

She nodded.

I went into the mud room and stripped. I was cold, the room unheated, and I stood above the midfloor drain. Nothing for it, though. I turned the hose on my body. A cold draft of water, a painted wave flushed me. I had thought ahead. Two towels from home. My clothes packaged in vinyl hung from a far hook. I dressed—lavender with white dots. Combed my hair, put on lipstick.

The women in the kitchen nodded approval. Lovely, they said, their sweat-charged bodies in professional rhythm. They shooed me out. It was all done, they said.

Martin became the jovial host. We acknowledged, we greeted, we embraced—all those cousins. But where do we sit? Always before, it was open seating. Free to join in small groups—cliques of the familiar. But it is easy, I called out. Alphabetical order by first name—and where the first names are alike—why, there is the added initial of the last name.

The place cards. I had worked so long on those. Each one, you see, was a four-line poem. Some partially in German, French, Yiddish, Latin. Some with ancient and bold words. My guests read them and discarded them or tucked them into pockets and purses before they gorged on food, slipped it into their mouths, clamped down dental-perfect teeth, coughed over diets, ate.

Hard to believe I had cooked that food. Some swore they recognized the hand of Good Eats or that traveling chef who did Arthur's anniversary last May. Hardly anyone was certain it had been me. Cousins Sandie and Beulah said the meal had been really interesting, although normally they didn't eat such rich food.

"I'm sorry," Martin said that evening. "I didn't mean to yell at you like that—in front of people. Anyway, I'm sorry. The food was terrific."

"Thank you."

He kissed me. He was tender and loving. We went to bed. Later, I lay in his arms, my head on his shoulder.

"I guess I understand about the food," he said. "The fact that you cooked it for all those relatives—it was kind of an act of love, wasn't it?"

"Not necessarily," I said.

The place cards. Some guessed. Six later wrote me notes of spleen and venom (see Box 76). Two thought their poems were meant as a joke. Ten called me up the next morning. Three on the second day. Randolph was among that group. "If you were a man," he said, "I would kill you."

Further reflections on packing, sorting, throwing out

I have come, it seemed, into the circle of my own being. Ruth rarely spoke to me, as if I were a ghostly presence. Paul was deeply angry. Martin left as soon as he arrived. So I wandered in solitary ways. I suppose I have brought this upon myself—but I had to. Otherwise, I could not have finished these tasks. Solitariness was really not that bad.

I wanted to return to the journal. Something must be written. For I remembered aprons. I bought butcher-style aprons and tied them around the waists of Paul and Ruth. What would you like to learn how to make first? Pâte à chou? Or ragout? The one with the messy white stuff, Paul said. Later, Paul said that he didn't care for cooking. It was his father's influence. Martin explained to me that maybe it was a gender thing, but a boy cooking just didn't sit well with him.

An old woman on the subway told me that cinnamon was a good totem with ancient roots. Sprinkle it on everything, the woman said. But barring that—eat mostly cold foods and beware the swelled belly.

Martin worried a great deal. When Paul was fifteen and Ruth was eleven, he worried the most. Due to the times. Look, he said, maybe we should check their rooms, search their drawers. What for? I asked. You're so isolated, Bernie, he said. You don't know—I mean you really don't know what's out there. The stories I hear in the office about drugs and more drugs. How do we know our kids are clean? They may have tried something, I said. But that would be all. Christ, Martin said. How can you be so sure? They are afraid of me, I said. Of my wrath, of my spirit, of my sense of who they are. Martin stared, then nodded. Yes, he said, because you're sick. I hadn't thought about that—they wouldn't want to hurt you. Yes, I can see that. I can buy that.

I never doubted that I was a good mother. I guarded the children with the fierceness of the animal. Still, I let them breathe. One day they walked away. And without regrets, I let them go. There was a time for me to serve as factotum, then a time for something else. And it was not wrong for me to believe that.

In the evening in the very middle of thinking about my own journal—I found Martin's journal—he never took it with him when he went out in the evening. So be it.

JOURNAL

——◻——

*Further entries of the journal
within a journal. The man gives
me no peace.*

EXPENSES—Journal

My oldest sister was named Mirla, then came Ada and then Ida. I never knew what came over my mother doing that. Anyway, I wasn't the spoiled baby brother. Mostly, I was ignored. But I watched them. Three thick girls chosen early for the volleyball teams, softball sluggers.

What I feared was that I would wind up in life with someone like them. Someone who looked like them—my sisters. Who were the men who got the girls with thin wrists, narrow ankles, youthful breasts?

Confidence came to me late. But then I did all right. I couldn't complain.

I have an address book with codes in it for different women. Makes me sound terrible, doesn't it? Only five women— furthermore, I have seen each of them only once. Except Lila. I don't know how Lila reached me as a client. Usually her kind of problem went to someone else in the firm. But there was a slipup—I got Lila. Anyway, I have always been convinced that life was a series of necessary coincidences.

*   *   *

This is the thought that oppresses me.

Among the three possibly worst moments in life, surely the worst must be to be in bed with another woman at the precise time when your wife died.

That thought bubbles like an erupting blister. It is ruining my life—it is both abnormal and symbolic. Because my thoughts run this through on a long-playing record. Later, I add and elaborate and fatten. So it ends that I am not just in another woman's bed but I am screwing that woman. I am fucking her, I am at the moment of penetration. I am possessed by a delicious liberation, a keening upward.

That's what the mind insists. In truth, as soon as the thought reaches me—I cannot make love. Never matter where, never matter with whom.

The first time, I managed. Difficult, but I managed. With Lila. Behind her store, an arena heady with the estrous smells of women and their clothes. We made love beyond the fitting rooms on top of a pile of dresses protected by a curtain hastily pulled from a rod. A cardboard *Closed* sign in the window.

How had I coped? I concentrated on Lila. Fought the rising, choking vision of Bernadette with face carved in ivory.

Now a smart man would have kept his mouth shut. Score one for the other side. "I had this terrible premonition," I said.

"What?" she said.

I revealed the thought.

She misunderstood. She knelt beside me, her kimono fell open, her breasts were small. She was thirty-seven but she had never had a child, never put on weight. "Oh honey," she said. "No one knows you are here—no one ever knows that. Not where, not the time."

She did not grasp the point. "If I'm here," I said, "and I'm making love to you and it is ten oh-five and I leave and find out that my wife died at ten oh-five—it would still be the same—whether or not anyone notifies me at the exact moment. The same."

I have given up the others. I don't know why. I only see Lila. We meet at her store twice a week. Then three evenings a week at her apartment.

Lila's apartment has plaster molding edging all the ceilings. Old-fashioned rococo. Her parents' apartment, rent-controlled, a legacy to her. A home to killer armoires and chairs with legs that descend to claws. Lila confessed that for the longest time she couldn't bring anyone to that apartment. Then one day she realized that anyone who would have cared about what she did was dead.

Lila made great coffee. She never spooned powder into hot water. She ground beans. I sat in her kitchen and we heard these boom sounds. Noises coming through the kitchen wall. A very old kitchen, wooden cabinets covered with centuries of paint. The noises came from the Russian immigrant family next door. A lady from ORT introduced them one afternoon. I was leaving and opened the door right into their faces. A bunch of frowning fat people. The lady from ORT called me Mr. Beck. This is Lila's husband, she said.

"I think they put a dart board on the wall," Lila said as she poured milk into a pot.

"Dart board? They must be throwing bricks."

The coffee was rich and she had made my cup extra sweet.

I can't stop thinking about yesterday, although the very thought made me feel as if parts of me have taken control or have become separate entities. Hiram said that was yielding totally to sex. Don't yield everything, Hiram said.

What happened was this. Lila and I were watching television, sipping Polish brandy. What was on? A standard comedy. Someone's family, with precocious and quipping kids whose homework was finished and whose life-style was up. A simple Simon story about a widower and three kids, the man in search of a new baby-sitter. One kid was small—an infant. Suddenly, Lila squeezed my upper arm. Look at that tiny child, she said. Imagine having a treat like that one. I said nothing, checked the time. She handled birth control. All day that hammered in me, flamed and bred.

So I was not in the mood for Mandel. I was packing my briefcase when Mandel came in. He had the office across the hall—he still wasn't a partner. What had he expected? Who truly forgot a scandal? He was tainted. It's snowing, Mandel said. Yeah, I replied. Know what, Marrkey? he said. Whenever it snows I think that I must go out and clean a path to my door so that my three daughters and my wife can freely come and go. It's a dream, an illusion. We have always lived in an apartment and never had to clean a path. In my car—in the trunk—I have a small shovel for digging out the car when I have to—that's how close I come to shoveling snow. Still, the feeling I have is that behind me as I shovel that path are the lighted windows of a house. I have never seen the building—yet I know that the windows are mine. Have you ever felt that way, Marrkey? No, I said, and I couldn't care less. Up yours, Mandel said, and left.

In my heart, what did I believe? Easy to say—an accountant lives with facts. I believed that eventually I would be found out and all this would be used against me, and everything misunderstood. This I believed. Who could keep a secret? Secrets cannot be kept. All secrets tumbled out. I have a secret, the child whispered, and then told. This was not deviant behavior. All secrets were always the same. Paternity or the commission of a crime or who the lover was or the man's true name. Who stole the money. Secrets, every last one of them, and the same today as last year or a thousand years ago. Just yesterday, I read in the newspaper how this murderer was caught despite an exemplary life and a secret that lasted twenty-five years. Twenty-five years—a quarter of a century—and still it came out.

The visitor

I recopied Martin's journal until lunch. I can no longer taste certain foods. Älois declared that a possibility. I didn't mind as much as I expected. A lot of life can fall away from you. At the age of five, the depth of my losses became known to me. Florence would not tolerate a variety of things. Chocolate had an odor. I cannot abide that stink, Florence said. And when it melts, hell to clean up. So I was forced to whisper to myself at night. Choc-o-late. Then I realized the three sounds. You could do something with that. Sounds.

For my seventh birthday I received a copy of *Webster's Collegiate Dictionary*. Crazy, Florence said. But for birthdays you could have what you wanted, if it didn't cost too much.

Much has been made of my education. Paul when he was twelve started in about that. Finish college, he said. Mothers do it. I have four friends whose mothers are taking classes either nights or afternoons. It will broaden your life.

Paul at age fourteen, rummaging in the hall walk-in closet,

found five college catalogs. Thattagirl, Mom, he said. Actually, I never sent for those catalogs. Maybe Ruth did.

My God! It was Nat.

Nothing, nothing was supposed to interrupt my journal time. He didn't telephone—he appeared at the door. The idea horrified me. I had put all these obstacles in the way of the world, and here it came. I thought of ordering him to go away, of threatening him, of a flat-out refusal to answer that jangling summons.

I stood behind the door, my pen in stab position.

"I'm not dressed."

"You're wearing your robe," he said. "You must be wearing your robe—almost every time I came, you were wearing your robe. I beg of you, Bernadette, let me in."

The anguish in his voice was the anguish of the self—nothing really to do with me. Nat keening for Nat. I opened the door. It was him in a wrinkled, weedy guise. He rubbed at myopically tearing eyes. He was cloaked in upset, his fingers had worn paths in his hair, his sweater—beloved garment—freshly stained.

"Forgive me, Bernadette. I knew I shouldn't come. I told myself that—Don't come! But I had to. Like an inner force drove me. Wrong—yes, it was wrong.

"I have consideration for you—for your health. I worry. But I have read and reread the poems—all night. All night, Bernadette. I called Helene. We must have more, I said. Do you know what she said?"

I shook my head.

"No! She actually said no. Bernadette, forgive me, but you have chosen wrong. *She* is not the right one. What does she know of poetry? A pimple's worth."

I stared at him. He had bled for what he wanted. Yes, he had bled. "Come," I said. "I'm having muffins and coffee." I led him into the kitchen. He sat and devoured food.

For some reason he equated the offering of food with acquiescence.

"What we need is a plan," he said, crumbs coating his tongue. "I am not rash. No matter what. Not rash. I understand that you can jump headlong into this and ruin everything. We need an outline, an approach, a time line. Not too fast. Not too slow. Not a buckshot approach. I believe that all your material should be cataloged, indexed, examined. Nothing discarded. Helene could be good at that. She is a born nitpicker. But she doesn't understand what could be ahead, Bernadette. I know she is blood, but she doesn't understand poetry. She may be a barricade to the future. She's a doppelgänger—your personal doppelgänger."

I urged Nat to eat more muffins. I poured fresh coffee.

I knew that he thought he had outwitted Helene. Stealthily, his foot reached out and rubbed against mine. What was my relationship to Helene—Blood? Who knew for certain if we shared blood. Ghosts, yes. Definitely ghosts.

"Do you want me to tell you something?" Nat said.

"Yes."

"Look, I know I shouldn't. But—well, Helene and I—it's not an affair. We had been together—alone—meeting at her house. Going over papers. It's a big house. Show you around? she asked. So I went. It happened. All right, we made love a few times. I suppose I'm telling you this so you won't think that I despise Helene—because I don't. On the other hand, I have to tell you this, too. I have become attracted to you, Bernadette. First, it was through the poetry—a literary attraction. But now—I know it is more. There—it's been said. Don't think that I will trouble you—because I won't. I respect you. And your poetry.

"But Bernadette—if the rest of your work is like what I've seen—I'll be able to send it onward. I plan a major paper for the

Modern Language Association. You could move from forgotten into known just like that." He snapped his fingers. "It has happened to others—I've seen it. Your work collected—I'll do the intro. Bernadette, at the very least make us coexecutors— Helene and me."

I sent him away. I sent him away jabbering with hope. I sent him away before he kissed the hem of my robe.

My clinical picture had always been cloudy—diverse. Almost subdivisions of symptoms. Clive would never permit me to read the chart. No, no, he said and wagged his finger. He was the only man I have ever known who could actually be said to wag his finger. Why no, no? My body outlined there in someone else's handwriting. I wish I could have swiped that chart and copied it—for the boxes. With a bit more time I'd ask Hiram. Get it, I'd say.

Sometimes my hands ached, my legs faltered. Ataxia? Tremors? Excellent descriptions can be found in accounts by Bourneville, Seguin, and Charcot. Ah, but they left certain things out. They left out the inside. The very inside. What it was like to be the sole possessor of those feelings. For when they were yours—they were yours. So the definitions are for the outside—the mutated outside as described by Älois. What came first—vibratory sensibility, cutaneous sensibility, or simply weakness of the lower limbs? Check the chart.

This was what I wondered about. I wondered what everything will look like when I am no longer here. I have known it as one way—when new truth made it another. Simple things. Yes, I referred first to simple things. Say, for instance, what I saw from the windows of this apartment. Look across the parkway. There.

A gray-blue two-story house. Suppose—just suppose that building was torn down, destroyed, razed. Then what I saw isn't there. Was never there. Who's to remember that it was there when seen from this window on this day at this time?

The couch will go. Already it yielded its cushions to despair. Someone (Lila, Ruth, Paul, Martin, Toby) will replace it. With something pale gray with a thin white stripe. All this that I now see and touch will be gone. People altered. The very air grown stale or clean. A new species of bird discovered flying north. A mutant fish with golden gills. A monsoon that changed topography. All new. Only a visionary will know how. New kisses, new fucks, new sensations.

Bernadette Amy Marrkey will lie moldering in the grave.

Her *Collected Works*, though, are absolutely unchangeable.

Damn Nat! The man literally ate away my time. Barely an hour left to myself—what must I do? The poems for the last box—more. "Window View" and "Three-Part Couch."

I forgot Shifton's friend. The dramatist. Don't think that I ever offered him my poems "To Mysterious B." No, I came home one evening and found Shifton and his friend drinking beer and eating leftover soufflé Rothschild. Shifton's friend had my notebook. I gasped, fumbled in my purse. I had no weapon.

"Hi," he said. "Listen, this yours?"

I nodded—a mute.

"Could be a play," he said. "Sometimes material is at a premium. Yes, I could adapt. The setting would be a boardinghouse in the Bronx where the girl goes to live. Thematically, kiddo, liberties are what adaptations are about—as long as the true substance is not lost.

"B also lives in the boardinghouse, of course—I see him as a kind of junior gangster. Young, uncertain—not yet hardened by experience. I admit that first I figured rape. I was going to have him rape this girl. But no—let's do the unexpected. We'll have her attempt the seduction. B—ever the American macho man— doesn't know how to respond to the sexual overtures—coming as they do from an obviously nice girl. Once, the girl even walks into his room and finds B in bed with another woman—Tillie. The girl tries to get into bed with them and is repulsed.

"But life remains life. She gets him in the end. She has charm, a white and enticing body. They become lovers. He cannot keep her. She is destined to have many men, to make her way upward, and away. Yet always a part of her cries for what could have been sweet and enduring—for B as shadowy American hero. She dies eventually—shot by a jealous lover. I think the play will definitely find an audience."

Deaths

This was what happened. Shifton vanished—no one knew where. The dramatist went to Hollywood. My source for "To Mysterious B" died. Florence called me up one day. The super's son passed away, she said. Bertram? I said. Yes, Florence replied. The parents took it very well. God's blessing, they told me. They were afraid they would die first, you know. Then who would take care of the boy?

There were more boxes. Always intended to have more boxes. But my thumbs ached and refused to bend to the will of the hands. Definitely a spectral quality to my body. I crumbled from wall to wall. The timing, though, was good. I did a touch of combining—and taped the last set of boxes. Aladdin & Sons kept their bargain and hauled them away.

I called their main office. Gave them Helene's address. How

much to deliver everything to the Island? The man whistled—quoted a figure. I wrote a check to cash and sent it to Hiram. For Aladdin & Sons, I wrote. Hiram is the executor of my estate—without bond. Helene is in charge of literary matters. They will mistrust and watch other.

My life should have been spectacular, don't you agree? Perhaps I could have borrowed from other lives. Don't think I didn't consider that. Made more of the murder—added the element of confession and dangerous accomplices. There should have been journeys. Instead, I can be accused of staying indoors.

My body has grown listless. It prodded at me with re-membrances. Did I consider that? Why not. Yes, I thought of becoming like some Roman empress—ending with a terrific orgy. Sexual adventures with, at the very least, the last men I have known. But my body, a reluctant conspirator, declined. My legs, then, will not ride the shoulders of those last men. The men will have to find solace in my poems. And what happened before.

This I did do. I wrote to Nat. You must act as Helene's assistant, I said. She is the literary executor. Treat her well—and you will be surprised at how she may respond. That, dear Nat, is all I can do. Blood is ultimately thicker. All decisions are now in Helene's hands.

I left a sealed envelope for each of my children. Not a good-bye note. How morbid. No, I have written for each a separate set of numbers—they should read the corresponding poems. There was good cross-referencing available—so they won't have to hunt or guess which one was meant. Those listed were the specific poems for Paul and Ruth to read. Those will tell them what they should know.

I called Clive. He was prepared. You're so brave, he said. The man's an idiot! Nevertheless, Clive called Alcott's. The day administrator was sending an ambulette. Martin packed for me. He wailed now from the bathroom behind the locked door. Oh no, he sobbed, oh God no.

Boxes

This is what I think. I imagine the expression on Helene's face when the boxes arrive—for, dear friends, I never told her the extent of my life. What had she expected? One box—perhaps five. They will arrive, borne on Aladdin's six-axle shoulders, a mountain range of boxes, a Chinese wall of boxes, a house of boxes. My life will fill the hall, tumble into the rooms, drop on the stairs. Helene will stand as watcher, mouth agape, hands clenched. Then, I am certain, she will cope.

For Death, That Old Houdini-Defier

My time is your time An old radio refrain
If my time is your time When then is my
time? Was it sneaking away, jitter-bugging,
looping the loop Did I play ring-around
with my time and all fall down Or
Was my time your time all the time.

The Maimed and Shortened Lover

Doctor, have you any advice for me
For I am about to marry forever
The maimed and shortened lover
He crawled into bed with me the
Other night. You've no choice
He whispered. A prick in time
Saves no one. Didn't you know?
Cunt you see that, he giggled.
We go together, he roared, tit
For tat. Didn't you know? It's
Lust to dust, my sweetpatootie.

Doctor, if it is true that the
Maimed and shortened lover will
Make an eternal husband, then
I must go. A bag of bones surely
Headed for the nocturnal pollution.
What's that? Go quietly, you advise.
Not me, oh lover, in the end perhaps
I have not really won. But still
I'll leave behind a lot of noise.